Berkley Titles by M. Leighton

The Wild Ones Novels

THE WILD ONES
SOME LIKE IT WILD
THERE'S WILD, THEN THERE'S YOU

The Bad Boys Novels

DOWN TO YOU
UP TO ME
EVERYTHING FOR US

The Tall, Dark, and Dangerous Novels

STRONG ENOUGH
TOUGH ENOUGH
BRAVE ENOUGH

BRAVE
Enough

M. LEIGHTON

BERKLEY BOOKS, NEW YORK

BERKLEY

An imprint of Penguin Random House LLC
375 Hudson Street, New York, New York 10014

This book is an original publication of the Berkley Publishing Group.

Library of Congress Cataloging-in-Publication Data

Names: Leighton, M., author.
Title: Brave enough / M. Leighton.
Description: Berkley trade paperback edition. | New York : Berkley Books,
2016. | Series: Tall, dark, and dangerous ; 3
Identifiers: LCCN 2015043701 | ISBN 9780425279489 (paperback)
Subjects: | BISAC: FICTION / Romance / Contemporary. | FICTION / Contemporary
Women. | FICTION / Romance / General. | GSAFD: Romantic
suspense fiction. | Erotic fiction.
Classification: LCC PS3612.E3588 B73 2016 | DDC 813/.6—dc23
LC record available at http://lccn.loc.gov/2015043701

PUBLISHING HISTORY
Berkley trade paperback edition / April 2016

PRINTED IN THE UNITED STATES OF AMERICA

10 9 8 7 6 5 4 3 2 1

Cover art: "Couple" by Deborah Kolb / Imagebrief.
Cover design by Lesley Worrell.
Interior text design by Laura K. Corless.

*For my wonderful readers who are brave even when
you think no one is watching. You inspire me.*

*For my incredible husband who makes me want to be brave even when
I'm not sure I can. You ground me.*

*For my God who gives me the strength to be brave even when
I feel like I can't breathe. You hold me.*

And for everyone who thinks they can't be brave today . . . You can!

ONE

Weatherly

I'm surprised that I know the way back to Chiara. It's been years since I've visited our family vineyard in the outskirts of a small Georgia town called Enchantment, but I find that I know the turns even before the navigation tells me which way to go. When I was growing up, it was one of my favorite places in the world. Winding roads, lush green hills and purple-gray mountains rising up in the background—it's like the best of every world, all in one spot.

Already I feel a little less claustrophobic just leaving Atlanta behind. Don't get me wrong. I love that city, but with my father and his old cronies bearing down on me, I had to get away. I can't very well come up with a plan to save myself if they're occupying all my time and hovering around every corner.

The lightly scented breeze whips through my hair like a lover's fingers as I slow my convertible to make the last turn. I barely creep along the serpentine road, taking my time to enjoy the sun filtering through the trees and the broken glimpses of row after row of grapevines. Being here feels like coming home. It always did.

Throughout my entire childhood, we would come here for two weeks every summer just before harvest. Dad would catch up on the vineyard business for the first couple of days, but then he'd relax with Mom and me. We ate meals together, we swam together, we played board games at night together. We acted like a normal family and I loved it. There were no pretenses to keep up, no important people to entertain, no pressures from the outside world. Just us in a mountain hideaway, protected by rows and rows of grapes.

Even now, I feel the stresses of my life draining away as I drink in the sweet scent of the air. It's as familiar as the bustle of city life, but as removed from it as east is from west. Although I haven't been here since before I went to college, time is already melting away as though I visited just last week. Here at the vineyard, little changes.

As I drive past the rows, a flash catches my eye. I slow to a stop and focus on a broad, sweaty back as a man drives wooden supports into the ground in front of a downed vine. I let my gaze travel over him. He must be new because I don't recognize the physique. And I think I'd remember if there had *ever* been a man built like this on Chiara grounds.

His shoulders are easily double the width of mine and he's probably almost a foot taller, just guessing. And I'm not short at five foot seven. As I start to pull away, I let my eyes linger on his impossibly narrow waist and hips, and the world-class ass that fills out the black denim.

I'd love to see if the face goes with the body. I'm very curious about him now, and about what the heck he's doing here. Maybe I'll run into him later. If I'm lucky.

I came back to Chiara looking for some peace and quiet, some time to find a way out. I would not be *at all* opposed to a handsome distraction, though. It's been too long since I've been able to want somebody just because I want them and not because of how they may or may not fit into my life. Maybe it's high time to go with my instincts. To go with someone who might be all wrong for me. To go with the passion. To throw caution to the wind.

As my dark, loosely curled hair flutters around my face, my optimism climbs with my speed. Maybe, just maybe, this little vacation will get a *whole lot* more interesting. It would be nice to get lost in something not planned and not political. Something real, something innocent to the ways of the world.

Is that too much to ask?

For my life, probably. But that doesn't mean I can't hope for it. Or try to have it. At least for a little while. A few weeks maybe.

When I pull up to the top of the circular drive, I shut off the engine and grab my smallest bag from the backseat. It has all I'll need right now—my toiletries and a change of clothes. I want to get the grime of the road off me before I unpack and get settled.

I glance at the ivy-covered stone front of the main house, a smile tugging at my lips. So many good memories here.

The front door is unlocked when I climb the wide front steps and test the knob. Maybe Stella is cleaning today. Although I didn't tell anyone I was coming (mainly because I didn't want my father to find me right away), she keeps the house ready at all times. That must be what she's doing.

"Hello?" I call when I step into the grand foyer with its Brazilian cherry floors, vaulted ceiling and antique chandelier. My voice echoes around me, but otherwise I hear no sign of life.

I set my bag at the foot of the winding staircase and head off past the formal dining room to the kitchen at the back of the house. "Hello? Stella?" I call again. No answer.

With a shrug, I make my way back to my belongings and carry them up the stairs to the room I've always stayed in. It's just one of the guest rooms, but it has a charming window seat that I used to curl up in a lot as a little girl. In my head, that made it mine, so that's how I've always thought of this particular room—as mine.

I set my bag on the thick, beige duvet that covers the bed and begin taking out what few things I'll need. As of today, gone are the "presentable" clothes. These are the days of spaghetti straps and sarongs, flip-flops and loose hair.

After I stow my bag in the closet, I eye the steam shower longingly, but as soon as my gaze falls on the oversized claw-foot tub, the shower is forgotten. A nice relaxing soak to soothe my stiff, road-weary muscles sounds like heaven.

I cut on the spigot and test the temperature with the backs of my fingers until it's a little warmer than what's comfortable, and then I start stripping. I grab two towels, a washcloth, my phone and my organic soap and set them on the chair that sits near the head of the tub. Then I climb in.

Air hisses through my teeth as the hot water stings my legs and then my belly. I let my skin adjust to the heat before I reach for my phone and turn on some music. I wet my washcloth, drape it over my eyes and then slide down in the tub. Within two minutes, I'm already feeling boneless.

I soak for a good thirty minutes before pulling the plug and draining half of the tepid water so that I can refill it with hot. I grab my soap and roll the silky bar in my hands, working up a rich lather to spread over my arms. The scent of almond and coconut permeate the air and I can all but feel it sinking into my skin.

I lather my hands again and set my fingers to my chin and neck, working toward my chest. I close my eyes, the image of the vineyard guy popping unbidden into my head.

I wonder what he might look like. What color eyes would go with a body like that? Something exotic, maybe. Something piercing. Something that would say he wants me without ever having to open his mouth.

My breathing picks up as my fantasy takes off in an unexpected direction. I massage the scented soap into the soft mounds of my breasts, dragging a fingertip around each nipple over and over, imagining what it might feel like to have the calloused touch of a manual laborer there.

"My birthday isn't for another week," a deep voice purrs, jarring me from my thoughts.

With a gasp, I sit up in the tub, covering myself the best that I can. I forget all about propriety, however, when I see the tall, insanely gorgeous man standing in the bathroom doorway.

Black hair, cut in a style just long enough to make him look rakish.

Gray eyes that are almost silver they're so light.

Olive skin that matches the sweaty back I saw less than an hour ago.

It's the man from the vineyard. His build and his coloring are unmistakable. As are the black jeans that he's wearing. He fills them out as perfectly from the front as he did from the back, only this side includes a thick, tantalizing bulge behind his zipper placket.

Holy. Shit.

"P-pardon?" I stammer, my brain a jumbled mess. Between the little fantasy I was indulging in, him catching me off guard this way and his incredible good looks, I think I might've forgotten my name, much less that I should be prudishly insulted right now.

Only I'm not.

I'm intrigued instead. Especially when he grins.

If smoke could smile, this is what it would look like. Dark, mysterious. Sexy as hell.

Holy mother! What is a guy who looks like *this* doing working in a vineyard?

"My birthday," he repeats in a perfectly modulated, cultured voice that sounds like chocolate and cinnamon. Deep. Spicy. Delicious. "Isn't that what this is about?"

"Ummm, no. I don't know anything about your birthday."

"Damn. I was gonna thank the hell out of somebody." His eyes rake my naked upper body and chills break out across my chest, reminding me that it's probably extremely inappropriate for me to be carrying on a conversation with a perfect stranger when I'm in the tub.

But other than propriety, which I'm evidently not *too* concerned about right now, I can't think of one good reason to ask him to leave. Not one.

"I'm Weatherly O'Neal. My family owns this vineyard. Who are you?"

One black-as-night brow shoots up. "I'm Tag. My family *works* this vineyard."

Every cheesy book and movie about a rich woman and the cabana boy (chauffer, gardener, handyman and a whole slew of other clichés) scampers through my head. Now I understand. Now I understand how it happens. Now I understand the draw. It doesn't matter that our stations in life are worlds apart. It doesn't matter that my father would have a conniption. It doesn't matter that it could never work out. All my body and my mind are thinking is that the way he's looking at me sets my blood on fire.

And I love it.

"Well, *Tag*," I say, enunciating the name that somehow suits him perfectly, "I guess I'll be seeing you around, then."

He's still smiling. I don't think he's stopped since he showed up in the doorway. "I look forward to it. Very. Much."

With that, he skims me once more with his smoky-silver eyes and then turns, very slowly, to leave.

When I hear the door to my bedroom click shut, the door I forgot to close, I rest back against the cool ceramic and exhale. I smile, too, as I think to myself, *Yep. This little getaway is going to be just what I needed.*

TWO

Tag

So this is Weatherly O'Neal, I think as I watch the stunning raven-haired beauty slide onto a lounger by the pool and tip her face up to the sun. She's wearing a tight camisole-type thing in red and a breezy wraparound skirt that shows off her long, slim legs when she sits down. Her skin glistens with a healthful glow after her bath. I can all but smell the sweet scent of her flesh from all the way over here.

It'll be a long time before I can get the vision of her out of my head, particularly the one of her in the bathtub. I watched her for a few seconds before I spoke. Her eyes were closed, her head resting against the curved edge of the tub, and her slim fingers were teasing the most perfect nipples I've ever seen. They were rosy and hard and my mouth waters just recalling the way they poked wetly from the lush mounds of some seriously great tits.

Damn.

I didn't get *as good* a look at the rest of her. Once I spoke and she sat up, all I could really focus on was her face. Heart-shaped, pale skin, plump lips just the right shade of pink. And her eyes . . . God, those eyes could make a man beg. If that body, with its round breasts, flat stomach and smoothly shaved *everything*, wouldn't do it, those eyes would. They're a rich blue. Almost violet. They have an exotic shape to them that makes her look like she's turned on all the time.

That, or she *was* turned on.

I grit my teeth.

Double damn!

Yeah, her arrival is definitely not going to make things any easier for me. Especially considering how she could play into my plans, plans I can't let her find out about. But nothing worth having is ever easy.

And I'd be willing to bet having her would be worth a *lot* of trouble.

I saunter down the dappled path to the patio that surrounds the pool. Weatherly's head snaps toward me the instant my boot hits the hard surface and alerts her to my presence. Her mouth drops open the slightest bit and, for a second, there's nothing but steam between us. Hell, I'm surprised the pool water isn't evaporating.

I don't stop until I'm standing over her, my shadow shading her face. She pushes her sunglasses up into the smooth sheet of her straight, black hair and focuses those amazing eyes on me.

"I'm sorry that I interrupted your bath," I say, pausing to inhale the decadent scent coming off her skin. "I'd have apologized at the time if I hadn't been so . . . *distracted*."

Her lips quirk, but just at the corners. "Distracted?"

"A bit, yes."

"Hmmm, what on earth had you distracted?"

She likes to play. God, this is going to be fun!

"The local . . . *scenery* changed today. It became much more . . . dazzling. Took my breath away, in fact. Made it hard for me to think. My manners went right out the window."

"That's understandable. I was a little, um, preoccupied myself."

"I thought you might've been. You looked deep in . . . *thought*."

Her lips spread all the way into a full-on smile this time, making her *even more* striking. The only sign of embarrassment is the telltale pink stains that appear on her cheeks.

"I was definitely deep. *In thought*."

The innuendo is as thick as the humid air seems to be. "Care to share what you were . . . *wrestling with*?"

"No, not yet."

"Not yet?" I ask. She shakes her head, mouth still curved. "Well, whenever you're ready to talk, I'd love to hear *allll* about it."

"I might take you up on that."

I nod. "Will you be eating in tonight?"

"I will, yes."

"Is there something particular you'd like? I can let Mom know."

"Anything that goes well with a Chiara red. I'm in the mood for red."

"I see that," I say, nodding to her red strappy top. "Anything else you're in the mood for that I should know about?"

She shrugs her shoulders, drawing my eye to the crease of her cleavage. "A surprise. Surprise me."

"Oh, I can definitely surprise you," I reply with an enthusiastic grin.

"Will you be joining me tonight, then? You and your mother, I mean?"

"Isn't it frowned upon to mingle with the help?"

"Nobody is here to care, is there?"

"Not a damn soul," I say. "Seven?"

She nods and lets her head drop back. The way she's staring up at me with that sleepy, sexy look on her face . . . the way her body language seems to be begging me to touch, to taste, to take . . . Holy God!

I nod and turn to walk away, only because if I stay any longer, I won't be able to resist.

THREE

Weatherly

I got ready too early. I'm far too anxious. The only *good* thing I can say about that is that I haven't thought about Dad and Michael even once. And that's a miracle!

I head for the kitchen, thinking I should at least go down and speak to Stella. I downplay the fact that I secretly plan to grill her about her son until he arrives. I find her stirring a pan of red sauce that smells like heaven.

"Hi, Stella," I greet loud enough for her to hear me over the overhead fan that's sucking most of the fumes from the room.

She turns a somewhat haggard yet still beautiful face in my direction. "Weatherly, it's been too long! Look at you, all grown up."

I walk over and bend to kiss her pale cheek. She's a tiny woman, probably not more than five feet or so. "It *has* been too long. How are you?"

Her hair is still mostly black and wound on her crown just like I remember, but her smile seems weaker somehow. Tired maybe. Of course, I guess it could be just that she's aged. It's been years since I've seen her.

"I'm fine, my dear. How have you been?"

I pause then shrug. "Okay." No need to burden this poor woman with all my issues. The fact that I even *considered it* for a few seconds is probably an excellent indication of my level of distress. Or my level of aloneness in all this. The people in my circles aren't the type of friends that I share with. At least not anything that matters.

"I don't suppose I've seen you since you went to college. Are you working?"

The embarrassing truth—God, how I hate sharing it. "No, I'm . . . still looking for the right job."

And I am. I have been since the day I graduated. Part of the problem is that I majored in business, which wasn't at all where my passion was. It was simply what was expected of me so that I would be better able to support my billionaire mogul husband when I landed him. Support as in keep his domestic affairs in order. Because in my family's circles, that requires a college degree. But since that hasn't happened, much to my father's dismay, no job that I've showed interest in has met with my father's approval.

"What is it that you *want* to do?"

I sigh wistfully. "I'd love to expand Safe Passage, but my father doesn't think that's a good use of money."

"Is that your children's charity?"

"Yes." I nod and smile. It makes me happy that she's heard of it.

It's such an important cause to me, one I wish I could further. "I plan to invest more when I get my trust." My funds are limited until I turn twenty-five. I've been holding out until then, until I can get out from under my father's thumb, but he threw the ultimate kink in my plan by announcing that I'll be marrying Michael Stromberg or my trust will be forfeited.

My father is a land developer and he ran into some financial trouble when one of his backers reneged on a deal. Stock prices for his company fell and their financial distress drew the eye of a larger company, Randolph Consolidated, that has tried to buy out the stockholders. However, rather than trying to work out a deal with Randolph, whom my father hates, he came up with a diabolical plan to merge with another developing company, Stromberg Holdings, through marriage. Marriage to *me*. Dad had no problem pimping me out to sweeten the deal. It's not even that *I'm* his only option; I'm just the easiest one. The one that's the least distasteful to him. It doesn't matter what *I* find distasteful. It's just about the money. Always the money. He's even using money to manipulate *me*, threatening to take my trust if I don't cooperate. He knows that I plan to use my trust to help the kids at Safe Passage, so I can't stand for my trust to be forfeited.

So far, his plan seems to be working. But I'm not ready to give up yet, which is why I came to Chiara. I just need time to come up with my own plan.

"I'm glad to see you doing something meaningful with your life." A gentle knock to the rest of my family? Possibly. The sad thing is, it's warranted.

As if on cue, my cell rings from the hidden pocket of my skirt.

I'd almost forgotten I'd brought it down with me. I take it out and see my mother's face displayed on the caller ID.

It's like she can read my mind.

"Excuse me, Stella."

She nods and returns her attention to the sauce while I make my way toward the study.

"Hello?"

"Weatherly, why must you be so willful?" Aurora O'Neal is usually much more circumspect. Her blunt disregard of pleasantries tells me just exactly how upset she really is.

"Hi, Mom. I'm great. How are you?"

"Don't be obtuse, Weatherly. You know I'm concerned about you. Always. That's why I'm positively baffled by your reaction to this merger."

"That's the problem, *Mother*. I don't want a merger. I want a marriage. To someone I at least *like*."

"Michael is a kind, intelligent, very handsome man. How could you *not* like him?"

"He's fine, Mom, but I . . . I . . . ." Michael *is* fine. For a friend. Or a business associate. Or one of my father's cronies. But I want more from a marriage.

"You can learn to love him, Weatherly. Just like I learned to love your father. Now I can't imagine my life without him."

"I'm glad it worked out so well for you, Mom, but this is not the way I want my life to go. I want to fall in love the *natural* way."

"And risk meeting the wrong kind of man? The kind who might break your heart?"

"Who's to say Michael won't break my heart?"

"This merger is a large part business. He would never."

I can't help sighing. "Maybe I want someone who will be good to me because he loves me and wants to keep me happy, and not because it might mess up some big financial deal that a bunch of rich men have cooked up at the country club over sixty-year-old scotch."

"Weatherly," my mother begins again, her voice laden with all the patience she can muster, like she's trying to reason with a difficult child. "Take time if you need it. Just don't take too long. Your father loves you, but he is convinced this is the best thing for you and the family. Don't push him on the trust fund. He *will* take it. And seeing that would break my heart. But this business with Randolph Consolidated is—"

"Why is everyone's happiness and financial stability *my* responsibility? How did that happen?"

"You're an only child. If I could've given your father another heir, this wouldn't be so important. You'd be free. There would be another option. But it didn't work out that way, sweetheart. Can't you just trust me that this is for the best? Because I promise you that it is."

"Maybe *I* know what's best for me, Mom. Did anyone consider that?"

"You're not a selfish woman. You never have been. I know you'll make the right decision." Her tone is certain, so certain it sets my teeth on edge. Is everyone *so convinced* that I'll succumb? That I don't have the intelligence or the backbone to figure out another way? That I can't devise a plan to keep the family intact without prostituting myself?

Well, to hell with that! To hell with them! I *will* find another way. I just need time. And maybe the nerve to call my father's bluff.

"Maybe it's time to be selfish, Mom. Maybe it's finally time. I'll talk to you later."

I hang up before she can say anything else and I immediately put my phone on silent. If I'm to get anything *at all* accomplished on this reprieve, I'll have to avoid talking to my parents. At least until I have some inkling of what I'm going to do.

I head back inside, making my way to the kitchen once again. I'm surprised to find Tag rather than his mother dumping dry pasta into a pot and tasting the red sauce. His hair is wet, the ends just long enough to curl around the collar of his loose white button-up shirt, and I can smell the clean scent of his soap above the spicy notes of oregano.

"You looked much different a few minutes ago," I say from the doorway, leaning one hip against the counter.

"Shorter? Older? Nicer?" he asks as he licks tomato sauce from his full lower lip.

"Definitely shorter and older, but I'm not sure yet about the nicer part."

"Oh, I think you are," he says with a wicked little half smile.

"Are you trying to tell me that you aren't nice?"

He shrugs his big shoulders as he sprinkles a pinch of something into the pan and gives it another stir. "I guess it depends on how you define nice."

"And how do *you* define nice?"

He turns his smoky-gray eyes back to me. "I don't think the thoughts I've been having about you could, in any way, be considered 'nice.'"

My mother and my current troubles are forgotten as heat creeps into my core like the lightest of caresses. It makes me feel careless. Daring. A little wild. "I suppose it would be rude of me to ask about those thoughts."

Ohmigod, what am I doing?

I know I'm playing with fire. Within minutes of talking to Tag today, I quickly surmised that he's dangerous. To hearts, to minds. Certainly to panties. Mine feel in danger of combusting just watching him, for heaven's sake. Which is unlike me. In fact, *all* of this is pretty unusual for me. I can't remember the last time I was so immediately and thoroughly intrigued by a man, or the last time I considered doing *anything* with such reckless abandon. I don't even *flirt*! Maybe that's why this is to tempting to me—it's not something I would ever do. *He's* not some*one* I would ever do.

And maybe that makes him perfect.

"I don't think it would be *rude* of you. Dangerous, maybe, but not rude."

"Dangerous, how?"

Tag wipes his hand on a towel and turns toward me. With his eyes on mine, he takes a few steps to close the gap between us. "Are you sure you want to know?" he asks. My body is like a tuning fork, reacting to the vibration of his gruff voice in a quiet shiver that moves all the way through me.

"No," I answer honestly, realizing that I'm probably *way* out of my depth with a man like this.

"Well, when you *are* sure, you just let me know. I'd be more than happy to . . . *educate* you when you're ready."

With him so close, I feel claustrophobic. But in the best possible way. His eyes are glued to mine, the silver of his irises appearing to flow around his dilated pupils like mercury. I can't look away, even though it's hard to breathe. But now, I'm not even sure I want to. I like the feel of him crowding me. I like the feel of his body heat radiating into mine. Plainly put, I like the way he makes me feel.

"What makes you think I need educating?"

"Maybe I'm just *hoping* that you do."

"I could always lie."

"And I could always believe you."

Stella's soft voice interrupts from somewhere behind Tag. "Is *this* why you were shooing me out of here?"

I hear her, but I can't see her. Tag is so big, his presence so consuming, I'm not sure the world even exists beyond the breadth of his shoulders.

Beautifully sculpted lips tip up at one corner before he replies to his mother. "No, Mom. I was just getting the bread."

Tag leans in to reach onto the counter behind me, his chest brushing mine and his arm grazing my hip. I hear the rattle of a bag and then he's leaning away, a ring of Italian *Ciambella* bread gripped in his long fingers.

When he steps away, air rushes back into my lungs as though he had consumed all the oxygen around me when he was near. I sag ever so slightly against the counter and plaster a polite smile on my face.

"I can finish," Stella tells her son when he returns to the stove with the bread. He holds it aloft, out of her reach.

"You need to rest. I told you I'd take care of this. But thank you for watching it while I showered."

She gives him a stern look, but she doesn't argue, and even now, I notice the unnatural pallor to her skin. "At least let me set the table."

"You don't even feel well enough to stay and eat. I'm certainly not going to let you do the work."

"But I—"

"Don't make me pick you up and carry you out of here," Tag threatens with mock severity.

Stella smacks her lips and dismisses him with a wave of her hand. Her small smile returns, though, when Tag bends his head to kiss her cheek and then physically turns her away from the stove, one big hand cupping her shoulder.

Stella exits slowly, more slowly than I remember her moving in previous years. Of course, it's been a while since I've seen her, but she can't be much over fifty. I would think she'd still have lots of spring in her step. But she doesn't.

When she disappears around the corner and out of sight, I drag my eyes back to Tag. He's got a long bread knife in one hand, slicing the ring in half. Although his expression is inscrutable from this angle, there's an air of melancholy in the kitchen now that wasn't there a few minutes ago.

"Is your mom okay?"

"Not really." His beautifully buttery voice holds so much sadness that my heart aches for him, this handsome man that I don't even know.

What the hell is wrong with me?

Although I'm curious, I don't ask for details. I simply wait to see if he offers any.

"She's got cirrhosis," he confesses softly.

I gasp. I can't help it. "Oh God! Is it because of—"

"No," he interrupts, shaking his head and turning to meet my eyes with his now dark gray ones. "No, it's not alcoholic cirrhosis."

I clutch my chest with my hand. "Thank goodness." My voice is awash with relief. Even though it wouldn't be my fault, I'd feel horrible if working here at Chiara, producing and tasting and enjoying wine all these years, had damaged her liver to the point of illness.

"She has Wilson's disease. She was diagnosed as a child and they've treated it for years, but they didn't catch it as early as they should have. Her liver is scarred. Failing."

Failing? That sounds . . . fatal.

"What about a transplant?"

"She has other health factors that make her a less desirable candidate for transplant. I offered her a portion of mine, but . . ."

"But?"

His laugh is wry. Bitter. "She won't take it. She's too damn stubborn."

"I-I'm sure she's worried about you, though. Being without a part of your liver."

"I'd give her half of *all my organs* if it would save her life," he says fiercely, his frown thunderous when he turns it toward me. It dissolves in seconds, though. As quickly as the ferocious lion showed up, he's gone, leaving behind only the Tag I've just recently met. Calm. Charming. Matter-of-fact. "But none of that matters if she won't take them."

I don't know what to say. It's easy to see that he's hurt by this situation, as anyone who loves a parent would be. I don't know much about transplants and compatibility and all that, but one thought comes to mind. "What about your father?"

I don't have many memories of Stella's husband, Joseph. I wasn't allowed out on Chiara grounds without my parents when we came each year, so I wasn't as familiar with the people outside these walls as I was the ones who worked inside. I guess that's why I knew Stella better than anyone. She took care of the house mostly. I knew she had a son, but I only saw him from a distance and I thought Dad had mentioned that he went into the military.

"He's dead."

Oh God!

"Tag, I'm so sorry. I . . . I . . ."

"Don't be. It's been a few years."

I'm ashamed that I don't know more about his life. His family has tended our vineyard for as long as I can remember yet I know so little about them. It's as though they weren't worth discussing in my family. Despite the progress made in the last two hundred years, class distinction still very much exists in some circles. I was born into it. Tag was, too, whether he knows it or not. And we are on opposite ends of the spectrum.

I clear my throat, not knowing how to recover the night at this point. "Did Dad tell me that you went into the military? Or did I just imagine that?"

"Yeah, I was in the Army for a tour."

I nod, relieved at the hope of a change in subject. "What did you do?"

Tag shoots me an odd look, one that brings the hairs on my arms to shivering attention. "I doubt you'd really want to know. And even if you did, I couldn't tell you much."

"Oh," I say flatly. I take that to mean that he *can't* talk about it, that he's done clandestine things, top-secret things. Maybe dark, dangerous things. I can't know because he won't tell me, but the possibility actually intrigues me. I won't press, though. I've made enough of a mess of tonight's conversation and dinner hasn't even begun yet!

Quietly and unabashedly, I examine him as he finishes up the last of the meal preparations, straining pasta and sliding a pan of buttered bread into the oven. I look at his hands—long of finger, broad of palm. Strong, capable. Although this man seems perfectly at home in the kitchen, or in the vineyard, or staring at me from the bathroom doorway, I can easily imagine him dressed in black, holding a gun to someone's head. He might even wear that same fierce look I saw only moments ago. Yes, I can imagine it all too clearly. This man is probably dangerous in many ways.

"Would you like to set the table? Everything will be ready in just a few minutes and then it will be your turn," Tag declares.

"My turn for what?"

"To tell me all your secrets," he says, his voice dropping down to a sexy whisper. And that's all it takes to shift the mood back to one of attraction that simmers as hotly as the red sauce bubbling on the stove.

"What makes you think I have secrets?" I ask, collecting plates from the cabinet so that I can avoid meeting his eye.

"Everybody has secrets."

"Then what makes you think I'd *tell them*?"

I feel the heat of his mouth at my ear as Tag leans into me from behind. "What makes you think you have a choice?"

When I turn to look at him, he's disappearing into the pantry, leaving me wondering if I have a damn clue what I'm getting myself into. Or if I even care.

FOUR

Tag

I hold Weatherly's chair as she slides into it. I hesitate to push it in because the enticing glimpse of her mile-long legs will be hidden from my view. I console myself with the thought that I'll get to see them again soon. With nothing covering them. With nothing covering *her*.

She smiles politely as I plate her spaghetti and offer her a piece of bread. Her eyes follow me as I pour her a glass of red, per her request, and then pour some for myself. I love that she's not one of those women who pretends she's not attracted when she sure as hell is. Something about the way she plays, even though I can tell it's not necessarily her nature, makes me think she could match me in passion. Honest, no-strings-attached, down-and-dirty passion.

"So, where would you like to start?" I ask, loving the way her eyes widen the tiniest bit with her discomfort.

She takes a sip of wine and then clears her throat before she responds. Very deliberate. I'm sure she was taught to think carefully before she speaks. I'll break her of that if she'll give me the chance. I want her to speak her mind, to tell me every erotic thought that passes through it, without even pausing. I don't know why I want so much to see her inhibitions die, but I do.

"What would you like to know?"

I arch one brow. "What I'd *like to know* and what you're *willing to tell me* are two very different things, I imagine."

"Then what do you think I'm willing to tell you?"

I can't help grinning. "So cautious. I'd love to see you let go. Do you think you might consider doing that, maybe just a little, while you're here?"

"I'm already letting go."

"How so?"

"My parents would disown me if they saw me dressed this way."

"And what's wrong with the way you're dressed?" I lean back, using this as an excuse to openly peruse her body. She's got an amazing build. Her round, high tits press into the purple knit material of her dainty top and her narrow hips and long legs are only hinted at in the thin, flowing black skirt with slits all the way up the sides. It would be so, so easy to push that fabric up, to press my lips to the top of her thigh . . .

My cock jumps eagerly.

Jesus! I have to quit thinking about that shit at the dinner table.

"This isn't appropriate for an O'Neal," she says mockingly in a deep, chastising voice, her eyes cast down as she looks into the bottom of her wineglass.

"Ohhh, I see. So, for you, dressing like a regular person is letting go?"

She shrugs. "Sort of."

"Not much of a rebel, are you?" I tease.

"Until now? No."

"And what makes you a rebel now, besides the clothes? And having dinner with an incorrigible rake?"

She grins and it brings out a dimple right near her mouth. Makes me want to stick my tongue in it. "An incorrigible rake? An *incorrigible rake*? Do you read historical romances or something?"

"Maybe one or two."

"Are you joking?"

"Why so shocked? What better way for a guy to become acquainted with the thoughts and desires of a woman? Especially when said guy is a horny teenager. With a mom who has a stockpile of those paperbacks."

"So that's your trick?"

"No trick."

"You think it worked?"

"I could say you tell me, but a decent man would never say such a thing, now would he?"

"Oh, surely not," she replies, the edges of her lips twitching.

I smile. Damn, she's fun.

I clear my throat and try to redirect my mind from its current dissection of what it would be like to undress her right now, lay her up on the table and devour every inch of her creamy flesh. "So, beautiful, rebellious Weatherly, how long will you be staying with us?"

"As long as it takes."

Fun and interesting. "As long as it takes for what?"

"Wouldn't you like to know?"

"I would, actually. Very much."

"And why is that? Why so interested?"

"Because you interest me. A lot."

"Why?"

"Because you ask a lot of questions."

"Is that all?"

"Oh, God no! Everything about you interests me."

"But you hardly know me. In fact, you *don't* know me."

"But I want to."

She nods slowly, her violet eyes never leaving mine. I can all but see the wheels of her mind spinning.

"You're running from something. Care to tell me what that is?"

Shock. That's what's written all over her face. Good old-fashioned shock. "Wh-what makes you say that?"

"I've run from things before. I know the look."

"Well, you . . . I . . . It's not . . ."

"Wouldn't it be easier to just tell me what it is rather than trying to make up excuses? You know you want to."

"I most certainly do not!" she denies vehemently, but I can also see on her face that she very much *does*.

"Liar."

"I am not. I—"

"Sometimes a perfect stranger can be a great sounding board. No attachments. No judgments. Nothing to fear. Just someone to listen. And maybe even help."

"Trust me, there's nothing you could do to help me."

"You'd be surprised by what I'm capable of," I tell her, deadpan. And she would. I've killed, I've stolen, I've pillaged and plundered. Well, sort of. But I've also saved and sacrificed, confessed and surrendered.

She starts to say something, her exquisite lips parting and then slowly closing again. "It's my father. He wants me to marry someone who's not of my choosing."

"A business connection, I presume?"

She nods once. She's looking down at her fork where she turns it up on its side and then rolls it to the other. Back and forth, back and forth. "He's a nice man, but I never wanted to marry someone for reasons other than love."

"Then don't."

"It's not that simple. My father . . ." Her sigh is deep and mournful. "I run a charity that's very important to me. A children's charity. To provide the hungry with food. He doesn't want to invest more money into it, but I do. I was going to invest some of *my* money once my trust fund matures when I turn twenty-five in a few months, but he's going to revoke the trust if I don't marry Michael before then."

In most of modern society, that shit doesn't happen anymore.

But in Weatherly's circles, and with men like William O'Neal? Who the hell knows *what* goes on?

"Why the rush? Why now?"

"Another company has been trying to get my father to sell a considerable amount of his holdings at less than market value because the stock has dropped. There have been some . . . financial problems in the last couple of years. But he doesn't want to sell. Now the other company is moving into a hostile takeover and this is my father's only way out. *Michael* is his only way out, or so he thinks."

"And does Michael want to marry you? Or is it strictly business for him, too?"

She shrugs, a vague movement of only one shoulder. "I suppose he does. He's always been . . . interested, I guess."

"I can imagine. You're an intelligent, well-bred, beautiful woman. What's not to like?"

"Wow! I've never felt more like a show horse."

"No, not a show horse. Just a very desirable catch, that's all."

Her eyes snap up to mine. They're shooting fire, violet sparks spitting out at me from around her wide, angry pupils. "And is that supposed to be enough for me? That *he* wants *me*? Is it so unthinkable that I would want to love the man I marry? That I would want to *want him*? To *like* him? That I would want to enjoy his company?"

"I don't think that's too much to ask."

"And yet . . . here I am, being forced into this like it's 1850."

"So you've come here to think of a way out, is that it? Is that the rebellion?"

"Yes. As pathetic as that is, that's pretty much it in a nutshell."

"Well maybe I *can* help."

"And just how, exactly, do you propose to do that?"

It's more her phrasing that catches me off guard than anything. And it gives me an idea. But that's another discussion for another day. Right now, I need to salvage the evening.

"I've been known to think strategically a time or two in my life. Maybe I can think of something. If not, maybe I can at least take your mind off things. Maybe just not being so overwhelmed by it will open you up to new possibilities."

I wink at her and her face slowly softens. I think she wants to abandon this topic as much as I do.

"New possibilities?" she asks, a smile running through her voice like a golden thread. "Is that code? Are *you* a new possibility?"

"Hell yeah, I am," I admit, pinning her with my gaze as I sip my wine. The sweetness pours over my tongue and I think to myself that she will taste just as sweet, just as intoxicating. I don't know how I know that, but I do.

She tilts her head to one side as she considers me. It's a subtly sexy move that hits its mark. "Are you like this with every woman you meet?"

"Like what?"

"So charming and flirtatious. So . . . forward."

"Am I being forward? I didn't mean to be. I thought I was just being honest." She narrows her eyes on me. Not really in suspicion, but more like she's trying to see inside my head. "Maybe you're just not used to honesty," I offer casually.

"Are you always so honest, then?"

"I try to be," I answer carefully, knowing that my honesty definitely has its limits right now. Some things are just more important. They have to come first. But I can't really tell her that either.

"Ah, so no promises of absolute truth?"

"I think promises of absolute truth are usually lies in and of themselves. Haven't you found that to be true?"

"No one has ever bothered to promise me the absolute truth before."

I set down my glass and lean forward, taking one of her hands from where it rests in her lap. "Then how about this? I promise to tell you the absolute truth about everything I'm feeling."

She leans forward, too, putting her face, her delectable lips, even closer to mine. "Why would you think that would matter to me?"

"Because if you stay here very long, there's going to be more between us, and I don't want you wondering if I'm feeding you a line of shit or not."

"Starting now?"

"Starting now."

"Then tell me, honest Tag, what is it you see happening here?"

"I see me wanting to kiss you the longer I stare at that incredible mouth. I see that you're curious about whether I will. And I see that kiss turning into something more."

"What's 'more'?"

"What do you want it to be?"

"My life is extremely complicated right now."

"Sounds like it. But *this* doesn't have to be. You intrigue me. Not because of your money or your father or what country club you belong to. Just you. The way you smile, what you're thinking behind those violet eyes, how your skin will feel under my hands. Maybe I'm just what you need right now."

"How will I know?" she asks softly, her face oddly vulnerable. Her big eyes hold her every insecurity and, if anything, I'm even *more* intrigued.

"Oh, you'll know, fair Weatherly. You'll know."

FIVE

Weatherly

With his swirling silver eyes sucking me into them like a vortex, Tag lifts my hand and brushes his lips over my knuckles. I feel his warm breath and the soft friction like a teasing caress between my legs. I've never met someone so . . . so . . . *potent*. Everything about him works together to form a powerfully persuasive concoction—his mesmerizing eyes, his cocky grin, his voice, his words, his sexily innocuous taunts. I'm not even sure he set out to seduce me, yet that's exactly what's happening.

Maybe I was in need of seduction. Maybe I was in such need of something so extraordinarily *not me* that I was ripe for the picking. For *his* picking. Or maybe this chance encounter is simply the intersection of all the right conditions coming together to create the perfect storm of emotion and attraction and opportunity. I don't really know, and the thing is, I don't think I really *want to*. Every-

34

thing in my life has to be given such thoughtful consideration—
how it will reflect on the family, how it will affect my future, how
controllable the end result will be. But this doesn't. This is just
mine. It has nothing to do with my family or my future. It's mine.
Mine alone. And I've never had anything that's just mine before.
Maybe that's why I'm throwing myself into this with such a marked
lack of thought and caution. It might be the only time in my life
that I can.

"So," Tag says, releasing my hand and leaning back. His face
settles into a friendly smile and he raises his fork to dig into his
food. "Tell me about this charity you're so passionate about."

And so I do. I tell him about Safe Passage, about the staggering
number of children in the Atlanta area who go hungry each day. I
tell him about the strides we're making in reaching more and more
kids, and how rewarding the results are. Conversation flows naturally from that. Naturally and effortlessly. Like we've known each
other all our lives, despite the fact that we only met a few hours ago.
As strange as it sounds, I'm more comfortable with him than I can
ever remember being.

"Are you two still in here?" Stella asks when she pokes her
head in from the kitchen.

Tag winks at me before he turns to speak to his mother. "I
can't get her to shut up, but you don't need to make her feel bad
about it, Mom." She waves him off with her hand and he chuckles.

"By all means, blame it on me," I say acerbically.

"She knows me better than to think I could be held here
against my will."

"I'm sorry if I've bored you going on and on about Safe Passage. I didn't realize how late it was getting." I'm genuinely surprised to see that it's nearly eleven.

"I've enjoyed every minute. I like hearing what you're passionate about."

How does he do that? Make every word sound devilishly delicious? He makes it seem as though everything that passes between us, no matter how innocuous, is intimate.

"Maybe next time you can tell me what *you're* passionate about."

"I'd be happy to."

There's a protracted pause during which my nerves begin to jangle. "Well, I suppose I'd better get to bed. It's been a long day."

"I'm sure you're tired," he adds. But he makes no move to get up. He just watches me with those disturbingly fluid eyes.

"Can I help clean up?" I offer.

"No, I've got it." He turns his head just enough to aim his next words over his shoulder. "Do you hear that, Mom?"

"I heard you, Mr. Bossy Pants," comes Stella's voice from the kitchen, a voice that sounds less than robust.

"I'll get it. There's a greater likelihood of her letting me clean up if *you* aren't in there. I'd have to wrestle her to the ground to get her to go to bed if you tried to help. And then she'd try to ground me like I'm fifteen rather than twenty-seven. You see how this could get out of hand, right?"

I smile. I can't imagine *anyone* giving this strong, charismatic man a hard time. Of course, he obviously has a soft spot for his mother, which I find incredibly endearing. Their dynamic makes me happy and a little envious. My relationship with my own mother leaves a lot to be desired.

I push thoughts of my family's shortcomings from my mind as I lay my napkin neatly on the table. "Well, far be it from me to get anyone in trouble."

Tag stands as well. "Oh, I think I'm already in trouble." His lopsided grin makes my bones melty.

"Are you always like this?"

"Always."

"Good to know," I say, hating that I'm hesitant to step away from the table. But I do. Because I must. "Well, thank you. For a wonderful meal and stimulating conversation."

He nods once. "Consider me at your service any time you need stimulating."

A laugh churns in my chest even as my cheeks flame, thinking that Stella might still be able to hear.

Walk away, Weatherly. Just walk away. Before you can't.

"Don't worry," Tag says, leaning toward me as I start to move past him. "She's not in the kitchen anymore."

"How do you know?"

"I heard the boards in the hallway creak when she left."

"Another power of yours, super hearing?"

"I have a lot of super powers."

"Such as?"

"You'll see," he says enigmatically. His eyes drop to my lips for a few seconds, making them feel throbbing and full. But then they snap back to mine and he leans away. "Goodnight, Weatherly. I hope you sleep well."

I draw in a deep, calming breath. "You, too, Tag. And thank you again."

"My pleasure."

I turn and walk away, but I can't seem to leave him behind. I feel his eyes on me as I go, burning through my clothes as though I'm not wearing any at all.

As I lie in bed, I wish I'd just taken the lead and kissed Tag. I wanted it. He wanted it. Neither of us did it. I know why *I* didn't do it, but why didn't he? Even after I've brushed my teeth and washed off my makeup, that one question still chases itself through my head. *Why?*

But for the chaos of my thoughts, it's absolutely silent in my room. That's why the knock, though soft, brings me bolting upright in my bed.

My heart is thundering so hard, my blood vibrates with each beat. "Yes?" I call out.

The door eases open with a long moan, one that is echoed within me when I see Tag appear. He takes one step inside, half his body bathed in the white shine of the moonlight slanting through the windows. "Can I come in?" he asks, his voice as mystical as midnight itself.

"Yes."

He slips through the opening, not bothering to close the door behind him. That's why I'm both at ease and slightly disappointed with his presence here. He won't be staying. He won't be stripping off my nightie and covering my body with wet kisses.

For some reason, that annoys me. He professes to want me, to be interested in me and intrigued by me, and yet . . . he hasn't even tried to kiss me. Why?

I should probably be glad that he's not trying so desperately to get in my pants. I mean, he is likely never in need of willing company, the thought of which sets my teeth on edge. But still, I'm strangely insulted that he's so . . . gentlemanly. Which is utterly ridiculous.

Yet, that's how I feel. Insulted. Challenged, even. He's so perfectly in control, as though he has set some pace that I have no say in. While the normal Weatherly wouldn't have a problem with that because she's accustomed to following the rules that others prescribe, *this* Weatherly—the rebellious woman who's throwing caution to the wind—is far from okay with it.

If he thinks he's in control of me, I guess it'll be up to me to show him different.

"Is something wrong?" I ask, slowly pushing the covers away and swinging my legs off the bed. He stops in the center of the room, his stance casual, his expression shadowed.

"No, nothing's wrong. I just forgot that I left my toothbrush in here."

"Your toothbrush?" I ask, coming to my feet and taking a few steps forward, just enough to throw my body into the wedge of moonlight with him. I push my long hair back, letting my fingers trail down my neck and across my collarbone. "Why would your toothbrush be in here?"

"Because the cottage is being repaired and your father said that it would be fine for me to stay in a room here until it's completed."

"So you chose *this* room?"

He takes one step forward. "It has the best view." Even in the low light, I see his eyes sweep me from head to toe. Whether in response to his unabashed scrutiny or to the game I'm playing, I don't know, but my nipples bead. I feel them strain against the slick material of my thigh-length nightgown.

"What's your favorite part?" I ask, my voice strangely coarse.

"The mountains. The view from *right here* is stunning. Their peaks are beautiful. Almost close enough for me to reach out and touch, it seems."

Oh *God*! I feel like groaning. Does he seriously do that on purpose?

I inhale deeply, sharply, my aching flesh pressing even further into the cool silk. I hear Tag's breath hiss through his teeth and I'm gratified that he's at least as *bothered* as I am.

"Are you sure nothing's wrong?" I ask again, taking one last step closer. We are nearly chest to chest. I have to crane my neck to look up at him.

"No, nothing's wrong. Everything is perfect. Just perfect."

Neither of us makes a sound or a move. I wonder if he'll kiss me. I wonder if he won't. I wonder if I have the nerve to do it if he doesn't.

And then I get my answer. At least one of them. I take a single step back and clear my throat. "Well, I'll let you get what you need, then." A vague invitation. Too vague? I don't know.

I turn and walk slowly back to the bed, bending over at the waist to straighten my covers. I feel the lacy hem of my nightie ride up the backs of my thighs, grazing the curve of my butt. I'd almost swear that I could actually *feel* the hot touch of his eyes on my hips and legs before I slip into bed.

I pull the covers up to my belly and rest my head on my pillow, turning to look questioningly up at him. He's watching me. Staring as though he's stuck in indecision. I don't know what I could do to move him in one direction or the other, so I simply stare back.

After several long, unnerving seconds, Tag nods and heads for the bathroom. I hear the cabinet open. I hear it close. I don't remember seeing a stray toothbrush in there when I put my things away, but to say I was distracted would be the understatement of the year. There could've been a rattlesnake in there and I might not have noticed.

When Tag reappears from the bathroom, he's empty-handed. "Mom must've thrown it away when she cleaned. I thought I got everything out when I moved my things, but . . ."

"So where are you sleeping now?"

"At the other end of the hall."

"Oh," I reply, my skin warming at the thought of him being so close. All night long.

"Well, if you need anything, you know where to find me." He backs toward the door and every cell of my body is screaming for him to come to the bed. *I need* you! *I need* you!

But I don't admit to that. Rather, I smile and say, "Goodnight."

"Goodnight," he returns, easing back out the way he came. It's right before he closes the door that I hear his soft, "Sweet dreams, fair Weatherly." And then he's gone.

I'm on my side with the covers pulled up over my shoulders, facing the door when it opens. The muted creak brings me out of my semi-sleep with pulse-pounding speed. My eyes adjust quickly enough to recognize that the short blonde walking into my room is *not* Tag.

I gasp, sitting up so fast the room spins for a second. "Who are you? And what the hell are you doing in my room?"

I think for a moment about what I might be able to use for a weapon if this girl is here to do me harm. Logic hasn't entered into the equation yet.

"Ohmigod I'm so sorry! I thought this was Tag's room. Sorry," she says, turning to tiptoe back out the way she came.

"Wait!" I snap, anger beginning to boil in my blood as realization sets in. The girl stops and turns her upper body back toward me. "You're here for Tag?"

"Yes. I didn't mean to bother you. I thought this was his room, but maybe I turned the wrong way. It *is* dark, after all."

Is it? Is it dark at two a.m., you brainless bimbo? I think venomously. Jealously.

"You've been here before, then?"

"A few times."

"Does . . . does Tag know you're coming?"

"He told me to come over tonight, but I'm running late."

I keep a firm hold on my jaw so that it doesn't drop open in humiliated outrage. "Well, you can find him at the other end of the hall."

I flop back onto the bed, turning away from the door and silently dismissing the interloper. No wonder Tag didn't try to kiss me. I guess since he was supposed to be seeing another woman within a couple of hours his sense of propriety stopped him. It *should've* stopped him a helluva lot sooner.

That is one messed up moral compass, I think.

I roll back over onto my back, throwing an arm over my eyes. How humiliating!

Wow, you're an idiot, Weatherly.

I've never fallen for cheap lines before. What the hell is wrong with me? Never mind that no one I know has the audacity to *throw* any cheap lines at me. I feel like a fool for believing one thing Tag said. I should've known a guy who looks like him would be *this* kind of person. An unscrupulous manwhore. A user and a liar and a cheat. An incorrigible rake, by his own admission! And I fell for it! God! And I hate that it stings so much.

I promise to tell you the absolute truth about everything I'm feeling.

Jesus, I'm an imbecile! No wonder my father doesn't trust me to make my own choice for a husband.

The thought brings my circumstances—all of them—rushing back to the forefront of my mind. I have *real* problems, problems that dwarf being temporarily sidetracked by a line-slinging ladies' man. Tag's despicable nature changes nothing, other than my silly intention of living in the moment for a change. I came here to get a plan together and that's exactly what I'm going to do. Tag be damned. I don't need him or his help or his sweet talk. And if he thinks he's *ever* going to be kissing these lips, he's got another thought coming!

SIX

Tag

I'm not surprised that I find Weatherly nursing a cup of coffee and a paperback on the patio. I'm also not surprised when she makes a point to ignore me the instant I step out. I know she heard me because she pulled her book in closer to her face, a clear indication that she doesn't want to be bothered.

Not that it matters. I'm going to bother her anyway. I know what she's thinking and I don't want her thinking it.

I saunter on over to the chaise she's lounging on and I squat beside it, near her right hip, and I wait until she acknowledges me. She doesn't for at least two full minutes, but I'm not deterred. If she thinks she'll outlast me, she's sadly mistaken.

Finally, with a loud and slightly petulant huff, Weatherly lowers her book and glares at me through the light tint of her sunglasses.

"Was there something that you needed?"

"Always polite," I say, unable to hide my grin. God, she's adorable! She's bristling, but heaven forbid she show it. Too much breeding for that, I suppose.

She makes no comment; merely arches one perfectly sculpted raven brow.

I clear my throat and continue. "I wanted to explain about Amber."

"Amber. Is that her name?" she asks, a marked bite to her frigid voice.

"Yes, that's her name. I told her to come before I knew you'd be here."

"And you didn't think *even once* to, oh, I don't know, maybe call and tell her not to?"

"Honestly, I didn't think about her one time from the moment I saw you in the bathtub yesterday."

That stops her. I can see it in the way her brow furrows and her full lips purse. "Why do I find that hard to believe?"

"I don't know. Why do you? You're incredibly stunning, smart, funny. I seem to remember listing these things off last night, but if you didn't believe I was sincere, I'm happy to continue."

The sun slicing through the trees illuminates her eyes behind the reflective glass. I can see that she's softening, but I wish she'd take them off. I want to see the color. That exotic violet blue visited me in my dreams last night. I want to see if they're the same brilliant color I remember them being, if the morning can do my memory justice.

She drops her book to her lap and gives me her full attention.

"Do you make a habit of leaving the doors unlocked and telling people to just come on in?"

I shrug. "We're way up here with no one else around for miles. Why not?"

"Well, I can think of several reasons."

"If it makes you more comfortable, I can start locking them at night."

"It would, thank you. And maybe if you'd have your guests arrive at a decent hour."

My lips want to curve, but I keep them straight and steady. "Absolutely. Anything else?"

"You might tell her that any self-respecting woman doesn't make two a.m. booty calls."

This time, I let my grin break free. "I'll be sure to pass that along if I ever see her again."

"Don't stop on my account. It's none of my business *who* you see."

"It is if you want it to be. In fact, I'd like for it to be your business."

"And why is that?"

"Because you're the type of woman who wants a man's undivided attention and I'd love nothing more than to give it to you."

She shifts uncomfortably. "I don't think—"

"I thought you were letting go, not thinking."

"That was before I met Amber."

"Don't give Amber another thought. I promise you that I won't."

Her frown gets deeper as she thinks. As she fights giving in. She wants to, I think, but she's torn. I just need to batter away at her resistance until we can get back to where we were last night when she was taunting me with peeks of her delicious ass bathed in moonlight. I didn't want to press her too soon last night. This is new for her. I get it. It's probably a good thing I didn't, too, considering that Amber showed up a short time later. But still, it's hard for me not to regret letting her get back into her bed. Alone.

Amber was more than happy to help me work off my fascination, but I wasn't interested. I had no trouble telling her no and sending her on her way. If I thought about that very much, it might worry me. That's not like me. But right now all I'm thinking about is the delectable, enchanting woman in front of me.

"She *is* gone, isn't she?" she asks dryly.

"I asked her to leave about five seconds after she showed up in my doorway. I was really hoping it'd be you and when I saw that it wasn't . . ."

"Why would you think *I'd* be showing up in your bedroom at two in the morning?"

"Wishful thinking, I guess. I couldn't stop thinking about the way you looked in that silky little thing you sleep in."

Her lips part, her cheeks stain. "Well I can assure you that I won't be showing up at your bedroom door anytime soon."

"I can wait."

I can tell when she straightens in her chair that she's getting ready to argue—just for the sake of her pride, of course—so I quickly change the subject. "How about a taste of a new grape I'm trying? They're Blanc du Bois."

"Isn't it a little early for wine?"

I straighten and hold out my hand as I smile down at her. "It's never too early for wine."

"You sound like my father," she says, closing her book and sliding her fingers over my palm.

"I sound like a winemaker."

"That you do."

SEVEN

Weatherly

Tag is a masculine force to be reckoned with. Dear God, when his attention is concentrated so solely on me, I find it hard to think about anything except him. The way his eyes seem lighter when he laughs. The way he glances at my lips when I talk and then licks his own, like he's thinking of tasting me. The way he tilts his head to one side when he's considering something I've said. The way he touches his palm to my lower back when we move from one place to another. Everything about him has this magnetic quality to it—his voice, his eyes, his laugh, his smile—and I'm drawn. Attracted. Fascinated, even though I'm still trying not to be.

I was ready to run recklessly into something with him. It felt immediately right and wild and rebellious. But when Amber showed up last night . . . well, that put things into perspective for me. While I might *want* to be a casual Amber kind of girl for a

49

few weeks, the reality is that I'm not. I don't like to share and I don't like the idea of being worn for a day and then tossed aside. Maybe it's my breeding. Maybe it's the way I was raised. Maybe it's my lack of a more normal childhood. I don't know, but there are limits to how much caution I can throw to the wind and still be able to live with myself. Last night, I found the first limit.

Still yet, I find myself increasingly willing to believe what Tag said—that he didn't even think of Amber last night. Not only do I *want* to believe it, I can relate to it. He has occupied a staggering amount of my brain space since he appeared in the bathroom door yesterday. Despite all that awaits me back in my Atlanta reality, I've thought mostly of him. Of this intriguing man and why he makes me feel the way he does.

"So that's why I thought maybe these would nicely complement the other varieties that we grow and bottle here," Tag says. "This grape is hardy, well-suited for this climate. And the wine is light and aromatic, an interesting addition to our bolder ones. Sometimes bold is what we need, but other times, a lighter touch is necessary." As he speaks, he watches me with eyes that have turned a stormy gray. Without looking away, he takes a single grape from the tray behind him. I watch, hypnotized by the velvet of his voice, as he rolls the grape between the pads of his fingers. "This fruit is firm and supple. The flavor exquisite. My mouth waters just thinking about it." Lightly squeezing, always rolling. My nipples pucker to stinging points within the confines of my lacy bra, almost as though he's rolling *them* between his nimble fingertips.

My eyes follow the plump grape as he lifts it to his mouth and slips it between his sculpted lips. I can practically feel the *pop* as the skin bursts and juice floods his mouth. His soft moan vibrates in the air around me, tingling over my skin, nearly triggering an answering rumble within me.

"Delicious," he whispers, the corners of his mouth curling up into a small grin as he chews. I drag my eyes up to his to find them sparkling down at me. "I bet you're dying for a taste, aren't you?" A blush stings my cheeks. He knows exactly what he just did to me, damn him!

"Isn't that what you brought me out here for? A taste?"

God, the innuendo . . . it makes my blood bubble right inside my veins.

"Indeed," he replies, unmoving, always watching. "I don't want to move from this spot yet, though."

"And why is that?"

"The way the light is pouring into your hair, the way it shines on half your face, you look . . . ethereal."

Air seems to swell in my chest, like a shiny red balloon slowly inflating, making it hard to breathe.

"Are those grapes to blame for your sweet tongue?" I ask a little breathily.

"*You* are to blame. I don't think I've ever met a woman more striking, more captivating."

We are standing no more than a foot apart and I'd swear that I can actually feel the gravity of him pulling me closer, begging me to sway in his direction. I stand up straighter, plant my feet firmer.

"I thought you might prefer blondes."

I regret the words the instant they leave my mouth. We were enjoying each other's company. Why did I have to go and ruin it?

Only it doesn't seem that I did. As he assured me that he didn't last night, Tag doesn't seem to give Amber even a passing thought. "I prefer *you*. Not brunettes or redheads or blondes or anyone so . . . general. What I prefer, what I *want*, is an exotic, dark-haired beauty who tempts me before she pushes me away, who tells me no with her lips and yes with her eyes. What I want is everything that's within arm's reach and all that is a thousand miles out of my grasp."

My heart is thumping wildly inside the bony confines of my ribs—a butterfly desperate to break free of her ivory cage. "She might not be so exotic once you get to know her. She might just be a sterling pedigree and nothing more."

"I don't care about the pedigree. To hell with pedigrees."

"In my world, they're all that matter."

"But you're in *my world* now. Here, the only thing that matters is whether or not you want me to kiss you as badly as I want to. Here, *we* are all that matter."

"And what happens when I leave here?"

"You came here to let go. Tomorrow doesn't have to matter until it arrives."

"You paint a tempting picture, Mr. Barton."

His lips twist into a lopsided grin. "I'm giving it hell, that's for sure."

"Am I going to regret this?" I ask, catching and holding my breath as he draws slowly, steadily closer to me.

"Not one damn minute."

When his face is so close it begins to blur, I half expect him to take my mouth viciously, violently. With all the crazy, inexplicable want that *I* feel for him. But he doesn't. He treats my lips just like he did the grape. He tastes, tests. Savors.

The touch of his mouth is firm yet soft in all the right ways. It brushes lightly over mine, back and forth, his breath tickling my flesh. I stand perfectly still, caught in the magic of the moment, the scent of him, the feel of him, the promise of him.

"Weatherly," he breathes, running the tip of his tongue over my bottom lip in a leisurely lick. "I don't think I've ever wanted something so much."

His mouth teases mine as he speaks, each word a delicate caress that touches my lips and then resonates through me in featherlight shockwaves.

His tongue traces a silky line to the corner of my mouth and then kisses that spot. "Open for me," he says.

I do. Instantly. He doesn't have to ask twice.

I part my lips and welcome Tag in. His mouth covers mine and his tongue dips inside, beginning as a tentative exploration. One hand sweeps up my back and curls around my nape, Tag's fingers weaving into my hair. Chills spread down my arms and I lean into him, sinking into his kiss like it's a pool of warm, inviting honey.

A soft moan escapes my throat. Seconds later, an answering growl vibrates in Tag's chest. And then I feel fire. The tilt of his head is the only warning I get before his other hand slides around my waist and crushes me to him.

Tag's lips become fierce. Hungry. His tongue becomes persistent. Persuasive. All the palpable chemistry between us ignites, exploding into the voracious devouring that I was expecting from the start.

I'm not ready for it to be over when he pulls away, panting as hard as I am. We're still mashed together from chest to thigh and I can feel the race of his heart, mirroring my own. "Holy shit!" he breathes.

"Wow," I whisper, feeling dizzy and off-kilter after those few whirlwind seconds.

Tag's lovely lips split into a smug grin. "Damn right. See how good we are together?"

I say nothing. I don't argue. Because I can't. There's simply no denying that there's something powerful between us. Maybe it's just physical. Maybe it's something more. I have no way of knowing and only one way of finding out.

Jump.

Dive in.

Let go.

It's inappropriate. He's all wrong for me. My father would kill me. But none of that matters. In *my world* it would. But I'm not in my world. Like Tag said, I'm in his. And here, *we* are the only thing that matters.

His lips take mine again, this time in a slower exploration, tasting *me* like he might taste a fine wine. Savoring. Relishing. Memorizing every deep, sultry note of my mouth. When he pulls away again, I nearly groan. I could spend the entire day kissing him, steeping in the way he makes me feel.

"Spend the day with me. Get to know me. Let me reacquaint you with Chiara. Let me show you."

"Show me what?"

"Show you everything."

My hesitation is brief. Very brief. He's offering me his time, his patience, his world. And I'm willing to take it all. Learn it all. Experience it all. "Okay," I say in immediate agreement. "Show me."

I stand at the bottom of the front steps, waiting, looking out at the beautiful landscape. Chiara is set in the lower third of Brasstown Bald. It's part of the Appalachian mountain range as well as the highest point in all of Georgia. The steep grade is perfect for raising grapes. The rain, characteristic of our hot, humid summers, just runs right off, ensuring that the roots of the vines don't rot. It also provides earth that is conducive to several varieties of grapes, as well as an ever-present breeze and some of the state's most amazing views. I drink in the gorgeous and unruly mountains, glad once more that I came here for refuge. They've always held a piece of my soul, much like Chiara herself has, and I feel the pull now more than ever.

I hear the high whine of an engine and I bring my thoughts back to what I'm doing here—waiting. I didn't know quite what to expect when Tag brought me back to the house, asked if I had some shorts and then told me to go change and meet him out front in ten minutes. But now, watching him pull up in the circular drive on the back of a mean-looking four-wheeler, I have all the clarification I need.

"Climb on, baby. I'm gonna take you for the ride of your life," he says with a mischievous wink.

My insides jump and twitch at what lies just beneath his words. I don't doubt for a second that every minute spent with Tag could qualify as the ride of a lifetime. He's wearing faded jeans and a white tank top that shows off his broad, tan shoulders, and his eyes are shielded by sexy sunglasses. Everything about him is alluring, exciting, mesmerizing. His looks, his words, his smile, his touch—together or apart, they pull me in like the earth pulls the moon.

Tag pats the seat behind him, his grin as dazzling as the bright, hot Georgia sun. Something tells me that even if my brain started firing off *no, no, no,* my heart would still propel my body forward. It seems to control my legs—making them move toward him, making them weak when I think about his kiss.

I swing onto the vinyl seat, noting the picnic basket strapped to the back. For about ten seconds, I indulge in a little fantasy about a romantic tryst in the mountains, but all thought disappears from my mind when Tag reaches back to grab behind my knees and pull me snugly up against his hips and back. His hands linger on my skin a fraction too long, just long enough to send a thrill up my thighs to land where I'm pressed against him.

"Can't have you falling off," he says, his fingers trailing slowly down my bare calves before he leans forward to start the engine.

He twists the throttle a couple of times before we lurch forward suddenly. I squeal, nearly unseated. Instinctively, I wind my arms around Tag's waist in a death grip. I feel his chuckle rumble through his back and into my chest more than I actually hear it. "That's better."

I hide my smile against the warm, smooth skin of his shoulder. I have to admit that I agree with him—this *is* better. Being so close to him, feeling so protected by him. It just feels *right* to be wrapped around Tag this way. I'm tall for a woman, but he's so much bigger and taller, I fit him perfectly. Like we were made for each other. I can't help wondering if he notices it, too.

I have to roll my eyes at my own sappy thoughts. In some ways, I feel like a teenage girl with a crush, a crush that drags the object of my infatuation into every waking thought and fantasy. I'll have to draw the line if I start writing *Mrs. Tag Barton* on napkins and notebooks, though.

We dart off down a well-worn path that cuts through a field that is slated for expansion. Tag stops and explains his vision for the new crop he wants to plant, reminding me of the grapes we tasted earlier. "I never got around to letting you taste some of the wine. *Some*body was tempting me with something even sweeter," Tag says with a playfully pointed look over his shoulder in my direction.

"Don't look at me! I was just there for the grapes."

"You were?" he asks, feigning insult. Then, without warning, he twists further in his seat, grabs my chin between his thumb and forefinger and kisses me again. It's short and hot and right next door to violent. It takes my breath away, and when he sinks his teeth into my bottom lip before letting me go, my entire lower half bursts into flame.

I gasp.

"Uhhh," he groans, swiping my lip with his tongue as though he's soothing away the sting. "I love the little noises you make. So damn sexy."

"That's what happens when you bite me," I say absently, embarrassingly breathless and addled.

"Then I'll have to bite you more often," he declares, leaning closer to nip gently at the skin along my neck. Chills spread down my arms and the muscles between my legs squeeze deliciously. When he pulls away, he's wearing a wry grin. "But I'll have to hold off until later."

"Why is that?" I can't even muster the composure to pretend that I don't want him to continue.

"Any more of that and I'm liable to embarrass myself." His grin is self-deprecating. Tag is clearly the kind of man who's used to a lot of attention and he doesn't seem like the kind to lose control easily. The thought that I might push him to that point makes me feel oddly powerful.

"We can't have that, now, can we?"

"Not when I'm trying to impress you."

"Why are you trying to impress me?"

"I'm not used to women like you."

"Women like me?"

"Yeah, women like you." I want to ask exactly what kind of woman that *is*, but Tag gives the corner of my mouth a quick kiss and then turns around in his seat, ready to take me to the next stop.

"This is probably new since you were here last," he says, pausing on the crest of a hill that looks down on twelve long, new rows of vines surrounding a half-finished cottage. I can already see the cozy comfort of it taking shape, though, right down to the wide porch that faces west, overlooking the steep mountainside.

"It's beautiful!"

"Thank you. I can't wait to finish it."

"You're building it?"

Tag turns a mildly outraged look on me. "Why is that so surprising?"

"I just didn't . . . I didn't realize you were a man of so many talents. That's all."

His expression melts into the sensually aware one I'm finding so unnerving. "Oh, you have no idea."

The sun is slanting in on half his face, allowing me to see his eyes behind his glasses. I see them flicker down to my mouth and then back to my eyes. "That kiss back there? That was the Blanc du Bois kiss. Light with some bite. But these are the new merlot vines. They're dark and deep in color, so any kissing here should reflect that, don't you think?"

He's leaning toward me very slowly, giving anticipation plenty of time to collect into a liquid ball in the center of my stomach. I'm so focused on his mouth drawing close that I don't even see his real intent coming. Tag grips me around the waist and hauls me around and into his lap, my legs automatically straddling him. Heat pours into my cheeks at my position, but I don't have one second longer to think about it before Tag is consuming me once again.

He drives his fingers up into my hair, holding me still for the crush of his mouth on mine. This kiss *is* different. It *is* dark and deep. Tag's lips open mine, his tongue shooting hot and ready between them. It licks relentlessly along mine, coaxing and convincing, begging me to give up all thought and control to him.

And I do.

I'm completely lost in sensation when his hands skate down my body to settle at my hips. His fingers dig in and urge my lower body closer to his, rubbing me along the ridge of his very obvious erection. I sigh into his kiss and his answering groan vibrates through the moist recesses of my mouth.

"Damn you," he growls when he wrenches his lips away. Before I can respond, Tag pulls me into his body again, grinding his hardness between my legs. I gasp, my back arching involuntarily. "You're gonna make me embarrass myself anyway, aren't you?"

"Th-this embarrasses you?" I ask, my core on fire with want. I don't even have the energy to feel ashamed or to second-guess what I'm doing. I wanted to let go, and the moment I did, Tag was right there to catch me. To catch me and to make sure that I couldn't think twice.

"To act like a damn horny teenager every time I see you? To have my cock come throbbing to life every time I think of you?" He releases my hips and I wish for a second that he hadn't, that we could sneak into the half-finished cabin and finish what we started. His boyish grin doesn't help to settle me down either. "It's not the most flattering thing for a man not to be able to control his own body when he's around a woman. But you're not just any woman, are you?" He studies me with those hypnotic eyes of his and I feel myself falling further and further under his spell. "You're a woman with a body made for sin and a mind full of delicate sensibilities."

"I don't have delicate sensibilities."

"I'd bet my life that you do."

"Well then maybe I don't want to have them while I'm *here*." And I don't. I don't want to be the same old Weatherly. The same old cautious, self-sacrificing Weatherly I've always been. This might be the last time in my life I'll have a chance to be who I want to be, to do what I want to do. I'll be damned if I'm going to waste it.

I reach for Tag's glasses, pulling them off so that I can see his swirling silver eyes. Even in the light, the pupils are dilated.

His expression isn't playful anymore. He watches me with all the seriousness in the world.

"Do you want to be a risk-taker, Weatherly?" he asks, his voice as dark and deep as the kiss and the merlot grapes. "Do you *really* want me to push you?"

My insides quiver. I nod, afraid that my voice will tremble with the last little bit of uncertainty that I'm hanging on to.

"Starting now?"

I nod again, my pulse picking up the pace.

Slowly, purposefully, his eyes never leaving mine, Tag raises his hand to my left shoulder. He slips one finger under the strap of my tank top and starts to ease it down my arm. I'm immediately uncomfortable, my instincts telling me to stop him, to cover myself. They remind me that we are out in the open and that I hardly know him. They tell me to stop him.

But his eyes tell me not to. They dare me to hold still and let him push me.

So I do.

Tag repeats the movement with my bra strap, tugging it down my arm until my breast sits in the cup like my flesh is being offered to him on the half-shell.

He drags his finger along the strap until he meets the lace of the cup. His eyes are still holding mine, daring me, pushing me. And then he pulls. One short, sharp pull that forces the material over the stiff peak of my nipple.

I gasp, responding to the action itself, the sensation of air and sun on my bare breast, the eroticism of what he's doing, out in the open, all the while watching me. We stare at each other as he brushes his thumb over me, each stroke resonating in my sex as though he's touching me there. Like I want him to. God, how I want him to.

Then Tag drops his gaze. I can almost feel it the instant it clicks to a stop on my nipple. My muscles tense, my blood boils, and the hiss of air through his teeth only exacerbates it.

He leans forward just enough to capture the tip between his lips, laving it with his tongue in a chaste way that makes me ache even deeper. I want to grab his head and force myself into his mouth, but I dare not. We are *still* out in the open and I am *still* trying to shake my sensibilities.

So I let him torture me with soft, slow circles and light, short licks until he lifts his head and rights my bra and tank. "Very good, fair Weatherly," he murmurs, licking his lips. "*Very* good."

"I told you," I tell him breathlessly, more than a little proud of myself.

"You did. But I'm not nearly finished with you," he states, reaching behind me and revving the engine. The grin that slides across his lips is pure wickedness. "Better hold on tight."

I realize with a shrill squeal, when he guns the accelerator and we take off flying back up the path, that he meant it literally and figuratively.

EIGHT

Tag

It's ironic that this woman, this woman who's been raised in the world that I so deeply resent, would be the one who makes me feel free from it. At least temporarily. We hate it for different reasons, of course, but I think that we can forget about it in the same way— by drowning it. Drowning it in this hot-as-hell attraction between us. And, soon, *drowning it out* with down-and-dirty sex. God, I can't wait. My teeth are on edge and my cock is hard as a damn concrete block just thinking about getting inside her. What she'll feel like and look like and taste like.

There's no question that she's on board with this. It's foreign to her, I suspect, but maybe that's why it works. She can be whoever the hell she wants to be while she's here with me. And I'm happy to let her. If we met under different circumstances, I get the feeling she wouldn't be nearly as friendly and amenable to spending time with me. Or if she were, her family wouldn't be. I know all about them. They're a big problem for me, in ways they don't even realize. But I didn't know all about *her*. At least not like I'm getting ready to. I'll know her inside and out, what she likes and what she loves before this day is done.

And it can't get done fast enough.

NINE

Weatherly

Before we could enjoy the rest of our trip and the picnic he'd packed, Tag got called away for some business he had to tend to down in Enchantment. I tried to hide my disappointment, but he saw it anyway. He threaded his fingers into my hair and held me still, his eyes pouring down into mine like a mercury spill. "If I didn't *have to* tend to this, I wouldn't leave you. I'd like nothing more than to spend all day kissing you. These lips . . . Jesus!"

He kissed me, making his desire for me clear, but it was his eyes that told me that he, too, was as disappointed as I was. When he released me, he backed away, his eyes on mine, his lips slightly curved. He only made it a few steps before he stepped forward to kiss me again, that time with more heat. But then he did leave, promising to find me when he got back. That was hours ago.

I thought Tag's business was Chiara, but considering the turmoil my family's holdings have been in during recent months, maybe he's been smart enough to make other investments along the way. Although charming to a fault, I get the impression that Tag is a shrewd businessman. His plans for Chiara, a vineyard that he has no control over, is a testament to his passion for the land, but also his head for growth and development.

The knock at my door is hushed, but I hear it instantly. Part of me has been resisting sleep, waiting, hoping Tag would come to me. I know it's insane—and slutty and irresponsible—to want to sleep with a guy that I hardly know and just met, but I don't want to think about that. I don't want to think *at all*. I want to feel. Just feel. For once, I want to do something that's only for me. No one else. I want to do something that's completely spontaneous, totally irresponsible and entirely questionable in every possible way. My mother would be shocked. My father would be angry. But for once, I want to consider only myself, what *I* want, what makes *me* happy.

Before I can call out in answer, the door creaks open and Tag slips in. He is shirtless, wearing only low-hanging jeans and nothing else. Not even shoes. As he walks, his abs clench, the stair-steps drawing my eyes down his belly to the dramatic cuts of muscle that disappear in a V into his waistband.

I sit up as he approaches. He doesn't say a word, just reaches for my hand. I curl my willing fingers around his and let him pull me from the warmth of my bed. My heart is hammering beneath my breastbone and desire is coiling inside my stomach. The time is at hand, the moment has arrived. It's do or die with this man I've known for a day and can't stop thinking about. Am I going to go down this road with him? Am I going to jump without weighing the risk? Without being able to predict the outcome?

I can feel in my bones that this is my last chance to change my mind. Something is going to happen tonight, and if I don't stop now, there will be no stopping later.

When Tag tugs on my hand, urging me to follow him back to the door, my feet know the answer before my mind does. They follow him without thought, without qualm. Without caution. And just like that, my decision is made. I'm going. And I'm not looking back.

Tag leads me silently through the house, down the stairs and through the kitchen to the back door, holding open the screen until I pass through. It hisses slowly shut behind me as we step out into the night.

A soft, warm rain is falling, but I barely feel it. Every nerve, every sense, every thought is focused squarely on the man in front of me, leading me. To where, I don't know, but I can't wait to find out.

We walk across the yard, the wet grass teasing my toes and tickling my ankles. Tag's hand is warm and solid around mine, his smile reassuring when he glances back at me. His face is shadowed in the pale moonlight, giving him an air of mystery that he doesn't need. He's already mysterious. Enigmatic in the way he has captured my interest so completely, so effortlessly.

The grass changes to smooth dirt as we pass into the first row of grapevines. My captor pulls me gently along until we are four rows deep, an island in the darkness of the night, and then he stops and turns to face me.

"Close your eyes," he whispers, his voice as velvety as the onyx sky above.

I obey without question, my breath coming in quick, anxious bursts.

"Now, take a slow, deep breath," he instructs. And so I do.

That's when I smell it.

It's sweetly aromatic with just a hint of sin drifting around the edges. The grapes scent the air with a fruity musk that is as delicious as it is sexy.

"They only smell this way when it rains at night. I don't know why, but it's like they come alive in the dark. In the warm, wet dark."

When I open my eyes to find Tag's stormy silver ones, the perfume roots in my chest. It grows there as though the bud of everything that is between us—the sweet, the sexy, the forbidden—is blossoming like a rose in the sunshine. Spreading its petals within me. Driving its thorns into me. Holding me. Trapping me.

"Say yes."

I don't have to ask what he wants me to say yes to. I already know. I think I might've known the instant he showed up in my bathroom doorway and stole my breath, my logic, my caution.

He waits. But not patiently. I can feel eagerness, anticipation radiating from him like sound waves from a speaker, tickling my senses, teasing my sensibilities. He wants me to say yes. I *need* to say yes, but still he's leaving it up to me.

I take one step toward him, bringing my chest flush with his, my stomach pressing to his all the way to the impressive bulge I feel below his waist.

"Show me," I murmur. The moment the words leave my lips, I feel him tighten against me, as though his every muscle is straining to get to me, but he's holding himself back.

Tag bends and sweeps me into his arms. I can see the wicked flash of his teeth in his tanned face before he says, "I hope you don't mind getting dirty."

Before I can answer, he drops to his knees and lays me gently on my back in the soft, wet mud. When he stretches out on top of me, I sink ever so slightly as though we are cocooned within the earth itself. Protected. I smell only the sweetness of the grapes, I hear only the muted patter of the rain, I see only Tag. *Feel* only Tag. It's as though, in this grove, on this night, we are hidden away from all the world.

Resting his weight on his forearms, Tag cups my face with his hands. In his eyes is all the desire I feel for him, harnessed carefully so that it doesn't lash out and hurt me. "You'll never look at these grapes the same way after tonight," he whispers. "I promise you that."

And then his lips find mine. They brush once and retreat, brush again and retreat. His tongue slips out to tease the crease of my mouth and his fingers hold my face prisoner. Not that I would want to escape. I want this with everything in me.

I can't resist sneaking out to taste *of him* with my tongue, too. He lets me line the inside of his lower lip, holds perfectly still so that I can explore him. I revel in the irresistible essence of him. When he's had enough, he draws my tongue into his mouth and sucks gently, sensually. I moan reflexively and, just like it did earlier, my reaction seems to unleash something within him. His demeanor goes from quiet curiosity to fierce need.

He drives his fingers into my hair and fists them, tilting my head just so in order that he can devour me. He wedges one knee between my legs, forcing them apart to accommodate him. The feel of his body pressed so intimately to mine is nearly my undoing.

But there's more. So much more.

As his tongue tangles with mine, Tag flexes his hips, rubbing the long ridge of his erection into the apex of my thighs. "I want you so damn bad I can't even sleep," he hisses between clenched teeth, as though his need of me is more than he can bear. And to be wanted like this . . . by a man like him . . . it sets free a burning wildness within me that I never knew existed.

I raise one leg to wrap around his waist, tipping up my hips to press into his hardness. He wrenches his mouth away from mine and levers his upper body away from mine, up onto his hands so he can arch his back and rock his cock against me.

I gasp, sensation running through me like the rain is running down my face. I close my eyes for a few seconds, exulting in the abandon that has taken over me. When I open them again, I see Tag staring down at me, hunger written all over his face.

He lifts one muddy hand and palms my cheek, dragging his fingertips down my neck to the thin strap of my nightie. He does it purposefully, passionately, like he's marking me, each streak the bold evidence of his possession.

He tugs down the strap, exposing one pleading nipple, baring it for his ravishment. And ravish, he does. With his hips circling against mine, he pulls my flesh into his mouth and sucks. Sucks so hard that I gasp again, unable to censor my body's response.

Suddenly, he sits up. He fists both of his filthy hands in the low neck of my top and jerks, splitting it all the way down the front. His chest heaves as he watches warm rain splatter on my naked flesh. It softly pounds my breasts and gently teases my spread folds. The wet stimulation coupled with the hot flames of Tag's eyes on me brings moisture flooding to the ache between my legs.

"No panties?" he asks, his voice gruff. "I love a dirty girl, but I want you dirtier," he growls, rubbing his hands in the mud and dragging them from the valley of my breasts all the way down my stomach. He stops just below my navel and soils his hands again, rubbing them in the mud and then grabbing my hips. Roughly, he digs in with his fingers and he pulls me toward him, bringing my body into sharp contact with his denim-clad erection again. "I want to see my hand prints all over you. When you look in the mirror, I want you to remember what it feels like to have my hands on you. My mouth on you."

He dirties his hands one last time and presses them to the insides of my thighs, spreading me further as he slides down between them. The first scrape of his tongue over my throbbing sex is like lightning. I jerk against him, my legs clamping around his shoulders. That only fuels Tag. He presses his open mouth to me, opening and closing, opening and closing, as though he wants to consume me. And I want to be consumed.

He licks with long, slow strokes and then sucks my clit into his mouth, his fingers digging into my butt to hold me still for his sensual assault. And when I can't take it for another second, writhing in the wet, slippery mud, he relents, moving down to slip his tongue deep inside me as if in apology for driving me mad.

Over and over, he licks and sucks, he teases and torments,

until I'm delirious with need, my skin a fevered blanket barely covering the nerves that are screaming his name. The light rain bathes my face, the sweet grapes scent the air and the heat of Tag surrounds me. I'm invaded by this moment, by this man. Invaded, body and soul.

As I spiral toward a shadowy peak that only my body knows, Tag pauses, releasing me as he sheds his jeans, cleaning his hands on them before he rattles a condom wrapper. I glance down at him, his eyes trained on me rather than what he's doing. They gleam like puffs of pale smoke in the moonlight, challenging the beauty of her half-full globe above. She is ethereal. *He* is magnificent. He is a pagan god preparing to take what's his. I am the willing sacrifice, laid at the altar of his perfection.

Water sluices down his wide chest, trailing over the ridges of his abdomen before parting to run around either side of his thick cock. My insides quiver as I take him in—so strong, so long, so proud. My sex squeezes in anticipation.

Tag rolls the condom into place, sheathing his massive length, and then places his hands on my knees. Gently, he presses them apart until I spread fully for him. Not once do his eyes leave mine as he crawls up my body to settle on top of me.

I feel the engorged head of him prodding at my entrance. My body sucks greedily at it, eager to have him inside me.

"I've thought about this from the moment I saw you washing these beautiful breasts in the tub," he says, sparing a light kiss to the swell of one mound before he continues. "I've thought about what it would feel like to slide my cock into you, of how I'd like to do it for the first time with the taste of you still lingering on my tongue. And now here we are," he says, easing the tip of his thickness into me. "It's just as perfect as I imagined it would be."

I hiss as he eases in a little more, stretching me, stretching me, stretching me, almost to the point of a bit of pain. He must know, too.

"A little pain never felt so good, did it, fair Weatherly? Do you know how I know that?" he asks, his voice dark chocolate. Rich cream. Black silk.

"H-how?" I pant, wanting him to stop, but praying that he won't.

"Because of these," he says, bending his head to swirl his tongue around one of my rock-hard nipples. "They tell me you like it. They tell me you want me to keep going. You do, don't you? You want to feel every bit of me? You want to feel me all the way inside you, don't you?"

Oh God! I squeeze my eyes shut, my body clutching and sucking at his even as he threatens to tear me apart.

Slowly, he continues, steadily pressing more and more of himself into me as his lips and tongue work magic at my breasts.

Lava is pouring through me and I'm drifting higher and higher on its hot wave. When Tag begins to rock against me, forcing himself a little deeper and rubbing my clit with the most delicious friction imaginable, the heat within me blazes out of control.

I gasp and moan uncontrollably, my tongue dry but for the rain that soaks its parched surface. Blood buzzes through my ears, blotting out every sound except for the purr of Tag's voice at my ear. "Are you ready?" he whispers. "Because you feel *so* ready."

All I can do is nod and hold on. So that's what I do. I curl my fingers into the mud and I wind my trembling legs around Tag's narrow hips, bracing for what's to come.

With one withdrawal that takes him almost completely out of me, Tag thrusts back in, filling me up so completely that it pushes air out of my lungs in a huff. He swallows my exhalation with a hungry kiss as my body gives up its fight and begins its tumble over the edge.

Tag rides me in hard, deep strokes, unrelenting. His tongue tangles with mine and I raise my fingers to dig into his back. He groans into my mouth when my body fists around his in one tight squeeze. He knows where I am. He knows where I'm going. He flexes his hips and grinds against me, forcing me higher onto the crest.

And then I'm lost. Splintering. Flying.

My body begins to ripple rhythmically around his and Tag yanks his mouth away. His eyes bore down into mine, surprise reflected in them. "Oh shit, I can't stop! I can't stop," he breathes desperately, straightening his arms and pumping his body into mine. "Weatherly!" he growls, arching his back sharply.

And then I feel it.

The first pulse of his orgasm throbs into me, throwing me back into a second release that sends electricity shooting all the way to my fingertips.

Ruthlessly, he pounds his body into mine until his tension eases. I feel it as his climax calms. The pulses come slower and slower and his rhythm changes to a long, deep push that presses my body into the mud. The sodden earth sucks at my back as Tag drags over my front, caressing every inch of my skin with his own.

Wetly, he slides over me, into me until we are both limp and drenched, covered in vineyard earth and filled with the delicious cocktail of our combined release. When he collapses on top of me, I close my eyes and listen to his ragged breathing, trying desperately to bring my own under control.

Every detail of this moment sears itself onto my brain—the fragrance of the grapes, the tap of the rain, the cool of the mud, the dark of the night. Permeating each of those fragments is the feel of Tag within me, his weight atop me, his desire moving through me. He holds the pieces together like a thread that weaves in and around every sight, every sound, every feeling.

Of all the things that I imagined this moment might be, of all the sensations that I imagined this moment might hold, this is more. So much more. It's more than I can process. More than I can explain. More than I've ever before experienced. Emotions assail me. Feelings assault me. Words fail me. Except for one. It loops through my mind in lazy circles, like a melted figure eight.

Wow.

Wow.

Wow!

I know that I'm not alone in this when Tag lifts his dark head and pins me with his languid gray stare. "Damn," he says simply, one corner of his mouth curling up appreciatively.

I can't help smiling. "That's just what I was thinking."

TEN

Tag

I'm a night owl, a light sleeper and an early riser. There isn't much that escapes my notice, awake or asleep. I heard Weatherly's car the day she arrived, despite my distance from the drive, just like I heard the car arrive this morning.

Last night, after I marked her ten ways from Sunday, I carried a wet, muddy, naked Weatherly back to the house and straight into the shower. I hated to wash my handprints off her. I liked seeing them there. A lot. But damn if I didn't like washing them off her almost as much. At first she just stood under the warm spray like she was too boneless to move, but as soon as my soapy hands found her big, heavy breasts, she wasn't so boneless anymore.

I've never met a woman who responds so intensely to my slightest touch, my softest whisper, my lightest kiss. But Weatherly does. Maybe that's why, even as I crept out of her room this morning, I was hard with the need for more. Maybe that's why I turned around and went right back inside, peeled the covers off her naked body and climbed back into bed with her. I don't think she was fully awake when I rolled her onto her stomach and pressed her down into the mattress. I don't think she was fully aware of what I was doing when I slipped my fingers inside her. But that might've been the best part. She was already wet, like she was just waiting for me to come back to her.

"Fair Weatherly," I'd whispered in her ear as I fingered her from behind. She'd moaned, raising her hips to give me better access. "Please tell me you're on some kind of birth control."

"I . . . I am," she answered breathlessly. I almost lost it right on the spot. "I-I'm clean, too," she'd panted. I told her I was tested regularly and everything was fine.

By that time, she was riding my fingers all the way to my knuckles and my hand was wet halfway up my palm.

"Oh God," she'd whispered, and I could feel her squeezing me tighter and tighter. That's when I pulled her hips up off the bed and eased my cock into her as deep as it would go. She came as soon as I entered her and I think I came about ten seconds later, with her milking me the whole time.

That tight little pussy . . . God!

I was still breathing hard, still buried balls deep inside her, when she fell back to sleep. That time, I *did* manage to leave and not come back. Now here I am, on my way back to the house after checking the east field for evidence of glassy winged sharpshooters, an insect that can mean death to an entire crop of grapes. They've been particularly bad in some areas this year and if they spread

Pierce's disease, it's all over but the crying. My mind isn't as focused on the grapes as it should be, though. I've been picking at a little corner of guilt that sprang up right after I left Weatherly. I can't help wondering how differently this would be playing out if she knew everything about me, about my past. Even about my present. But I can't tell her those things. At least not yet.

That's when I heard the motor. Now I'm watching dust puff up behind the rear bumper of the silver car, wondering to myself who the hell brings a Bentley up into the mountains. Even William O'Neal, Weatherly's father, has enough sense not to do that.

A vague sense of dread and irritation seeps in to suffocate the satisfaction and contentment I'd been feeling since leaving Weatherly's room. Something tells me I won't like what I find when I get back.

And I don't.

I hear voices when I walk through the kitchen. One of them is Weatherly's. It's barely recognizable. It's stiff and cool, although still remarkably pleasant despite it. I'm already bristling at whoever decided to intrude upon our morning before I even walk out into the foyer.

I clear my throat when they're within view. Both Weatherly and the guest, the guy with whom she is obviously familiar, turn toward me. On her face is fear. Fear and the same dread I was feeling on the walk back to the house. She still looks like the beautiful creature I left sleeping in her bed, only now she has this cornered look about her, like a predator found her while her protector was away. That much is easy to see.

I tear my eyes away from her in favor of assessing the threat. The man she's talking to reeks of money. Everything from his two-hundred-dollar haircut to his thousand-dollar shoes speaks of power and influence. I would estimate him to be in his early forties, the touch of gray at his temples making him look distinguished rather than weak. His blue eyes are as shrewd and sharp as the lines of his tailored black suit, and his diamond cufflinks sparkle when he extends his hand.

"Michael Stromberg," he says, his polite yet distant voice cutting into the tense silence.

I don't hurry to reach him. I saunter slowly across the marble and stop closer to Weatherly. I reach out and cut my palm across his, giving it a hard squeeze and two sharp pumps before releasing it. When I retrieve my hand, I have to cross my arms over my chest to keep from drawing Weatherly against my side like I want to do.

"Tag Barton. What brings you to Chiara, Mr. Stromberg?" I ask boldly. I have no right to question anyone, of course, but I don't give a damn.

"I'm here to see Weatherly," he replies, his statement as much a challenge as it is an answer.

I glance down at the woman in question, the one who is now looking up at me with panic in her eyes. The quiet grows around me. It snaps and snarls and writhes with antagonism from Stromberg and supplication from Weatherly.

Her sparkling amethyst eyes are begging me to save her, even though I doubt she thinks I can. And I want to. Damn, how I want to.

That's when it hits me—how to solve all sorts of problems in ten short seconds. If only Weatherly will go along with it.

There's risk in doing it this way, but risk has never mattered to me. What's worth having that isn't worth taking a risk for?

So I go for it. Because that's just who I am. I am my father's son.

"You can speak freely in front of me, Mr. Stromberg. My fiancée and I have no secrets."

I'd swear I could hear a pin drop all the way down in Enchantment.

ELEVEN

Weatherly

I'm so stunned at first that I just stare up into Tag's handsome face, wondering what the hell is happening behind his winsome smile. My mind stutters along. I was still in a sluggish stupor from Tag's loving when I came down to find Michael in the foyer. All I wanted to do was turn around and go back upstairs, back to the sore yet satisfied place I woke to.

"Weatherly?" comes Michael's questioning voice. When I don't answer, he becomes more insistent. "Weatherly!"

That brings me to razor-sharp focus for some reason. He sounds so much like my father, that chastising tone all but ordering me to pay attention, do the right thing, make the right decision. *For the family.* Always for the family.

It's for that reason that I cling to the life preserver—or at least the time extender—that Tag threw to me. The lie springs easily to my mind and pours quickly from my lips, too quickly for me to have second thoughts.

"Michael, I'm sorry. I was going to tell you. That's why I came up here. I knew I had to get some things straightened out. Figure out what I'm going to do."

"You mean to tell me that you're *engaged* to this man?"

I nod hesitantly, wondering *now* what the hell is happening behind *my* winsome smile. Only I'm not wearing a winsome smile. I imagine I'm wearing something closer to a hideous cringe. Dear God, what have I done?

"Since when? Why didn't your father tell me?"

"Probably because he doesn't know."

Michael's eyes narrow suspiciously. "And I'm supposed to believe this?"

That strikes a nerve. I struggle to keep my voice calm and well modulated, like a good O'Neal would. "Why wouldn't you? Why wouldn't you believe that, after a lifetime of following *to the letter* rules set over my life that I had no say in, that I'd want to do something rebellious? That I'd want to have something of my own, that my family had nothing to do with, no knowledge of? Why is that so hard to believe?"

I'm satisfied that I held on to my cool with both hands, yet still let Michael know in no uncertain terms that I'm not going to be walked all over this time.

"Because that's something a silly girl would do, and you are no silly girl."

"No, I'm not, am I? I never have been. Not even when it was acceptable, expected even, to be a silly girl. I've never been able to just be myself. I've always had to be what everyone else wanted me to be."

"Until you met me," Tag says quietly from my side. In my impassioned debate with Michael, I'd almost forgotten he was there. The man who is, at once, offering me the means to save myself and hang myself, depending on which way this goes.

But he's right about one thing: He hasn't wanted me to be anything other than what I showed up here being. Not once. He only wanted me. Just Weatherly.

"Until I met you," I reply softly.

"Well, it will be very interesting to see what your father has to say about this when he gets here."

My heart pumps blood that now feels like cold concrete throughout my entire body, cementing my muscles and freezing me where I stand. "My father is coming?"

"Yes. He wanted to surprise you."

Oh, I'm surprised, all right.

"How did he know I was here?"

Michael's gaze shifts from me to Tag and back again. "Maybe he knew of a reason you'd come here."

That might make sense to Michael, but it doesn't to me. This engagement is all of three minutes old. There's no reason for my father to think I'd come here. Although I *have* always loved it, I haven't been to Chiara in years.

"I don't suppose I'd be entirely surprised. That man seems to know everything," I say, my tone more than a little dry. All my life, there was no escaping the all-seeing, all-knowing eyes of William O'Neal. It appears that, in all these years, nothing has changed.

The silence that follows drags on until it swells and surges through the room, threatening to drown me in an ocean of unsaid things.

"Michael, I . . . I'm sorry," I offer. And I am. For all his similarities to my father, he really *is* a nice guy and I really *do* believe that he cares for me. As much as one can care for someone who is merely a business arrangement, a business arrangement that one happens to find physically attractive, that is. "I never meant to hurt you. I just . . . I always wanted to marry *for me*. Just for me. I needed time to figure things out."

I'm sure he is under no delusions as to what I'm figuring out. He must know that my choice is between a man I (presumably) love and a man who is the better fit for my family. While in most of Western society the decision would be a no-brainer, in my privileged, cutthroat world, nothing is quite so simple.

Michael's smile is polite and tolerant, much like a father who is struggling for patience in dealing with his willful daughter. And that's what our dynamic would be—I'd be going from one controlling man who expects me to never buck my place in our world right into the arms of another who feels the same way. The expectations are the same for all the wives of men like this. It's bred into us. And we are bred into this world.

"Fine, if that's what you need to come to the right decision, you have it. If you'll show me to a guest room, I'd like a shower to wash away the grime." He makes a point of glancing at Tag, as if to say that *he* is the reason for the grime rather than his trip here from Atlanta.

"Of course," I say, extricating myself from Tag's hold. I hadn't even realized he'd pressed up close to my side and slid his arm around my waist. I felt so comfortable there, it felt so natural there that I hadn't even noticed. Which is odd because thus far I've been inordinately attuned to his every move. Maybe it's because, at this moment, I needed comfort. And that's what he was providing.

"I was just on my way upstairs to our room. I can show him on my way," Tag offers with a pleasantly innocent smile.

I swallow hard at the "our room" part, but manage to keep a calm curve to my own lips. "Oh, well thank you."

My last glance at Michael shows that he is in no way pleased by this turn of events, but he says nothing, merely picks up his bag and follows Tag up the stairs. Even now, it's all about the show, the breeding.

I watch until the two men disappear. My unease worsens and I wish now that I'd at least offered to go along. Wondering about what's being said up there is incredibly unnerving.

Ten minutes pass with excruciating sluggishness. When ten turn into fifteen, I start pacing. As I make my way to the kitchen and back again, my thoughts begin to slip automatically into hostess mode despite the "let it go" attitude I arrived with. I'm thinking of what refreshments to offer Michael and what to suggest for lunch. And dinner. And every meal on every day, all the way up until my father and his crony depart.

I'm just about to pick up the phone and dial for Stella when I remember her color and her failing health. I can't very well ask her to tend to the house and the cooking and ask her to see to our guest when she's all but dying.

I take out my cell phone and start trolling the Internet for a replacement service down in Enchantment. I'm just about to dial when a knock sounds at the back door. It's odd for *anyone* who's unfamiliar with Chiara to be going around back.

I find a pretty, petite redhead in neat black pants and a stiff, spotless white shirt standing on the steps. She's clutching a clipboard to her chest.

"May I help you?" I ask, opening the screen door as well.

"I'm Cher Young. I'm from Concierge Services in Enchantment. Is Mr. Barton available?"

What in the world?

"Um, yes, of course. Please come in." I step back into the kitchen as the woman enters. "Let me get Tag for you."

"Get Tag for who?" Tag asks, strolling in just as I turn. He looks heart-stopping in a white button-up shirt, faded jeans and hair still wet from his shower. He smiles at Cher, rolling his sleeves up his tanned forearms as he approaches. "Tag Barton," he explains, holding out his hand.

"Uh, Cher Young. Y-you called about some housekeeping and gourmet services, I believe." I almost feel sorry for the young woman. She looks as though she's having trouble thinking at the moment. She's trying not to stare and failing miserably. Of course, I can't really blame her. Tag is truly one of the most gorgeous men I've ever seen. Ever.

"I did. Thank you for coming so quickly." He turns his smile on me. My knees get weak accordingly. Damn the man! How does he do that? "This is Weatherly O'Neal. She's the lady of the house. She's had some unexpected guests. One is here now and more are on the way. She'll be the one to give you instruction on what meals she wants prepared and what housekeeping services she'll be in need of."

"Yes, sir," Cher says, still grappling with her composure. She blinks several times when she looks down, as though she's stared too long at the sun and is trying to rid her vision of the residual bright spots. "I, uh, we can certainly take care of whatever needs you might have. We are full service and offer twenty-four-hour coverage if you'd have a need of—"

"I don't think we're in that bad a shape. I think day and evening coverage should suffice, don't you, Weatherly?"

Is that laughter I see in his eyes? Does he find my discombobulation amusing?

"I agree. I think we can make do with someone in the mornings and again in the late afternoon to prepare dinner and such."

Cher nods. "We're happy to provide that. I just have a few details I'll need and then I have some paperwork for you to look over."

"Of course, I—"

The bang of a car door out front has me stiffening all over again. That has to be my father.

Tag, ever observant, notices immediately. "Go," he says, tipping his head toward the foyer. "I'll take care of this. You can make a list of what you want for tomorrow. Cher and I can take care of today."

I'm torn. I need to go greet my father, but I want to stay and work out the details with Cher. The last thing I need is for the household to appear to be falling apart because of Tag's sick mother. My father is already going to be very unhappy about this situation. The last thing I need to do is give him a reason to toss them all out the door.

I have to admit to wanting to hang around in here because of Cher's overly bright smile, too. As Tag explains what he'd like prepared for lunch and dinner (which actually sounds quite delicious), Cher watches him with stars in her eyes. She keeps taking deep breaths, which only draws attention to the ample chest straining against the linen of her shirt.

I curse the stab of jealousy as I make my way out of the kitchen and into the foyer to greet my father. I stop just before I step out into his line of sight and take a cleansing, calming breath, reminding myself that I'm a grown woman and this is *my* fate we're dealing with, too.

I feel more prepared to face William O'Neal after my ten-second pep talk. My smile is perfectly polite and unruffled when I step out into the foyer. "Hi, Dad," I say, catching my father just as he steps through the door.

"Weatherly, Weatherly," he says, shaking his head, his tone rife with disappointment.

He has no idea just how disappointed he's going to be on this trip, I think to myself as I give him my cheek.

Let the games begin.

TWELVE

Tag

Cher is interested. Very interested. I can see it in the way she licks her pouty lips so often. I can see it in the way she sat up a little straighter, just enough to emphasize her plump tits, when Weatherly left the room. I can see it in the way she smiles at almost everything I say. She's being professional for the most part, but if we were meeting under different circumstances, I seriously doubt she'd be this discreet. I've known a hell of a lot of women like her. At this point, I can pick them out of a crowd. And while on any other day I'd probably make some arrangements to meet up with her later—or, hell, even take a little detour to the broom closet as I show her around the house—the only thing on my mind right now is Weatherly. With her in my head, I find it hard to really notice *anyone* else.

She's out there by herself trying to deal with her father. I've thrown a twist into the already-complicated relationship they obviously have. When he finds out about me, she's going to have an even bigger mess to clean up with him. He'll think I'm all wrong for her. She probably thinks so, too. Deep down, anyway. The problem is they're wrong about the things that make me inadequate for her *in their eyes*. They have no idea about the *real reasons* I'm wrong for her.

THIRTEEN

Weatherly

I haven't had a chance to speak to Dad privately since he got here. Our ten-second run-in standing in the foyer was quickly interrupted by Tag touring Cher through the house. He winked at me as he passed, and nodded to my father, but otherwise, he didn't pause in his chatter with the redhead.

"Who is that?" my father asked.

"Tag. You've met him before."

"Not Tag. I know Tag, for chrissake. The redhead. Who is that?"

"We are hiring a service to take care of the cooking and the housekeeping while you and Michael are here. Stella isn't well. She doesn't need to be tending to us right now."

At least my father had the good grace to appear worried and to express some concern. "Isn't well? What's the matter? It's nothing serious, I hope."

I went into a very brief explanation of her condition, to which he merely nodded and agreed that hiring out her duties was best. Before I could ask for a word in private, Michael had descended the stairs and, from that moment on, my time has been completely monopolized.

My father's desire to matchmake is at the root of it, no doubt. He probably suggested that he and Michael come up here so that we could get to know each other better in a more relaxed setting. And when Dad gets something in his head, it's nearly impossible to change his mind or alter his course. He's like a dog with a bone.

His first suggestion was that he take Michael on a tour of the buildings on the grounds. I was more than happy to let them have at it, but my father *insisted* that I go, too, citing my childhood love of Chiara and Michael appreciating my "enthusiasm." Politeness is too deeply ingrained in me to do anything more than simply smile and graciously agree, so that's what I did. No reason to make this any more uncomfortable and disagreeable than it already is. Or is likely going to get, once my father finds out about Tag.

We returned to find lunch set up on the east veranda. I wondered what Tag was up to, because I haven't seen a glimpse of him since he came through with Cher right after Dad arrived. I didn't have time to look for him, though, because my father called for the Jeep right after we ate. I thought maybe I'd see Tag when he brought it around, but it was just sitting at the top of the driveway, empty, with the keys in the ignition.

I sat in the back for the Jeep tour of the vineyard, enjoying the breeze coming through the open rear windows. It was when we passed the merlot field that the ache began.

As though I was experiencing it all over again, I could close my eyes and remember with perfect clarity every kiss, every touch, every word that transpired between Tag and me last night. He was right—I'll never look at those grapes the same way again.

Thankfully, the tour is over. I quickly excused myself to shower before dinner and took a moment to search the house for Tag. Again, he was nowhere to be found. Not even Stella, resting in her rooms at the caretaker's cabin, knew where he might be.

I stare at the bed as I strip off my clothes. My skin is sensitive. Tender, almost. And the ache that I've carried since the fields deepens to a need that throbs and pulses all the way through me. I moan softly at the pleasure/pain of thinking about Tag, of his hands and his mouth on me.

What the hell is wrong with me?

I don't bother with gathering clothes. I just head for the bathroom, hoping that a cool shower might ease my discomfort.

I turn on the spray and step in immediately, gasping at the shock of the cold water on my heated skin. I had an allergic reaction to antibiotics once when I was a little girl and this is what my skin felt like—as though even the air was too much stimulation. Only this, *this* is centered around my core. Every drop of water, every run of liquid down my body causes a reactive squeeze between my legs, a plea for release.

I grab the soap and roll it in my hands, determined to ease the discomfort any way that I can. I can't go through the evening this way. I'll just have to take care of things myself and hope that fixes me.

I barely hear the soft click of the shower door open and close. It isn't until I feel Tag's hands at my heavy breasts that I cry out. I'm surprised, yes, but the feel of him touching me, when I need it so, so badly, is enough to reduce me to a writhing mess in his arms.

He is pressed snugly to my back, his face tucked into the curve of my neck and his arms wrapped around me from behind. He rubs and tweaks and teases my nipples until I'm grinding my butt into the unforgiving granite of his erection.

"You missed me today, didn't you?" he whispers, nipping at my earlobe with his teeth. Even that seemingly innocuous action sends a bolt of electricity shooting to my sex. "Did you think about me when you rode through the fields? Did you ache from having me inside you so much last night?"

I nod, my mouth hanging open as I take in gulps of air and try not to bring the house down with all the sounds that are bubbling up in my chest.

One of Tag's hands slides down my wet stomach, pushing between my folds to slip a finger into me. "Were you thinking about having me here? About having my cock in you, stretching you tight?"

He thrusts his finger deep inside me, the pad of his thumb rubbing my clit with the action. Reflexively, my body ripples around him. My knees nearly buckle, I'm so close to orgasm.

"Oh, it's like that, huh?" he murmurs, crooking his finger inside me and slowly dragging it out. "I think I have just the thing for you."

I don't ask what he means. Honestly, I don't care as long as he doesn't stop touching me. Today has been torture without him, the memories of his touch enough to drive me mad with desire. I've never *needed* someone's touch this way. But I *need* Tag. I need to feel him inside me. I need to feel him wrapped around me. I just *need* Tag.

Gently, Tag turns me to face him. He bends down in front of me and hooks his arms through and around the backs of my thighs. I gasp when he pulls me off my feet. I feel like I'm going to fall backward; I wasn't prepared for him to pick me up. But I don't fall. Tag turns as he stands and presses my back into the cool shower wall, pinning me there with my legs wrapped around his head.

I don't have time to question what he's doing, because the moment I feel his tongue spear into my crease and circle my clit, my climax rolls through me like thunder. All I can do is hold on, my fingers fisting rhythmically in Tag's silky black hair. He works his mouth over me, his tongue, his teeth, prolonging my orgasm until I'm breathless and the room is spinning every time I open my eyes.

Before the spasms have subsided, Tag pulls my wet back down the wet wall, readjusting me in his grip until my legs are wrapped around his waist and his face is mere inches from mine.

"I hope you saved some for me," he says softly just before he takes my mouth and slams his cock into me.

He swallows the loud moan that escapes my throat upon his penetration. Never has anything felt so good as Tag buried so deeply inside me. There is only a flash of discomfort as I still stretch to accommodate him, but it's gone as quickly as it came, leaving only intense pleasure behind.

My body wrings his length with his every thrust, and with every thrust he triggers more wringing. It's an endless cycle of orgasmic delight that ends with Tag's desperate whispers in my ear, whispers that promise he's going to come and that he's thought all day about coming inside me again.

His words thrill me. The idea that he wants to pour himself into me this way, the idea that I hold a piece of him deep inside my body is so intimate, so erotic I wonder if I'll be able to think of anything else for the rest of the night.

When Tag finally releases me and lets my legs slowly straighten, he cups my cheek in his big palm and kisses the corner of my mouth.

"All through dinner, I want you to think about me, about how my warm come is still way up inside you. And I," he says, tracing my upper lip with the tip of his tongue, "I will be thinking about this shower, about how you came on my face with your back pressed to the wall."

I'm already getting breathless again when he takes my lips. His kiss is a mixture of satisfaction and promise and something fierce, like he wants to mark me as his own before I leave this room. It reminds me of what he said about seeing his muddy handprints on my body. He's possessive, and for some reason, as antiquated as the thought is, I like it. I want to be possessed by him. I want to be his and no one else's. And I love that he seems to want that, too.

Yes, I needed this. I needed *him*.

FOURTEEN

Tag

I hadn't planned on joining Weatherly, her father and her would-be fiancé for dinner. I figured there would be enough of a blowup without my help. In fact, Weatherly and I didn't even discuss it. We didn't exactly have food on our minds as much as we did other delicious edibles. But after I left, and the more I thought about that cool shower and her come in my mouth, the less appealing dinner without her became. Turns out that my idea of torturing *her* with thoughts of us ended up torturing me just as much. Besides, as far as they're concerned, she's my fiancée. My place is at her side, whether they like it or not. And until she calls off this charade, she's mine and Stromberg better damn well get used to it.

Now I find myself dressed in a silk shirt and slacks, headed toward the dining room for a fashionably late arrival to a dinner I wasn't invited to attend. My smile is one of anticipation, both to get under Stromberg's skin, but also to sit beside Weatherly and touch her oh-so-casually with fingers that were buried inside her only a short time before. That thought alone gives me much satisfaction.

When I stop in the doorway, all three people at the table glance up at me. William looks perplexed, Michael looks aggravated and Weatherly looks nervous yet deliciously flushed. I don't have to be a mind reader to know what she's thinking. In fact, if I think about her thoughts too long, I'll probably end up having to excuse myself. My dick seems to have lost its head when it comes to Weatherly. She can make me hard faster than a cowboy can say "spit." Damn the woman!

"Good to see you, Tag," William offers when the silence becomes uncomfortable. "What brings you here tonight?"

"Dinner. If that's all right," I say, glancing at Weatherly.

"Why wouldn't Weatherly's fiancé be welcome at the dinner table?" Michael interjects, one dark brow jerking up in challenge. I nod my head in a mute *touché*.

William's face starts to redden the instant he processes what was just said. "Weatherly, what's the meaning of this?"

"Um, well, I wanted to tell you about it in private, but we've been on the go since you got here."

"Tell me what?"

"Tag and I ar-are engaged."

To William's credit, he doesn't freak like I half expected him to. He just gets quiet. Very quiet. But it's easy to see by his rigid posture and the vein standing out in the center of his forehead that he's livid.

Finally, he glances to Michael and offers a tight yet pleasant, "Excuse us, please."

Then William gets up, tosses his napkin on the table and stalks out of the room, giving me an "eat shit" look as he passes.

I stop Weatherly with a hand to her arm when she reaches the doorway. "Will you be okay by yourself? I can come if . . ."

"I'll be fine," she says, impulsively rising up on her toes to give me a quick kiss. I'm sure that pisses both men the hell off, but I don't give a damn.

William stalks on ahead and when Weatherly would pull away to follow him, I reach up to hold her to me for a few seconds longer. I don't know why, but I want her to know she isn't alone in this. And I want her asshole father and his bag-of-dicks friend to know that Weatherly isn't alone, too.

When I let her go, she leans back and stares into my face, her violet eyes sparkling up at me like twin amethysts. In them, I see caution and dread, but a ferocious determination, too. That makes me smile.

I bend to whisper in her ear. "Maybe you should stop thinking about our shower for a few minutes. You might need all your concentration for this."

Two pink spots infuse her cheeks and it's all I can do not to drag her back upstairs and make her forget that there's anyone in the house besides us.

"You are a wicked, wicked man, Tag Barton," she scolds softly, licking her bottom lip when she moves her glance down to my mouth. "Your face cleaned up nicely by the way."

She moves to walk past me and I turn to watch her go. When she looks back over her shoulder and grins, I think to myself that this woman might be more of a problem for me than I ever would've guessed.

FIFTEEN

Weatherly

"You'd better have an excellent explanation for this prank, young lady," my father says the moment I shut the door to his study.

"Dad, I've told you all along that I want to marry for love, not for business or convenience."

"And *I* have told *you*— Wait, so you're telling me that you're *in love* with this person? Just how gullible do you think I am, Weatherly?"

"Why is that so unbelievable? What do you know about my life other than what you choose to fill it with?"

"So you're going to stand there and tell me that you're in love *with the help*?"

"Oh, so that's what this is about. You're not nearly as upset that I'm engaged to someone else and didn't tell you as you are about the fact that he's not up to your high standards. Is that it?"

"Don't make *me* out to be the bad guy here. I'm just trying to do what's best for you, for our family. Like I always have. I've never been selfish and I didn't raise *you* to be selfish."

"God!" I say in exasperation. "Why is it so horrible, so unthinkable, so *incredibly selfish* to want to marry for love? This *is* America, right? Arranged marriages *did* go out with the cavemen, right?"

"It's not like Michael is some kind of barbarian who will treat you poorly, Weatherly. For chrissake, he's worth four hundred million dollars and he'd see to every comfort you could ever even dream of."

"But that's not all there is to it, is it, Dad? This isn't about what Michael can do for *me*."

His eyes narrow on me. "I've worked my whole life, made sacrifices you'll never know anything about to build this business into what it is today. And the instant someone threatens it, threatens the very foundation of who we are as a family, and *you* can do something to help, this is how you respond."

"Don't be so dramatic! This isn't about our safety or our freedom. This is about money. And power. Plain and simple. If Randolph Consolidated takes over, you'll be out and that's eating you alive."

"You listen to me, young lady, I *will not* have my daughter marry a common laborer just because she doesn't agree with my politics. Let's not forget, *darling*, that it's *my* business, *my* money that has funded your precious charity all this time."

"Which you've refused to continue helping as a means of extorting me into doing what you want."

"Make no mistake, Weatherly, if you want to play hardball, I can exert much more pressure than just pulling your trust fund. Don't tangle with me, young lady. I didn't get to where I am without learning how to bend people to my will when it suits my purposes."

I feel my chin tremble. How has it come to this? That he is so uninterested in me as a person, *as his child*, that he would seek to hurt me just to get what he wants? I've always known I was nowhere near the top of his list of priorities, but that he would play dirty with *me*, his own flesh and blood? I guess I never knew just *how low* I fell on that list. "I'm sorry that this particular pawn has grown up to be such a disappointment to you, *father*. I thought you'd eventually see it my way because you love me and you want me to be happy. I can see now how very wrong I was."

With that, I turn on my heel, fling open the study doors and make my way back out to the dining room. "Tag, can I have a word please?" I say from the doorway.

He's in the middle of a sip of wine. He sets down his glass and pushes away from the table. "Of course." He turns to nod at Michael. "Stromberg."

"Barton," he cuts back, disdain dripping from his voice.

Tag grins at me as he approaches. To be the caretaker of a vineyard, he sure seems to hold his own with people like my father pretty well.

I don't say anything when he reaches me. I simply turn and make my way toward the kitchen. I can't hear Tag's soft footfalls, but I know he's behind me. I can feel his silvery eyes traveling the length of my back and butt as I walk. I stop by the fridge for the dish of leftovers from lunch. I hand them to Tag so that I can grab a bottle of wine and two glasses as we pass.

Wordlessly, I make my way out the back door and around to the Jeep, which is still parked in the driveway. I climb into the passenger side and look back at Tag, who is standing a few feet away, watching me. "Well? You got me into this. The least you can do is get me out of here."

He holds my eyes for a few seconds, long enough for me to feel guilty about lashing out at him when he was only trying to help, but then he nods and walks around to the driver's side and climbs in.

"Where are we going?" he asks, setting the dish of food on the console between us.

"How about that half-finished cabin with the great view? I'd like to wake up to that sunrise in the morning."

"Oh, it's like that, huh?" he asks with a knowing grin, repeating his earlier phrase.

"Yeah, it's like that," I answer.

"I've heard stories about girls with daddy issues. I hear they can be pretty wild." There's a playful glint in his eyes that eases my tension. I feel the tightness that had gathered between my shoulder blades melt away like a sliver of ice in the hot sun.

"Maybe we can get that four-wheeler out later tonight."

The smile he gives me is bright enough to light up the darkening sky. "Woman, I gotta hand it to you. You brought your daddy issues to the right guy." Tag gives me a wink as he fires up the engine. I lean my head back, content to watch him drive. It only takes me a few seconds to realize that I feel a little better already. William O'Neal has never made me a priority. Why should I give him so much room to hurt me?

As we pass the rows that we crossed over during the rain last night, I feel the throb of memory begin low in my belly. Meeting Tag might be the thing that saves me. Nothing has ever distracted me from my life as much as he does. His face, his grin, his kiss— they seem to be lurking around the edges of my mind all the time now. And when I let him in, he can easily crowd out other things that I worry about. He's a powerful influence.

When we reach the partially finished cabin, Tag takes my hand to help me out and then up onto the porch since there are no steps yet. I stop just inside the door. The interior smells like fresh-cut wood and clean mountain air. I inhale deeply, letting the scent wash away the remainder of my cares.

Tag gives me the unofficial tour, showing me the roughed-out rooms, guiding me with his vision of what it will look like when it's complete. "I'm surprised that Dad agreed to this."

"Why is that? It's a great way to expand the business and to bring people to Chiara."

"I can see that, but he's always been sort of protective of this place. I don't know why."

"Well, this isn't hurting anything. Only helping it. I'm sure he knows that when he looks at the bottom line. The old cabin had been renting often, which is why it needed renovating."

"You've got a good head for business, Mr. Barton," I say, turning toward Tag.

"Yes, I'm quite the visionary," he says quietly. "And right now, I'm having all sorts of exquisite visions."

He reaches out to brush the backs of his fingers down my cheek. His pale gray eyes look darker in the night. They sparkle like onyx in the low light of the moon filtering in through the mostly open back of the cabin.

"You are? Pray tell." Even though we've made love several times, still my body is vibrating with anxious anticipation. Already, I know that look and I respond instantly to the promise it holds.

"Are you very hungry?"

"For what?"

One side of his mouth quirks up. "For leftovers."

"Not particularly."

"Good. I'd hate to starve you."

When his mouth descends onto mine, all thought of food and Chiara and our unwanted guests drift away on the lightly scented breeze. Tag undresses me at the edge of what will soon be a bank of floor-to-ceiling windows overlooking the sloped fields and gorgeous mountain views. He peels off my clothes and adores every inch of my skin in the lone wedge of silvery light.

When he lays me gently on my back and kisses his way down my stomach, I stare up at the swollen globe of the moon until I can focus no longer, until nothing exists except the thrilling touch of this man between my legs.

Hours later, after we've explored each other, eaten all the leftovers and drank all the wine, we lie at the edge of the opening. My head is on Tag's chest and the only sound other than our breathing is the steady beat of his heart.

"We can't sleep here," I say, breaking the silence.

"Why is that?"

"If we roll over too far, we'll roll all the way down the mountain."

His hold on me tightens. "I won't let anything happen to you. You're safe with me."

I wonder at his words as I gaze out over the whitewashed field below. "My father can't understand why I would even consider *not* marrying Michael when he's the answer to our prayers."

"Not to play the devil's advocate, but maybe he's just willing to do anything for his family. Some men would go to any extreme for the people they love."

Although I find his remark a bit peculiar, I don't comment on it or ask what lengths *he'd* go to for the well-being of his family.

"Maybe *some* men, but not him. I have no delusions about where I fall on his list of priorities." I sigh, hating that I brought my father and my worries to this peaceful sanctuary. "If it weren't for the kids at Safe Passage, I wouldn't even be worrying about this. I don't worry about what will happen *to me*. Or to Mom and Dad. I'm sure he has enough money stashed away to live well for the next hundred years. But the kids . . . If he cuts *me* off, he cuts *them* off."

"Is he really that much of a bastard?"

"If it means getting what he wants? What *he thinks* is best? Yes. He is. He was always absorbed with his work, with becoming more and more powerful, but it wasn't always this bad. Things were better when I was a little girl. We had some good times, especially here at Chiara. Before he became so driven. But the more he *got*, the more he wanted. And the more he *wanted*, the more ruthless he became until he got it."

"Then we'll find a way to work around him."

"We?" The thought makes my heart shiver in delight. I don't know why, but it does. Maybe it's because Tag seems so capable and it would be wonderful if he *could* fix this. Or maybe it's just the thought of him *wanting* to help me. That pleases me. Probably more than it should.

I feel him pick up his head to look down at me, so I lift mine and meet his luminous eyes. His lips curve into a lopsided smile. "Yeah. We. Unless you don't want me to get involved."

"No, it's not that. It's just that . . . No," I finally say, returning his smile. "No, I like the 'we.'"

"So do I." He kisses my forehead and we rest our heads back down. Tag drags his fingertips lazily up and down my bare side. I drag mine lazily up and down his bare torso.

"So, you'd do pretty extreme things for the people you love?" I ask when the quiet has settled back around us like a soft, invisible blanket.

"There's nothing I wouldn't do for the people I love."

"You were raised in a very loving home, I guess."

"I was."

"Tell me about it. Tell me about your family."

My head rises and falls with his chest as he takes a deep breath and lets it out. "My dad took this job before I was born. Moved Mom and me here when I was just a baby, to live full-time in the caretaker's quarters. This place was all I ever knew for most of my life. I grew up with my hands in this dirt, surrounded by Chiara grapes and Chiara wine."

"I wish I'd known you then," I admit quietly.

I feel almost cheated that I was kept so far from the "common" people, as I'm sure Dad thought of them. While I was enjoying a luxurious family retreat in the mountains, Tag and his parents were working the fields that kept this place running. *They* are the backbone of Chiara, not my family.

"I saw you several times over the years. You were like a beautiful princess, kept in the highest room of the tallest tower, far away from the common folk." I doubt Tag knows how accurate that statement actually is. "I never dreamed the little girl that I saw from a distance would grow into such an amazing woman."

I hide my smile against his muscular pectoral. "I saw you from a distance once or twice. It's probably a good thing they never let me get too close. I bet, even then, you'd have fascinated me."

"Oh absolutely," he says without one hint of doubt. I laugh and look up at him. He's grinning down at me.

"I'm sure you were every bit as humble back then, too."

"Of course."

"When did you leave?"

"I enlisted in the Army when I was nineteen. I'd had enough of working the vines and just wanted out. I met some great guys, saw the world. Did a lot of different . . . things."

I don't ask what those "things" are; I just wait for him to continue. When he doesn't, I prompt, "And?"

I feel a sigh swell in his chest. "And then Dad died. Mom couldn't work these fields, of course. I knew your father would have to hire someone else, maybe even a family like ours, which would inevitably mean that Mom would have to move. I couldn't stand the thought of that, so I came home a year after my first tour was up. Been back here ever since."

"Do you regret it? I mean, if he hadn't died, would you have come back?"

"Honestly, I don't know. But I don't regret it. Now that I've seen what's out there, Chiara is as precious to me as it always was to my parents. This is my home. These fields, these grapes, *this life* . . . it's part of who I am. And I'll do anything . . . *anything* to make sure there's a place for us here."

I feel the frown work its way onto my brow. "Is that why you're helping me?"

There's a short pause before Tag moves with the speed of a snake's strike. He has me on my back, pressing me so quickly into the clothes on which we rest that it startles a squeak out of me.

"I want to help you because *I want to help you.* Yes, I do want for my mother to be able to stay in her home for the rest of her life, no matter how long or short that might be, but I also want to help you. No one likes for their fate to be decided by someone else."

He says the last with such passion, it spurs more questions. "But what happens when this is over? Aren't you afraid that Dad will have you and Stella removed?"

"As ruthless as he is, or as he talks at least, I'm not sure he'd actually be able to throw my mom out. She's cared for him, his family and his home for half his life. Me, on the other hand? There'd be a greater likelihood he'd toss me out on my ass, but then he'd have to find someone *immediately*, someone experienced and competent and familiar with this type of terrain, and have them trained in a matter of weeks. Harvest is just around the corner. It's crucial that things go smoothly. I think he's too smart to be that impulsive. I think he'll bide his time and keep trying to manipulate you through your charity. But in the end, I think it's a distinct possibility that we can both get what we want."

"And you're willing to bet all that you have here?"

"I am. Because I'm not betting on your dad; I'm betting on me. On my ability to read people, on what I know and what I want, and the lengths I'll go to get it. William O'Neal is still a smart business-man when you take emotion out of it. I'm betting on being able to rationalize with him if it comes to that, help him see what I have to offer. After all, he owns these fields, but I've worked them my whole life. And I've got plans for this place, plans that he'll like if he'd listen." He stares down at me, raising a hand to brush my hair behind my ear. "In short, yes. I'm willing to risk it. It's a risk, but a calculated one. And the possible rewards are . . . *compelling*," he says, smiling devilishly down at me.

Looking up at Tag, at his swirling eyes and his breathtaking face, I lose the ability to think clearly. All I can do when he settles his hips between my legs is gasp, my questions and concerns evaporating from my mind like water from a pool on a hot day. The only thing I can think to say is, "I hope helping me is worth the risk, then."

"From the first time I saw you, I've thought of little else. And, God help me, from the instant I got to taste these lips," he says, dipping his mouth to mine in a kiss that makes my head spin and my body melt. "From the instant I got to touch this skin . . ." He glides his hand from the swells of my breasts all the way down my side to my thigh, which he tugs on until I wrap my legs around his waist. "From the *damn second* that I got to feel this body . . ." he whispers, easing his rigid cock into my welcoming heat on a deep groan, "I knew, *I knew* I was a goner. You're worth the risk. I'd be willing to bet my life on it."

"But why?" I ask breathlessly, barely able to hold on to rational thought with him buried inside me this way. "Why me?"

I *have to* ask. Of all the women—all the young, beautiful, plentiful women—why me?

"If I could figure that out, you wouldn't be under my skin, now would you?"

I half laugh, half moan when he withdraws and then pushes back in a bit harder.

"But if I had to guess," he says, tracing a path up my throat to my ear with the tip of his tongue.

"Yes?"

"I'd say you're a witch. Because you've bewitched me. I just can't seem to get enough."

You've bewitched me. I love the sound of that.

As he whispers the last into my ear, he flexes his hips and steals my breath. After that, all conversation ceases to matter.

SIXTEEN

Tag

Weatherly is fast asleep on our clothes. Well, most of them. The majority of her creamy skin is covered in my silk shirt, but everything else is beneath her. I manage to extricate my slacks from under her right leg without waking her. As I pull them on, I stare down at her—at the beautiful face turned toward the rising sun, at the slim arm tucked under her head, at the spill of dark, thick hair spread out behind her. Damn, she's gorgeous.

Is that what's getting to me?

I quickly discard the theory. I've slept with gorgeous women before, so it can't be *just* that. So then what the hell is it?

The answer: I don't know. I don't know *what* it is or *how* it is; I only know that *it is*.

Just standing here watching her is giving me a major hard-on.

And she's sleeping, for God's sake. I wasn't kidding when I told her that I can't get enough of her. I really can't.

I debate waking her up the fun way, but decide instead to creep to the house and get some breakfast to bring back to her. And *then* we'll have another round of "fun," before the rest of Chiara wakes up and our love nest isn't so private anymore.

I carry my shoes out into the grass before I put them on to traverse the dew-covered field. At the house, I sneak in the back door, fairly certain that if William and Michael are up, they'll be having breakfast in the dining room. Men like them don't eat in kitchens. And I'm right. It's deserted except for the same fiftyish woman who was here yesterday afternoon.

"Good morning," I say as I make my way around to the pantry. I set about collecting a thermos, some Styrofoam cups and a small picnic basket, which rests beside the one I took on the four-wheeler and never used. I fill a clean dish towel with warm croissants and fill a plastic container with thick slices of warm ham and bacon. Lastly, I put a few cubes of cheese in a cup and pack it all into the basket.

When I glance up, the chef is eyeing me with something that looks like amusement.

"Breakfast in bed," I explain.

"A bed *outside*?"

"The best kind," I answer, grinning at her. She merely cocks a brow and resumes stirring a pot of . . . something. I bet those sharp blue eyes don't miss a thing.

I set the basket on the counter and take the back stairs up to the room we share to use the bathroom and clean up a little before heading back. I'm standing, bare-chested, in front of the bathroom mirror brushing my teeth when I hear the door open. I smile, my hunger forgotten when I think about spreading Weatherly out on the bed and eating *her* instead. But when I rinse my mouth and step out into the bedroom, all I see is Cher. Naked except for her fiery red hair, which is obscuring part of her very ample breasts.

I stop, obviously surprised, and stare.

Before I can ask any questions, Cher makes her way over to me. Her hair shifts as she walks, giving me peek-a-boo glimpses of hard, pink nipples.

Oh shit.

"I think you might have the wrong room," I say, retreating a step when she reaches me.

"No, this is *definitely* the right room. Your friend told me exactly which one you sleep in."

"My friend?"

"Rogan."

"Rogan," I repeat. Damn him! He *did* send me a woman for my birthday. I wasn't kidding when I told Weatherly I thought she was a gift from him.

"How did he talk *you* into this?"

"We cater events for the studio all the time. I've known Rogan and his girlfriend for a while now. I asked if he knew you, told him we were doing some work up here. He told me it was your birthday. And what you wanted. I thought we'd be the perfect fit, since it just so happens that I want it, too."

She rakes her short, clear-painted fingernails down my chest as she says this.

"Look, I'm sorry that you went to all this trouble, but—"

Her smile tells me it was no trouble *long* before her lips do. "Believe me, this will be all my pleasure."

I figured. I knew it when I first met her. Like I said, I can spot these women a mile away.

She leans into me, pressing her tits up against my chest and dragging the nipples from left to right. I wrap my fingers around her upper arms and push her gently away. I'm debating the best way to blow her off without pissing her off, if for no other reason than to keep this from getting any more awkward. Unfortunately, I'm still thinking when Weatherly opens the door and walks in.

Even though her hair is tangled, even though her clothes are wrinkled, she's still mouthwatering. She still pulls my attention, my *desire* like no one ever has, especially with her eyes flashing like violet flames. For a few seconds, all I can think about is how much I want her.

It's when the two bright red spots appear on her cheeks and her mouth drops open that I realize what her beauty caused me to miss initially. That fiery little spark in her eyes and that hot little flush to her cheeks aren't the result of lust. She's mad. Mad as hell. And I know exactly why.

"This isn't what it looks like," I begin, releasing Cher who is desperately trying to cover herself.

"I'm so sorry, ma'am. I thought we were alone."

Weatherly turns her blazing eyes on Cher. "You thought you were alone? Does that really make a difference? Do you have *any clue* how inappropriate this is? Are you *trying* to lose your job?"

Cher blanches visibly. "No, ma'am! The guy, Rogan . . . his

friend . . ." she tries to explain, hiking her thumb over her shoulder at me. She inches her way toward the clothes thrown over the back of an armchair in the corner as she continues in a stammer. "He . . . he assured me that this was okay. It's . . . it's . . . I'm a birthday present."

Weatherly watches her with thinned, furious lips before she turns that withering look on me. "Well, I sure hope you enjoy your present."

And with that, she turns on her heel and calmly exits the room. I have to grin when she closes the door rather than slamming it off its hinges, which is what *I'd* want to do. What I imagine that *she* wants to do, too. But a woman of her breeding would never make such a scene. It almost makes me want her more. I've seen firsthand the kind of fire she's capable of, fire that seems to leap to life at the touch of my fingers or the lick of my tongue. But she can obviously control herself when she wants to. The fact that she doesn't use that control when it comes to me . . . that she doesn't want to . . . or that she *can't* . . . Damn, that's hot!

I glance at Cher on my way after Weatherly. "You won't lose your job. I'll make sure of it. Just get dressed and get back to work."

I don't catch up to Weatherly until she's walking proudly out the front door. I don't know where the hell she's going, but I love that she's going without thought of the two men who are watching curiously from just inside the dining room.

"Weatherly, wait!" I call as I barrel down the stairs. That only makes her speed up. I catch her before she can descend the steps out front, taking her gently by the arm to stop her. "At least give me a chance to explain."

She whirls around, eyes spitting purple sparks. "Don't bother," she hisses through firmly gritted teeth. "I saw all the explanation I needed."

She yanks her arm free and marches down the steps. With an exasperated shake of my head, I follow. "Damn it, Weatherly, do you really think I'm *that* stupid? *That* shallow?"

"Obviously you are," she answers without turning around.

I lunge for her before she can get to the garage, to her car. "We can talk about your opinions of me later, then, but you can at least give me five minutes now."

"You don't deserve five minutes," she bites off, making me smile again.

I don't respond to that, but launch right into my explanation. It seems that the fair and beautiful Weatherly has a bit of a temper. "I asked you when I saw you in the tub that first day if you were a birthday gift."

That gives her pause. I feel it in the way the supple muscle of her arm relaxes a little.

"Remember? And that's all this was—a stupid birthday gift from my numb-nuts friend. Cher was just playing along. I didn't touch her, I swear."

"I *saw* you touching her."

"Oh good God, you know what I mean. I didn't touch her *that way*, nor did I have any intention of touching her. You can ask her yourself if you don't believe me. I was right in the middle of trying to let her down without embarrassing her when you walked in."

That gets another rise. Weatherly spins toward me. "Without

embarrassing her? Without *embarrassing* her? I think she had *more than embarrassed herself* . . . quite sufficiently, in fact, by that point."

"It was just a misunderstanding. No reason for anyone to get fired or beheaded or any dicks to be cut off. Because that's what it looks like you're thinking right now."

I cover my junk with one hand.

Still no smile.

I see the indecision in her eyes, though. I see the rational, reasonable woman returning, although I love this hot-blooded one, too. I'm not normally a fan of jealous women, but for some reason, I find that I very much like this one.

"What the hell is going on out here?" William O'Neal bellows from the front steps.

My shoulders sag. *Shit.* I don't even turn to look at him. I'm not worried about him right now. I'm worried about Weatherly.

"Don't let this mess things up between us," I tell her softly. "I had nothing to do with that. I swear it. I have no interest in her. Which will probably worry me later," I add.

Weatherly's brow furrows. "Worry you? Why?"

"Because I'm not in the habit of turning down hot women who throw their naked bodies into my arms."

"Then why did you?" she asks, an edge returning to her voice.

"Because she's not the hot woman I want. You're the only woman I can even *think about*. I have no interest in touching anyone else. Touching or kissing or spending time with. I told you that you've bewitched me, and hell, woman! I meant it."

"Why do you make it sound like such a bad thing?"

"Because I don't like not being in control. And you make me

lose control. You're all I can think about. And every time I start thinking about you, I feel like I'm gonna lose my damn mind if I can't get inside you. Or put my hands on you. Or press my mouth to yours."

Her expression changes. I recognize the look. I see it the instant she goes from angry to hungry. Hungry for me, for what's between us. I know it because I feel it, too. It's all I *can* feel, it seems like. That should bother the shit out of me, but this woman is under my skin. Jesus Christ, how she's under my skin. And I just told her as much, which is a first for me, something else that's out of character for me. Then again, Weatherly O'Neal is proving to be all kinds of firsts in my life.

When I start to step closer to her, desire shifts back to concern. Her mouth cracks then closes, and then cracks again for her to speak.

"Don't hurt me, Tag. I wanted to let go. I'm *trying* to let go, but I'm still not a woman used to this. To *you*." Her eyes . . . they glisten with sincerity. With the soft plea. They're trusting me to be a man of honor.

Guilt stabs me in the chest. *Don't hurt me, Tag.*

She's so honest, so vulnerable. I know it's hard for her, which makes me admire her all the more. Most people aren't brave enough to admit weakness. Maybe that's why, *on her*, it doesn't seem like weakness at all. Just courage.

I bring the tip of my finger to her trembling lower lip. "I swear on my life that I'll do my best."

And I will. I'll do my best not to hurt her. I just hope to God I haven't already broken that promise.

SEVENTEEN

Weatherly

What in the name of all that's holy have I gotten myself into? I think as Tag reaches for my hand and laces our fingers together. It's an intimate, comfortable gesture that two people who really *are* engaged might indulge in. But we aren't. And I'm terrified that this ruse is going to start feeling too real. If it hasn't already.

Tag brings our entwined fingers to his mouth and kisses my knuckles. "Let me bring you a no-longer-warm breakfast. Let's start over. The right way. The way I intended for this morning to go," he says, staring deep into my eyes. I feel myself falling helplessly into his stormy gaze. Falling, falling, falling until I'm lost in the tornado once more. He does it so effortlessly—pulls me in. It's not all his fault, though. Part of the problem is that I find myself wanting to fall. Badly. I find myself wanting this to be real, wishing this could be my chance at happiness, happiness that has nothing to do with money or power or holdings or business. I want those things to be mine. All mine. I want Tag to be mine. That's why it nearly leveled me to see him holding a naked woman in his arms.

I nod and smile through the memory, tearing it up like a piece of paper and letting the tiny slivers slip through my fingers to be carried away by the wind. I don't want them anymore. I don't want to think back on that. Ever again.

Tag turns, eyes still on mine, half grin still on his face, and tugs me back toward the house. He doesn't let me go. All the way back to the house, he holds me. My hand with his. My eyes with his. And that's *more than* fine with me. I don't want to look at my father, who I know is still standing on the steps. I can feel his angry energy like cold air blowing through my soul.

He won't be ignored, though. When we mount the stairs and move to pass him, he reaches out to grab my arm, stopping me and forcing me to meet his disapproving eyes.

"Don't do this, Weatherly. Don't throw away your future on a whim."

"This isn't a whim, Dad. This is my life."

"You're telling me that you love him?" he asks, tipping his head toward Tag but not deigning to look at him.

I inhale deeply through my nose. "Yes. I love him."

I feel Tag's fingers twitch around my own, squeezing them a little tighter. I don't know if it's panic or what, and I don't look at him to find out. Although I know it's insane since we only just met, really, but I don't want to see him shudder or shirk away from that word. It feels too right, *too true* when I say it aloud, even though it's just what I had to tell my father.

Dad flings my arm away. "I raised you better than this. Better than *him*. He's a common field worker, for chrissake," he hisses, his voice dropping slightly as though he knows what he's saying is in poor taste, regardless of his feelings for my engagement to Tag. "I'm sure he's a fine enough man, like his father, but he'll never be able to take care of you. This is exactly, *precisely* why I didn't want you making this decision for yourself."

"So you're not even going to pretend that my happiness matters in all this?"

"You don't have the first idea what will make you happy, Weatherly. You've been sheltered your entire life. But I won't shelter you anymore. If you do this, so help me God, I won't protect you."

"I never asked you to," I tell him, raising my chin defiantly and holding his gaze. "Stay if you want, but don't think that your presence here will change my mind. It only strengthens my resolve."

With that, I nod once and turn from my father, walking stiff-backed through the door and into the house.

"I'm sorry you had to hear my father say those things. He has no idea who you really are. He's just . . . he's a . . ."

I hear the soft rumble of Tag's chuckle. "Sticks and stones, Weatherly. Sticks and stones."

I let the conversation drop, unwilling to let my father mar one more second of my time with this man.

Tag sits up suddenly, resting his hand on my bare stomach. "Come down to Enchantment with me today."

I love the excitement on his face, even though I'm sort of exhausted by it. After an orgasm-filled, nearly sleepless night, a dramatic morning, the world's most romantic picnic on my bed, and then incredibly slow, sensual sex, my energy level is at rock bottom.

Yet, as I look up into Tag's handsome face, as I lose myself in his swirling silver eyes, I feel my enthusiasm return. This man, this gorgeous, charismatic, highly desirable man, wants to spend the day with me. Why would I *not* be enthusiastic about that?

"For what?" I ask. After such an emotional hour or so, I don't want to seem *too* eager. Even though I am. I think I've revealed quite enough of myself to Tag for one day.

"I want you to meet some of my friends."

I'm immediately skeptical. "The ones who sent Cher?"

He cringes visibly. "Yes, but that's why I want you to meet them."

That seems backward, but whatever. And truth be told, I'm interested in Tag's friends, in his life outside this place.

My hesitation must make him think I need convincing. "While yes, Rogan is the one who sent Cher, he's really a great guy. He's just got a . . . different sense of humor. He's like a brother to me, though," he confesses, his expression turning serious. "We were in the military together. Spent several years in Delta Five together. Right up until I had to come home. He's saved my life more times than I can count. We've *all* saved each other's life dozens of times. He's as much family as my mom is."

After hearing that, a team of guerilla warfare experts couldn't keep me away. "Sounds like a trip I don't want to miss."

"Oh, so *that's* what it takes to convince you," Tag complains, flopping down on top of me. "It wasn't enough that you get to spend the day *with me*." He bends his head to capture a nipple, worrying it with his lips and tongue until it comes to a tingling, begging peak.

"It's not that at all," I tell him in an already breathy voice. "It just took a pretty tempting offer to get me to leave this bed today."

He lifts his head and pins me with his gleaming gray eyes. They're so pale they seem almost backlit in the olive expanse of his face. "Well, when you put it *like that*, I don't want to go now. I didn't realize staying in bed all day was an option."

I can feel the pressure of his growing erection against the inside of my thigh. "I think that should *always* be an option," I respond, my heart melting as quickly as my bones beneath the passionate intensity of his gaze.

"Mmmm, the perfect woman," he says, trailing his hand down my belly to my simmering center. "Just perfect."

My last thought is that I guess Enchantment can wait for another hour or so.

I might be sheltered and well bred, but I doubt there's a woman with a pulse who doesn't know who Kiefer Rogan is. MMA champ, Hollywood up-and-comer, playboy charmer—his face has littered dozens of magazines and gossip sheets since he started dating vacuous starlets. I had no idea that *Tag's* Rogan was *that* Rogan until we pulled up in front of a gorgeous, contemporary home in the gated hills of Enchantment's "little Hollywood" subdivision. I was immediately uncomfortable and wished that I'd opted for staying in bed after all. But it was too late to back out, so I let Tag drag me up the geometric walk to a tall front door.

The beautiful woman who answered Tag's knock, however, was not at all what I was expecting. I took to Katie instantly. I doubt I've ever met a more down-to-earth, relatable person than Katie. While she's extremely pretty with her rich auburn hair and her twinkling blue eyes, she also has some scarring down the side of her neck. While it doesn't detract from her in the least, I admire the fact that, in the world of glamorous perfection in which Rogan obviously lives, she is comfortable with who she is, flaws and all. I'm sure it helps that Rogan adores her. It was obvious from the moment he trotted up behind her at the door, kissing her scarred neck and smiling happily at us from over her petite head that he thinks she hung the moon.

"Tag, good to see you, man," Rogan said, pulling him in for a bear hug.

After the two men released each other, Tag then leaned in to kiss Katie on the cheek. "He still hasn't managed to run you off, I see."

Katie smiled and twisted to look up at Rogan over her shoulder. "He's never getting rid of me."

"Not if I have to chain you to my bed," he'd answered. His expression had taken on a wicked look. "Wait, on second thought, try to leave. I wouldn't mind chaining you to the bed for a few days."

Katie had playfully ribbed him in the stomach. It was plain to see that they're incredibly well suited and happy together. My heart stung with envy from that point on.

Now, however, as I get to know them both over imported beer

and homemade pizza (made in a brick oven built into the outdoor fireplace by the pool), I find that I'm thrilled for them. Just thrilled, even if I'm never able to have something so wonderful in my life.

"How did you two meet?" I ask from my place beside Tag on a two-person wicker loveseat. It's situated in a grouping on the patio by the pool. With all the lush greenery surrounding us, this space has the feel of a tropical paradise. It's much different than the pools we've had all my life. They were always rectangular and formal, bordered by rows of columnar cypress trees, like sentries standing guard over my life. But this, *this* is informal and natural and relaxed. It's everything a pool should be, everything a pool should *feel*. I know it's weird to get hung up on a pool, for goodness sake, but it seems to parallel the way I feel about the life I've always had versus the life I've always wanted.

"She was my makeup artist at the studio while I was filming my short part on *Wicked Games*. It was love at first sight. At least for me. She was a harder sell."

Katie starts shaking her head. "Don't believe that. I could hardly speak the first time I saw him. I was a mess."

"If she'd had a grain of damn sense, she'd have noticed me groveling at her feet, but she's as hardheaded as they come."

"I had reason to be a little skeptical. I mean, what would a gorgeous guy like *you* want with a scarred girl like *me*?"

"I never saw the scars. Still don't," he says softly, tilting his head to kiss her neck again. It's quite possibly the sweetest thing I think I've ever seen. It seems he's determined to show her how much he loves her, scars and all, with every breath he takes. Every look, every word, every smile between them is like a confession. A declaration. A promise.

Once again, I feel a pang of envy. When I glance over at Tag, he's watching me, his face an inscrutable mask. I smile and he winks at me, getting my butterflies all stirred up. Just like that. Easy peasy. Like it always is where Tag is concerned.

Tag's arm is draped along the back of our little couch. With his eyes on mine, he drops his hand to the back of my neck and tunnels under my hair until I feel the skin-on-skin brush of his fingertips. They draw lazy circles, first small and then widening, sending chills racing down my arms. It's as though he's touching me everywhere at once. Or at least that's what his eyes are saying. They're reminding me of what it feels like to have his hands on me, his lips, his mouth, but they're also reminding me of his words. *You've bewitched me.* But right now, with him gently touching me, with him intently watching me, I'm not exactly sure *who* bewitched *whom.*

The sun is on its way to setting before Rogan and Katie escort us to the door. "I wish you'd stay for dinner," Katie says, hugging me to her like we've known each other forever. That's how I feel, too. It makes me a little sad to think that I might not ever get to see her again. After all, Tag isn't *really* my fiancé.

"I wish we could, too, but we need to get back. There are guests at the house."

"Oh, at the cabin?" she asks, her eyes lighting up.

"Yes, have you been there?" I ask. That would be odd.

"Enchantment's about as big as a thumbnail. Everybody knows everything around here," Rogan supplies with a smile.

"Come up and see me sometime, man," Tag says to Rogan at the door.

"Stay home some, dude, and I will."

The two men shake hands and Tag kisses Katie's cheek again. Rogan pats my shoulder. "I'm glad you got the hermit to come down, Weatherly. And, uh, sorry about the birthday present I sent. If I'd known he was off the market, I wouldn't have done that."

"Please don't apologize. There's no way you could've known. Tag and I . . . we . . . we only . . . we haven't known each other very long."

Rogan glances at Tag where he stands slightly behind me. He grins before turning his attention back down to me. "I don't think that matters."

I feel my face flush with pure pleasure. It's not like Tag uttered those words, but Rogan's statement still feels like affirmation. Or maybe just hope.

Impulsively, I lean in and kiss his cheek. "Thank you. It's a pleasure to meet you. Both of you."

I find that it's hard to turn away from the smiling, happy couple. In my life, in my *world*, I don't come across very many genuine people. I find that I'd very much like to, though. My parents' marriage was more like a delicate, exquisite piece of blown glass. On the outside, it was perfect and shiny, the weaknesses only visible from the inside. They were never big on displays of affection, so I sort of always just assumed that they loved each other. They both said as much. But being able to actually *see* the love between two people, to be able to feel the glow of their happiness like warmth from a fire . . . that's the kind of love I want. Not the cool, cultured kind I was groomed to have. The messy, wild kind that I'm only just now dreaming of.

When Tag has helped me up into the Chiara Jeep, which we brought because we had to go get it from the half-finished cabin where we spent the night, I impulsively kiss him, too, only his I deliver on his perfectly firm-yet-soft mouth.

"What was that for?" he asks when I lean back.

"For bringing me. I had fun today."

"I liked seeing you happy," he says simply before shutting my door. I don't know what to make of that, or if I should make anything of it at all. Some small part of my heart wants to, though. It wants to believe that, against all odds, this could be something more. That *we* could be something more.

The problem is, I've never been a gambler and I'm not sure I even know where to start.

EIGHTEEN

Tag

I'm distracted all through dinner, even with Weatherly by my side. The call that I got while Weatherly was in the shower only added to the distraction that she, herself, provides. The information that my associate gave me was a game-changer. *Is* a game-changer. My question is: How does it change the game? How far am I willing to go? It's questions like those that have taken my head out of the conversation when William O'Neal summons it back to the table.

"Would you like to weigh in, Tag? Or don't you have any reason to follow the stock market?" He's wearing a smirk that makes me want to jump across the expanse of polished wood and strangle the shit out of him.

Stromberg adds to it with his pathetic attempt at covering his laugh with a cough. It's fine if they want to get their kicks at my expense. We'll see how that works out for them in the end.

I let a smile play over my lips. It's easy to keep my cool when I know what I know.

"I dabble," is my only response.

"What else do you 'dabble' in, other than dirt?" Weatherly's father asks. He's making very little effort to hide his contempt. In fact, I don't know why he bothers.

"A little of this, little of that, but you're not really interested in my answers, are you?"

"Pardon me?" William O'Neal asks, his smug expression turning to one of thinly veiled anger, as if to say he's affronted that I'd dare take a tone with him.

"Let's be honest. You're looking for ways to reveal me for the ignorant commoner that you think me to be, exposing my 'real self' to Weatherly so she'll see the error of her ways and run into the arms of your handpicked man. Isn't that about right?"

There's an eerie absence of sound, like the whole wealthy world is holding their breath as they wait for my inevitable social beheading.

He surprises me with his candidness. "I'd be lying if I said that results like those wouldn't please me. It's no secret that I want what's best for my little girl. And as much as you obviously have to offer society," he says, his lips twitching over his droll comment, "I feel that she could do better."

"So pairing her with a man twice her age who wants her as a trophy wife and business arrangement is what you deem 'best' for your only child?"

"Pairing her with someone who has the means and the knowledge to care for her for the rest of her life *is* what's best for her."

"Regardless of how she feels."

"Weatherly is young and impetuous. She'll thank me for this one day."

It infuriates me how he degrades her right in front of her, as if she has no feelings at all. I don't know how she turned out so well with this asshole for a father.

"And what if she never does? What if she blames you instead?"

"She won't, but if you think you know her so much better than I do, then marry her. Right now. Show her that you love her for her and not for her money. Because she'll be destitute if she marries you. Promise her that you'll care for her and your children on the salary you make here, a salary that wouldn't even afford an engagement ring, for chrissake. I'll even make it easy for you. You'll have this job for as long as you want it. I won't fire you for ruining my daughter's life. At least that way, I'll know she has a roof over her head."

I'm not normally a particularly capricious man, especially when I can't identify and account for the consequences of my actions. Yeah, I take my pleasure where I can get it, but there's little risk. I make sure of it. And my business affairs are always well planned and researched. I've never let someone push me into anything that I didn't want to do. Not William O'Neal. Not even Weatherly O'Neal. I know what I'm doing, even if they don't.

"You know, *Mr. O'Neal*, I really would've expected a man of your intelligence and business acumen to be a better judge of character, but I suppose that's *my* mistake." I lean up in my chair, staking Weatherly's father to his chair with my gaze, and I invite, "Look into my eyes and tell me that you're fool enough to think you can goad me into doing something that I don't want to do."

He leans forward and glares right back at me. "I'm hoping I can goad you into leaving my daughter the hell alone."

I stand so quickly my chair rocks behind me, nearly tipping over. I place both hands flat on the table and I bend slightly forward so that he can hear my low voice plainly. "Rest assured that this decision will be up to your daughter, because I'm damn sure not throwing her away to the selfish whims of her jackass of a father."

For the first time since he started with his barbs, I look to Weatherly. She's sitting, still and quiet, in her chair watching me. As I walk around the end of the table and approach her, her amethyst eyes shine up into mine with something between excitement and amusement and maybe a little awe. I bet she doesn't see people stand up to her father very often.

I reach for her hand, bringing it to my lips. I kiss the very spot where a ring should be. That was an asinine oversight on my part. "How about that ride on a four-wheeler?"

Her lips twitch up into a small grin even as her pupils dilate with anticipation of what's to come. She knows what kind of a ride I mean—the kind that we spoke of last night.

"I think that sounds like a spectacular idea," she says, standing.

"Gentlemen." I smile and nod at both William and Michael. "Don't wait up."

NINETEEN

Weatherly

I'm shaking. Whether from the conflict at dinner or the idea of what's to come with Tag, I don't know, but I feel like I might spontaneously combust.

I hear the unmistakable whine of the four-wheeler engine as Tag races from the farthest building, up the path toward the main house. I descend the steps when he hits the concrete of the driveway. He stops and holds out his hand, which I take as I climb on behind him. His head is turned toward me as I situate my legs on either side of his slim hips, so I meet his eyes when I go to wrap my arms around his waist. I pause when I see him looking at me. His eyes are bright and bottomless in the glow of the moonlight, full of something that makes my insides shiver. He leans forward just enough to kiss me, a soft brush of his lips over mine. I'm not sure what the gesture says, but my heart interprets it as something amazing and trembles with delight.

He turns and hits the accelerator, and we speed off toward the upper field and the mountains beyond. I don't know where he's taking me; I just hold on and enjoy the ride. There's something heady and unpredictable about being with Tag. He's a different kind of animal and he lights up the sky of my bland, uneventful existence. I think I'm becoming addicted to his particular brand of wild.

The night is hot and sticky around me despite the breeze rolling out from between the trees up ahead. It intensifies the scent of Tag's skin. It exaggerates the feel of his body between my legs. Everything from the passing landscape to the moon in the sky seems . . . better. New. Exciting. Nothing like what my life has held up to this point.

Tag drives us straight into the forest, darting around trees so quickly it almost makes me dizzy. It's easy to see that he's traveled this path a million times before, while I've never been in the forest once in my entire life. He has lived free from the moment of his birth. I've lived in captivity since the moment of mine.

The path forks and Tag takes the right curve, sending us climbing up a small incline and then dipping sharply down on the other side. Tag continues until the trees suddenly part, revealing a waterfall nestled in among the crags and hollows of the mountainside.

Water spills roughly over the rocks like liquid silver, and when Tag cuts the engine I hear the distant hiss of its flow. I stare out at the view with my chin resting on Tag's shoulder. Something about the moment is familiar, as though we've been here a million times. Together. Although we've only really known each other a few days, it's as though we've known each other forever.

"Come around here," Tag says quietly, his voice as rough and beautiful as the waterfall. I start to ease off the bike, but he stops me. "No, like this." He holds his arm up and urges me to climb under it and then into his lap. I'm thankful that the skirt I'm wearing is loose.

When I'm settled with my legs wrapped around his waist, Tag clasps his hands at my lower back, his eyes shining down in to mine.

"Marry me," he says quietly.

"Pardon?"

His lips pull up into a gorgeous smile that shows his perfect white teeth and reminds me why he is so irresistible. "I said, 'marry me.' Please."

I grin. "That's what I was waiting on. The 'please.'"

He says nothing at my sarcasm, just continues smiling. But when he does speak again, so softly that I have to strain to hear him, it echoes through me as if he'd shouted the words. They stir something deep within me. "Marry me, my fair Weatherly. I want you to marry me. I want you to be mine."

I'm stunned and breathless and thrilled. It's completely insane and totally, inconceivably crazy, yet I want to say yes so much it hurts. I don't know why. I don't know if I'm nuts. I don't know if it's stupid and impulsive and irresponsible. All I know is that it *feels right*.

But I have to ask . . .

"Why? Why would you want to marry me? What's in it for you?"

Tag unfolds his hands and brings them around to my front. Slowly, he unbuttons my sleeveless shirt, revealing my lacy bra underneath. "Well, there are these. These are in it for me." He leans forward and sucks one nipple through the thin material. Heat pours into my panties.

He's not finished, though. His hands continue down my stomach, onto my thighs where they slide back up, under my skirt. Pushing my panties aside, his fingers find my entrance and he eases them inside. He presses hard and deep, his three digits rubbing me from the inside. "And this. This is in it for me."

As he works magic from within my throbbing center, his eyes never leave mine. "B-but this is just sex," I tell him on a pant, even though I don't believe that at all. At least not for me. But I'm quickly losing interest in the conversation.

"Is it? Is it just sex when you're all I can think about?" he asks, nipping at my bottom lip with his teeth before pulling it into his mouth. "Is it just sex when you do this to me every time you cross my mind?" He unzips his pants and frees the broad head of his erection. I can see a single drop of semen glistening on the smooth crown. "Every time you walk into a room, open those beautiful lips, capture me with those dazzling eyes?"

Curious, I reach between us and run my finger over him, swiping up the drop of moisture and bringing it to my lips. I lick the tip, savoring the flavor of him as I bring my eyes back up to his. They're darker now, serious. Vicious almost.

Without warning, Tag crushes me to him. My bones shift. My muscles give. My flesh concedes.

We are chest to chest, my aching breasts smashed to his firm pecs as he winds his arm around my waist and lifts me. My breath sticks in my throat when I feel him prod at my wet and swollen opening.

"Does this feel like just sex to you?" he growls, slamming me down on him so hard I cry out, arching against him. He picks me back up and does it again, throwing me straight into the wild, tumultuous throws of orgasm. "That's more than just sex. That's perfection," he whispers, pumping his hips up into me as he moves me on his length.

I hear his loud groans in the fuzzy back of my mind as my body tosses me on the furious waves of release. I feel him spasm within me. I feel him pour out into me. I feel him swivel his hips as if to enjoy the feel of it inside me. "There's no better feeling than my come inside you. Marking you. Staking my claim. Making this pussy mine," he hisses against my neck, lips and teeth and tongue nipping me as he speaks. "Tell me this pussy is mine. Tell me nobody else can have it. Say it. Say it!"

"It's yours. All yours," I moan and mutter, my mouth dry and my throat raw. "My pussy is all yours."

His low roar resonates in my ear at the same time that I feel the sharp pulse of him inside me, a last spurt of warmth shooting up into me. It's as though he really is marking me, sealing our deal from the inside, and the thought of it, the idea of it, is enough to send another bolt of pleasure rocketing through me.

"Marry me," he whispers, his lips pressed to my throat, his heaving breath searing my skin. "Say you'll marry me. Not because I'm an out, not because you're trying to stick it to your father. Marry me because you need me as much as I need you. Marry me because you want my mornings as much as I want yours. Marry me because you want the afternoons and the nights, the smiles and the tears, the good and the bad. Marry me because you want all of me. Like I want all of you. All of you, every day. Every. Single. Day. Say you'll be mine."

I consider one answer. It's the only one I want to give. So I do. God help me, I do.

"I'm already yours, but I'll marry you anyway."

When Tag's lips find mine again, there's a sweetness to them, a reverence that causes my eyes to fill with tears of pure, radiant joy.

"This is what's in it for me," he breathes against my mouth, cupping my face so that his thumbs make lazy passes over my cheekbones. "You. Always."

I know in this moment that there will never be another man like this one. I'll never find someone who fits me like Tag does, who thrills me like Tag does. Who can love me like Tag just did.

I wake to an empty bed. After that phenomenal experience on the four-wheeler, Tag drove us back, slowly weaving through the trees and casually cruising through the fields. Something quiet and comfortable had settled between us. The house was asleep by the time we returned. We crept up the stairs to my room and washed each other off in the cool spray of the shower before crawling between the crisp sheets and falling straight to sleep, my head nestled on Tag's chest, his arm wrapped around my shoulders.

I wonder briefly where he went, but when I roll over, my body is so pleasantly achy and sore that I forget my curiosity for a few minutes and just revel in the memories of his touch. I've had a few boyfriends in my life, boys (and in some cases men) who fit the criteria of an O'Neal match. I even really liked one of them. His name was Robert Cohen and he took my virginity. There was a time, in my young mind, when I even fantasized that he might grow up to be "the one," even though part of me realized that was very unlikely to happen. Turns out Robert was gay, he just hadn't come out yet. I think on some level I knew, but it was much nicer to pretend.

After Robert, there was a guy in college who I thought I had great chemistry with, especially after we had sex. Turned out that he had too many mommy issues for me, though. And as good as the sex was, I never imagined it could be like this. I never dreamed I could come alive for someone this way. Tag is just different. With him, *I'm* different. I'm someone I've always wanted to be. And he's like someone I've always wanted to be with, even when the idea of him was almost too taboo to even consider. For an O'Neal anyway.

But here we are.

Together.

And we're going to get married.

I smile. I can't seem to help myself.

I carry that smile with me all through the day. And the next ones, too. Despite my father's glaring and despite Michael's openly disapproving looks, I smile, basking in what's happening between Tag and me.

We spend our days together, in the fields, in the cabin, in the woods. Or in my room. The grapes are getting closer and closer to readiness, and I feel like I'm ripening right along with them. All my life, I've never really felt like I'm flourishing until now. Until Chiara. Until Tag.

Tag and I breakfast by ourselves and take packed lunches wherever we go. We talk and laugh and make out like high school kids who can't keep their hands off each other. We share long looks and sometimes short naps like we don't have a care in the world. And for the moment, it feels as though we don't. It's as if trouble has been suspended, disallowed entry into our happy little bubble, and I for one am going to enjoy every damn second of it.

At dinner, Tag does a great job of keeping conversation focused on Chiara, and when it's not, we talk softly among ourselves, leaving my father and Michael to do the same. They don't, though. Mostly, they just glower at us.

And then there are the nights. God, just thinking about them causes my sex to shudder hungrily. Sometimes I think I could lie next to him 24/7 and never get tired of the feel of his touch, of his kiss, of his body working magic within mine. And when he's not around, like now, it's as though I can't quite get comfortable with life until I see him again.

I jump when my phone rings. Surprisingly, I'd almost forgotten it was in my pocket. I grabbed it out of habit after dressing, before I headed down here to the lanai. It hasn't made a peep in days and I haven't checked it in just as long. It's a tie to the outside world (and the problems therein) that I really would rather forget about. The fact that it's my assistant's number rather than my mother's tells me that my father hasn't told her about Tag yet, which gives me a nice little reprieve.

I stare at the number. I feel the weight of my trust-held-hostage bearing down on me as I move my finger over the green TALK button. As much as I'd like to stay in my happy bubble of oblivion, I can't ignore my biggest responsibility, so I answer the phone.

"Hi, Deana," I answer politely, coming to my feet to walk to the edge of the water.

"Hey, Weatherly, sorry to bother you, but I have some news I thought you'd be interested in."

I can clearly picture Deana's dark brown eyes sparkling in the rounded contours of her pretty face. Her cheeks are youthfully chubby, even for her twenty-six years, which gives her a perpetually mischievous look, like a chipmunk up to no good.

"What's that?"

"We got an anonymous donation to Safe Passage."

I'm not sure what makes that noteworthy. We do very well with donations, but it would take ten times the *number of them* to keep us moving in the direction that I've been planning toward. The direction that would be a breeze if I could get my trust.

For the first time since all this talk of engagements and marriages, the reality of my situation hits me. If I marry Tag, I'm dooming all the kids that I planned to help. Yes, Safe Passage could still do great work, but it would be a greater, broader, more massive effort if it had a few million dollars more.

Guilt and indecision strike. And they strike hard.

"Let me call you right back, Deana," I tell her quickly, hanging up and stumbling back to drop down onto the end of the chaise I just vacated.

I can't marry Tag. My father is right. That would be the most irresponsible thing in the world. Not just for my family in light of the Randolph takeover, but for the kids as well. I can't put my happiness before the needs of starving children. Ultimately, my mother was right. I'm not a selfish person. At least not selfish enough to throw away millions of dollars that could feed thousands and thousands of hungry kids for years to come.

Why do I feel like crying? This was all basically a ruse from the very beginning. It's not like I'm losing the love of my life.

Right?

Then why does it feel that way? Why does it feel as though I'm giving up something rare and precious and wonderful?

The soft pad of shoes across the patio work to pull me out of the miserable vortex I was sinking into. I glance up to see Tag striding toward me, a pleased half smile drawing his lips up at the corners.

God, he's amazing! Everything about him is perfect. At least for me. He appeals to me on a deep, soulful level, not just a physical one.

"You waiting for me, gorgeous?" he asks, bending to set his fists on either side of my hips so he can press his lips to mine. As always, a wildfire is kindled within seconds, leaving me well on my way to breathlessness.

"What if I was?" I ask, torn between the dark cloud of my circumstance and the bright sun of Tag's presence.

"Then wait no more. I've come to save the day," he says playfully.

I can't help smiling. "You have? And how do you plan to do that?"

"Well, I'd like to start by whisking you away on my four-wheeled chariot. I've got something to show you."

The temptation to leave trouble and worry and inevitability behind for just a little while longer, just a few hours more, is overwhelming. I reach up to wrap my arms around Tag's neck and bring his face back to mine. "Take me away, kind sir," I whisper, pressing my lips to his again.

This feels right. It feels like nothing can harm us or affect us when we are together, touching. Tag straightens, pulling me up with him and wraps his arms tight around my waist. I love it when he does this. He holds me like he doesn't ever want to let me go, like he's daring anyone to try and take me from him. So possessive. So thrilling.

"Better stop that now, fair Weatherly," he says softly when he drags his lips from mine. "Or else the only place we'll be going is upstairs."

I giggle, feeling like a teenager again. "You aren't supposed to give me choices like that. I might choose the wrong one."

"Okay, how about come with me now and *then* we'll resume kissing. And go upstairs. If we can make it that far. If not, all I can promise is that I'll try to find some soft grass."

I grin up at him. He grins down at me. "Deal."

I squeal when he sweeps me up into his arms and carries me across the patio, around to the front of the house where his four-wheeled chariot awaits. He throws his leg over it and sets me across his lap in front of him. I lower my arms, winding them around his waist as I lean my head against his strong, wide chest. There's literally no place else in the whole world I'd rather be.

The engine throbs to life beneath us and Tag punches the gas, sending us careening down the path toward our cabin. Since that first night we spent in the half-finished structure, we've both called it "ours." And considering how many times we've made love there *since then*, it's fitting.

Tag doesn't stop at our cabin, though. He takes a left and heads up the mountain, toward the forest. I close my eyes, not worrying about where we're going. I'm content with the feel of the sun on my face, the wind in my hair and the heartbeat tapping under my ear.

I know when we enter the woods. The temperature drops by about ten degrees and Tag slows considerably. He drives us back to the edge of the drop-off, the one that overlooks the waterfall, where he stops.

The view is not quite as mystical in the daylight, but it's every bit as stunning. The sun pours down into the crease in the mountain face, kissing every treetop and turning the waterfall to a million-sparkling-diamond-fall. Other than the hiss of water on rocks, the only sounds that interrupt the blissful silence are the soft whisper of the breeze teasing the leaves and the distant chirp of some birds.

"I missed something the other night," Tag says from behind me. I pull my eyes from one miracle of nature to another, equally spellbound when I gaze up into his flawlessly formed face.

"I don't remember you missing *any*thing on *any* night," I tell him with a shy smile. Sometimes, I can't believe we are this intimate. Although he never comments on it, I know I still blush occasionally.

"Well I did. And I'm here to correct my oversight."

Tag eases out from under me, leaving me sitting sideways on the four-wheeler. He pauses for a quick second, his face a breathtaking mask of what looks like anticipation, before he reaches into his pocket for a small box and then drops to one knee in front of me. My heart stutters to a stop in my chest and the backs of my eyes burn like fire.

Ceremoniously, he slowly snaps open the lid to the velvet box, revealing the most incredible ring I've ever laid eyes on. The center stone is an enormous round diamond, cut perfectly to capture every possible facet of light. It's flanked by four small amethyst ovals, slightly offset so that they appear to be wings. Below them are diamonds of a similar shape, which form the body of the butterflies. The stones are graceful, the placement subtle, making the ring simply breathtaking. And my breath is taken.

"Tag, it's . . ." I don't even know what to say. I just follow it with my eyes as he takes it from the tiny cushion and places it on my finger.

"Amethysts for your eyes. Butterflies for your freedom. Diamonds because you're mine," he says softly, just before he kisses the ring where it rests on my finger. "I'll ask you again, my fair Weatherly. The right way. Will you marry me?"

Tears flood my eyes. I want to say yes more than I've ever wanted anything except Tag Barton himself, but I can't. I just can't do that to the kids that I've worked so hard to help. Thousands of them depend on Safe Passage for their nourishment, and thousands more depend on us for breakfast at school or food on the weekends.

"Tag, I . . ." I can't bring myself to say no. The word just won't fit past the boulder lodged in my throat. It seems everything I've ever wanted is right here, kneeling before me, asking me to be his, yet my father still manages to stand in the way. He knows me so well. Too well. He knew where to hit me where it would hurt the most. And he did.

My phone bleeps from my pocket. An incoming text. I take the signal as an excuse to gather my composure before I do what must be done. "Pardon me," I mutter, taking it out and sliding my finger over the screen. It's a message from Deana. Evidently, she got tired of waiting for me to call her back.

Oops.

> **Deana:** Five million dollars.
> **Me:** Five million dollars? Am I supposed to know what that means?
> **Deana:** SOMEONE DONATED FIVE MILLION DOLLARS.
> **Me:** WHAT? WHO?
> **Deana:** Maybe this guy I met at a fund-raiser who was looking for a good write-off. But who cares? SOMEONE DONATED FIVE MILLION DOLLARS!

I stare at the screen for several long seconds, my heart pounding as I read and re-read the words. Someone donated five million dollars. We've always had a handful of generous donors, but no one has ever given an amount substantial enough to allow the charity to function without my help, without my money. Well, technically Dad's money, I guess. And that was never a problem until recently. Maybe Deana's guy came through. Maybe someone else heard of us and felt the need to help. I don't know. I don't know and I don't really care. Whoever it was and whatever the reason, someone donated five million dollars to Safe Passage.

Five. Million. Dollars. Dollars that buy my freedom.

With this money, we'll be okay *without* my trust money. That means that the kids won't suffer no matter what I do. That means that I can marry Tag.

Because, God help me, I want to.

I toss my phone aside, not caring when I hear it drop to the ground on the other side of the four-wheeler, and I throw my arms around Tag's neck. I can't dial back the brightness of the smile that wreaths my face when I give him my answer. "Yes. I'd love to marry you, magnificent Tag."

I don't think of the kids, the money or the butterflies again for quite some time.

TWENTY

Tag

As much as I wanted to lend Weatherly a hand with her shower, I knew I needed to check on Mom. I haven't seen her since late last night.

The caretaker's quarters is basically a tiny cottage located at the rear of the property, right at the edge of the oldest of the Chiara vines. Its dark, aged brick matches that of the main house, only this structure is about one-sixteenth the size. Although the inside is quaint and functional, consisting of a small kitchen, a sitting room and a good-sized master bed and bath, the wide porch off the back is my favorite part. It overlooks the fields, something that I used to hate, but have since grown to appreciate.

When I was a kid, the sitting room was actually *my* room, but after I left for the military Mom converted it back to its original state and gave my bed to a needy family she knew in town. That's why I was staying in the guest cabin when I first got back after Dad died. Not that I would've been comfortable sleeping in the room next to my mother. Not with a social life that's as . . . *active* as mine has always been.

It actually worked out perfectly since Mom got sick. She has a place that she can relax in peace and quiet. I have privacy. Well, I *had* privacy. It wasn't until the cabin started renting again that it became a problem. Luckily, since the owners are rarely here, William didn't have a problem with me taking up residence in one of the spare rooms in the main house. It's when he got a complaint about the plumbing that I suggested we remodel. He was agreeable. For the most part, I don't think he gives a shit about this place as long as the wine's good and it continues making him some money.

I knock on Mom's door before I enter the kitchen. It smells like garlic, which leads me to believe she made herself some lunch. Although I've been having the kitchen staff bring her meals as well, I'm glad that she *felt* like cooking and that she *felt* like eating. "Mom?"

No answer, so I go peek in her bedroom door to see if she's sleeping. It's empty. If she's not there, she's out on the porch. It's one of her favorite places, too.

I find her knitting a blanket that she's been working on for a year, it seems. She's humming to herself and I notice that her color looks pretty good today. Less . . . yellowed. My heart twists a little in my chest.

I went on dozens of missions, did things that will haunt me to my dying day, but watching my mother die a slow death in front of me is by far the hardest thing I've ever had to do, ever had to see.

Although her color looks better today, her end will still be the same. It will come, and it will come painfully. And it kills me that there's nothing I can do to change that. That's why, if it's the last thing I do, I'll make sure she can at least spend her last days in the only home she's known for half her life.

"You have to be the slowest knitter in the history of the world," I tease, bending to kiss her cheek before I take the rocking chair beside hers.

"This is a labor of love. It can't be rushed."

"A labor of love? Who's it for?"

She reaches over to pat my cheek. "Who else but my boy?"

I eye the soft pastel colors. "You *do* realize that I'm twenty-seven, not seven, right?"

"Maybe you won't be the one using it."

"Well, if you're making it for me, who else would be using it?"

"Maybe you'll have a baby to wrap it around one day."

An image of Weatherly rubbing a belly rounded with the child she's carrying—*my* child—rolls swiftly through my mind and I smile.

"Okay, I can see that."

Mom puts down her knitting and fixes her pale blue eyes on me. "Is it Weatherly?"

"Is what Weatherly?"

"The one you just imagined."

"Who says I imag—"

"Ah-ta-ta. Answer me."

She always knew when I was lying.

"What if it is?" I ask good-naturedly.

I thought we were still playing until she reaches over and curls her fingers urgently around mine. She squeezes them so tightly, her hand trembles.

"Don't you make decisions that will affect the rest of your life because of me. Don't marry her just to get this place."

"How do you know—"

"I know you tried to buy this place. I know he turned you down. Now I see you running around with Weatherly, and I'm hearing things. I can put two and two together."

I frown. "That doesn't mean—"

"No, it doesn't. It doesn't *have to mean* anything, but I know you, son. I know how you love—with your whole heart. You won't listen to reason. Won't let anything stop you. Won't let anyone get in your way. But I don't want you doing things like that for me. If you marry that girl, marry her because you love *her*, not because you love *me*."

I take her thin, cool hand in mine, wondering briefly if it was ever this frail before. It seems that I could crush the bones if I squeezed even a tiny bit tighter. "This is your home, Mom. No one will ever force you out of your home just because you're sick."

"This place was my home, but it was also my job. You can't expect them to keep me around out of the goodness of their heart. When I'm no longer useful, they'll find someone who is. I knew it all along. But that's life, son. That's business. This is still *just a place*. I can make a home anywhere. As long as you come by and see me from time to time . . ."

"But this is where you lived with Dad. It's where all of my childhood memories are. I'm not going to let anyone take that away from you."

"Tag, I'm telling you," she says warningly. "Don't do this for me. Don't. Please."

I give her my brightest smile and gently pat her hand. "Why don't you worry about finishing that blanket before the second coming and let *me* worry about the rest? I've got this, Mom. I've got this."

TWENTY-ONE

Weatherly

Twenty-one days. It's been twenty-one days since Tag put a beautiful ring that probably cost him his whole life savings on my finger and asked me to marry him. Not a day has gone by that I haven't been certain that I'm insane, that I haven't been certain that *he's* insane. But neither has a day gone by that I haven't been, at least when I'm in his arms, the happiest that I've ever been.

The more I learn about him, the more compatible we become. We have so much in common in some ways—our love of the land and the grapes, our bond to family whether good or bad, our connection to Chiara—but in other ways, we are very different. He's a risk-taker. I'm not. He's a free spirit. I'm not. He's willing to give up his life to help his mother. I feel like I've given enough to help my father. Our differences, however, seem to bring us even closer. It's hard for me to find anything that I don't like about him. Or

156

even love. The way his eyes sparkle when he watches me walk toward him, the way he reaches for my hand like it's automatic, the way he kisses me so often like he's drawn to me without realizing it. The way his laugh seems to rumble in *my* chest, like he's actually becoming a part of me.

If we weren't getting married, I would probably worry more about falling in love with him. I would be afraid of giving my heart away to someone who might break it. But now, I don't think much about it. I just feel. I just go with it. And it feels wonderful!

At first, I was content to just be able to spend my life with someone to whom I was so desperately attracted. But now, more and more with every passing day, I feel as though I'll be spending it with my soul mate, with someone I'll love for the rest of my days. Because I do love him. I think I have for a while now. I only hope he will one day love me in return.

I *do* think about that sometimes—what if I fall in love with Tag, but he never learns to love me the same way? But I try not to let those thoughts take root in my mind. Right now, it feels like we're *both* falling. And there's hope in that.

We were going to elope because my father is so against this union, but my mother had a cow and convinced him that we should at least have a small ceremony so that he can walk me down the aisle and she can see her only child get married. He grudgingly agreed to that. I think for a while he kept thinking it would all fall apart and he wouldn't have to worry about it, but it hasn't. *We* haven't. Tag and I have spent every day together, every night together, too, and we are even happier as the days go by.

Dad and Michael left Chiara two days after Tag gave me the

ring. I don't know what Dad has cooked up to replace the way he expected my marriage to Michael to affect the company, but I feel sure he's got something up his sleeve. As long as it doesn't involve me, though, I don't really care what it is.

Mom came to visit after that, ostensibly to talk me out of the "ludicrous notion" of marrying beneath me. It only took her three days to see that she wasn't going to make a bit of headway. That's when she went home and talked to Dad about a real wedding. Since my charity received the anonymous donation and I no longer have to rely on my father's money to keep it afloat, they have no leverage to force me into or out of a marriage. As I'd always dreamed, I got to pick who I want to spend the rest of my life with.

And now, here we are. My wedding day. I went from the prospect of marrying Michael, a man I had zero feelings for (unless vague disdain counts) to marrying a man I can't wait to wake up to every morning, all in the span of a month. It's surreal, but in the best fairy-tale kind of way. Even my friends are envious, especially when they met Tag. I think then they understood how things could've happened so quickly and how I could be so happy.

I haven't seen Tag since last night. He left my room two minutes before midnight so that he wouldn't risk seeing me on our wedding day. We decided to have the ceremony here at Chiara. It seemed fitting somehow. He could've spent the night anywhere, but I'd be willing to bet he's at our cabin. It gives me chills just to think about it.

My closest friends and family are all waiting for me downstairs, as is Tag. Mom hired a decorator from Atlanta to come and make the grounds and the main house wedding-beautiful, and it is. I peeked over the upstairs railing this morning and it nearly stole my breath. This small, intimate wedding is more perfect and more fitting than the grandest of events could be. For me, anyway. And for Tag.

A soft knock at the door has my stomach clenching into a nervous knot. One of my best and oldest friends, Shannon, my maid of honor, pokes her expertly coifed head in. "It's time." Her smile is bright and beautiful, if a little envious. She has no qualms about marrying for money and very much looks forward to her impending nuptials to Avery, the son of one of her father's associates. Shannon *is attracted to* Avery, though, so her situation isn't as . . . distasteful as mine was.

She leaves the door ajar and walks away, probably to get in line at the top of the stairs. Seconds later, I hear the harpist begin her first song, the one that the wedding party will enter to. The one that comes right before mine. My stomach flutters and I get up to walk to the heavy, floor-length mirror that leans up against the wall in the corner.

I see Weatherly O'Neal. She looks the same as she's looked every time I've seen her for the last month, only today there's a shine in her purple-blue eyes and a slight flush to her cheeks. Her black hair is drawn into loose curls artfully arranged on top of her head. The few tendrils left dangling frame her small smile, a smile that doesn't betray the way her heart soars. She was bred to remain calm and collected during stressful times. Times like these. But *I* can see it, though. I can see the change—the happiness, the hopefulness. *I* can see that she fell in love with the most unlikely of men in the most unlikely of ways. And *I* can see that, despite the convenience of the arrangement and its questionable origin, she is thrilled to be walking down the stairs, down the aisle toward Tag Barton.

I make my way out of my room, along the hallway that's dripping with bunches of white roses and purple wisteria. It smells like heaven. It *feels* like heaven.

My father awaits me at the end of the hall, standing at the top of the stairs. His face is expressionless at first, but when his eyes rake me from the top of my veiled head down to my richly beaded, A-line, Sarah Burton gown, he softens. Minimally, but still he softens. When I reach him, he turns to face the stairs and holds out his arm for me.

I don't want to start an argument, but I hate the thought of walking down that aisle and not telling him how much it means to me.

"Dad . . . I . . . I wanted to thank you."

"For what?" he asks, eyes still trained straight ahead.

"For walking me down the aisle. For giving me away. To Tag. I know you don't approve, but . . ."

Long seconds elapse before he sighs. I see it more than I hear it. His puffed chest visibly deflates.

"You deserve better. Is it so wrong for me to want the best for my daughter?"

"No," I admit. "No more than it is for me to want to be happy."

"I only wanted to keep you protected and cared for."

"That's something that you can't spend the rest of your life worrying about, Dad. I'm grown. This is what daughters do. And their fathers worry about them. But they try to make it work."

"I'm not most fathers."

"And I'm not most daughters. I'm an O'Neal. Can't you just trust that you raised me right and be happy for me? Just this once?"

Finally, he drags his eyes over to mine. Reluctant, but willing. It's a first step, anyway.

"I'll try."

I hate to press my luck, but while I'm at it . . .

"And Tag. Do you think you could take it easy on him? Just give him a chance?"

"Weatherly, I—"

"What if you're wrong about him, Dad? What if he *is* the best thing for me? Would you really want to take that from me? To risk ruining it? Everything we *both* ever wanted for me, for my life?"

He studies me. Closely. Quietly. Almost as though he might find answers or assurance somewhere in my eyes. So I do my best to give him what he's looking for.

"I'll try," he says again, but this time I believe him. Something about the small smile that curves one side of his mouth tells me that he's finally admitting that this is happening and that maybe, just maybe, he should make the best of it. "At least he knows how to make good wine. Looks like we're gonna need a helluva lot of it."

I laugh softly. From William O'Neal, this is the best I'm going to get.

Impulsively, I stretch up on my toes to kiss my father's expertly shaved cheek. This is the man I remember from my childhood and that little glimpse makes this day all the more perfect. "That's more like it, Dad."

As we look into each other's eyes for a few more seconds, our truce is cemented. I'm marrying Tag because I want to. Because I'm falling more and more in love with him every day. Because I think we can be happy. Maybe not rich, but happy. And that's worth more to me than millions of dollars, especially now that my charity is taken care of. And my father is walking me down the aisle. This is as close to perfect as I'm likely to get.

The familiar, traditional wedding march begins to play and I hear the shift of clothing as everyone in the room below stands to their feet. I wind my shaking hand around my father's elbow and he reaches up to place his fingers on top of mine. Together, we begin our descent.

Guests start to come into view as the staircase sweeps toward the formal living room. Most are smiling, all are standing, facing us. I see them, but I don't *see* them. My eyes and my mind are waiting breathlessly for one man to appear.

And then he does.

My foot touches the floor, my father and I turn, and there he is. Tag. Standing at the front of the aisle, flanked by his friends on one side and the minister on the other. I'm aware of all these other details, but still, *he* is all I see.

His raven hair gleams like black ink in the afternoon light and his pale eyes shine like silver moonbeams from the chiseled planes of his face. There's a smile in them, much like the one that graces his full lips.

His wide shoulders and trim waist are displayed perfectly in a brilliantly cut black suit. The creamy white of his shirt matches my dress as though it were taken from the same swath of silk. His big hands are clasped lightly in front of him and he never takes his eyes off me as I approach. It's as though we are the only two people in the room. No guests, no musicians, and no air. Just us, in a beautiful vacuum adorned with fresh flowers.

We stop a foot away and my father ceremoniously takes my hand and transfers it to Tag's waiting palm. I turn to him before he can go. "Thank you, Daddy," I say, not having called him that since I was a little girl. It was something playful between us when I was growing up—he'd call me Weathervane and I'd call him Daddy. And then we'd both smile and he'd ruffle my hair. It was how he said "I love you" and how I told him that I knew. And I did, back then.

Surprisingly, his dark blue eyes mist just before he leans forward to kiss my cheek. "Be happy, Weathervane."

My happiness is doubled as I watch him move quickly away to sit beside my teary mother. That was his way of saying that, no matter what, he loves me. Still. Always.

And I'll take it.

Tag's fingers squeeze gently around mine and I step forward to stand at his side. I sneak a peek up at him as the minister begins. He's looking down at me, unabashedly, smiling. I wonder if the happiness that he wears so easily right now could be because of me. I hope and pray that it is. I hope and pray that he won't one day regret his capricious decision to marry a woman he hardly knows just to help her out. Or just because they have phenomenal sex. I hope and pray it's more. So much more.

With his shimmering eyes fastened to mine, Tag raises our joined hands to his lips. He presses them firmly to my knuckles and lets them rest there for several long seconds before he drops them back to his side and turns to face the minister.

We listen in silence to his words and when it comes time to repeat our vows, Tag surprises me with vows of his own.

"Some of life's most beautiful things come at unexpected times and in unexpected ways. I never expected to meet you, here of all places. I never expected to feel the way I feel about you, now of all times. I never expected to be standing here with the most breathtaking bride I've ever seen, me of all men. I promise to give you every part of me that I can, from this day forward."

He kisses my hand again, right over the ring that he placed there just a matter of weeks ago. And when he lowers it again, I feel his thumb brush back and forth over my skin, like he's marking me—always marking me—giving me another physical reminder of this day, of this moment. But he needn't have bothered. I won't ever forget this day *or* this moment. Not for as long as I live.

When his voice has stopped reverberating through my soul, the minister moves to finish the ceremony. "Do you, Taggart Gregory Barton, take this woman—"

"Wait!" I interrupt impulsively. My heart is trampling my lungs from the inside, but I can't let this poignant ritual go on without confessing how I feel. It just seems wrong to start our life together without being totally honest with him. Without fear, without hesitation, without deception.

"I love you," I whisper, my throat clogging around the admission. I swallow hard and force my eyes to hold on to his. "I've been falling more and more in love with you every day. The longer I'm with you, the harder it is to imagine my life without you. I'm not here for any reason other than you. Just you. And I want you to know that I'll put you first in my life. Before everyone and everything else, you come first. I don't have anything else to give you, but I can give you that. I can give you *me*. Always."

Time slows, spinning in a hazy circle around us, blurring out the rest of the world. Tag's silvery eyes turn dark and stormy. I know that look. I don't know all the things that it means, but I know how it makes me feel. It makes me feel loved. Wanted. Like I'm the only girl in the universes that he can see.

Tag raises his hands to cup my face and inches closer until his nose is almost touching mine. "Say it again," he breathes.

My pulse thunders. My lungs freeze. My hands tremble. "I love you."

And then he's kissing me. Like we aren't in front of a crowd. Like we didn't just ruin the ceremony. Like we are the only two who matter.

And I kiss him back.

Because we are.

A muffled *whoop* and the resulting laughter draws us back to where we are and what we're supposed to be doing. Tag lifts his head and smiles down into my face. I glance behind him to an innocent-looking Rogan, whose wink at me is his only admission of guilt as the whooper.

The minister clears his throat, drawing my eye back to him. "Taggart Gregory Barton, do you take this woman to be your lawfully wedded wife?" he begins again, as if there was never an interruption in his service. I slide a sidelong glance over to Tag. He's still smiling at me. And I'm still falling deeper in love.

TWENTY-TWO

Tag

"What's going through that beautiful head of yours this morning?" I ask Weatherly as I come up from behind to wrap my arms around her waist and lay my chin in the curve of her neck. I love how she tips her head to the side. I love how she arches back into me, like a cat rubbing her slinky body against my leg.

"That of all the great vacations I've been on, of all the exotic places my family has traveled to, I've never seen a sunrise like this one."

"It's the company," I mutter, dragging my lips over the smooth skin of her shoulder.

"It is?" she asks, a smile in her voice.

"Definitely. Being with me makes everything better." I let one hand slide down her bare, flat stomach to the elastic band of her panties. When I feel her crease and slip a finger inside, I find that she's already wet. *Her* readiness is all it takes to inspire *my* readiness. With a light groan, I press my cock against the curve of her ass as I explore her more deeply. "And don't bother denying it. I can *feel* how much you agree."

"I wouldn't dare deny it," she assures in a breathy voice that makes me want to bend her over the balcony railing and let her bask in the view of Tuscany as I pound into her from behind.

"Good, because you'd be a liar," I tease, licking the lobe of her ear before I sink my teeth into it.

"I'd never lie to you," she pants, working her hips over my hand.

That cools my ardor a little. I believe her when she says she'd never lie to me. She's better than that. But I'm not.

Not that I've *lied to her*, per se. I just haven't told her everything. Omission isn't lying.

Or at least that's what I keep telling myself.

"Weatherly, there's something I need to tell you." As soon as the words are out of my mouth, I wonder why the hell I said them. I have to think this through. I can't let my feelings for her mess up everything. Too much is at stake. But I *do* have feelings for her. Strong ones. Stronger than I expected to have, especially so soon. But admitting them would be a disaster. I can't do that yet. And when I do, I don't want there to be these secrets between us, things she can't know anything about at this point. When I tell her I love her, if that's what the hell this is, then there won't be anything else between us. Nothing to stand in our way.

My movements have stilled, so Weatherly reaches behind me to dig her nails into the side of my thigh as she rubs her plump little ass against my cock. "Can it wait?" she asks softly.

My balls tighten and thoughts of lies and omissions, of guilt and burden fade away into the early Tuscan sun.

"Do you *really* want to be doing that *here*?" I ask, pulling her tighter against me as I look around at the few other villa balconies. They're all empty, the French doors shut, the curtains drawn. "Someone could easily look out and see us."

As a spot of moisture is forming on my boxer briefs, I'm praying she'll say she doesn't give a shit and beg me to take her right here, right now.

Her pause is so brief I might've imagined it. "I don't care if you don't care."

That's all the permission I need. With my thighs pressing against the backs of hers, I nudge her upper body forward until she's resting her forearms along the cap of the railing. I lean back only long enough to jerk her panties down over the curve of her perfectly rounded cheeks. I take out my cock and rub it through her slick folds before I drag up between those cheeks to coat the crease with her own juices. I dip back down and ease into her slowly, inch by inch, until my shaft is buried all the way to the balls in the silky fist of her body. I close my eyes and revel in the feel of being so deep inside her. I open them again to watch as I pull out. "Ah hell," I groan when the light hits the wet sheen on my cock.

That's when my intentions of giving her an easy morning ride leap off the balcony and fly away with the exotic birds.

"Remind me to thank Rogan for this trip," she murmurs between quiet, breathy moans.

That's the last time either of us speaks until I carry her limp body inside a few bone-melting minutes later. But as I lie beside her, stretched out behind her as she sleeps, the guilt returns tenfold. What the hell am I doing to this incredible woman? And will she hate me when she finds out?

TWENTY-THREE

Weatherly

Some part of me is very nervous on our return to Chiara. The way we were during the time we spent here, and even when we left two weeks ago for our honeymoon, was quite different than the way we are now. We are married. Husband and wife. Looking out at an eternity together. An eternity of normal life. What worries me is the fear that Tag might find that "normal" is actually "boring."

One of the part-time Chiara workers, Sam Wyman, drops us off at the bottom of the front steps. He was kind enough to pick us up from the airport and bring us home.

"You two go get settled. I'll get your bags."

"Are you sure, Sam?" Tag asks.

He nods, his smile genuine. "I'm sure. Go on, now."

Tag startles a squeak out of me when he sweeps me up into his arms and carries me up the steps. "What are you doing?" I ask.

"Carrying you over the threshold."

"I'm pretty sure the steps aren't part of the threshold."

"I'm hedging my bets," he responds, bending to push open the heavy front door. "Besides, I like any excuse to have you in my arms."

He carries me through the door then kicks it shut behind us and stands, holding me, in the foyer. "Welcome home, Mrs. Barton."

His eyes flash with a happy affection that warms me all the way to my toes. My heart soars with hope and optimism. Maybe this can work. Maybe this can really, really work.

"Why thank you, Mr. Barton, my handsome husband," I reply, batting my eyelashes at him.

His smile slowly fades to a gentle curve of his lips. "Say it again," he requests quietly.

"Mr. Barton, my handsome husband," I repeat obediently.

"Says my beautiful wife," he whispers, pressing his lips to mine in a sweetly chaste kiss that shoots all the way into my soul.

"Let me look at you two," comes Stella's voice from the dining room doorway. She must've been waiting for us.

Tag turns toward her and starts to set me on my feet, but she stops him, bringing her praying hands to her mouth. I can plainly see the tears in her eyes. "Don't put her down yet. I want to remember this."

He doesn't move a muscle, just stands still for his mother. She stares at us, trying to control her tears, for at least two minutes. Content to remain in Tag's arms forever if need be, I let my head rest on his shoulder. In a featherlight touch, he brushes his lips over my hair. The gesture is intimate and familiar and achingly tender. And it brings a smile to my mouth that I wouldn't even *begin to know* how to fight. The pleasure comes from somewhere deep inside me, a place where all the hopes I've carried since I was a little girl have lived quietly dormant all these years. Once I was old enough to see what my family expected of me, all my wistful dreams shriveled up and slept.

"You're happy, aren't you?" she asks softly, her eyes silently pleading.

"I am," Tag replies, his words rumbling through his chest and into my ear.

She closes her eyes in relief, and when she opens them again, they are fixed on me. "You, too?"

I don't hold back. I raise my head and I let my happiness shine from my face. "Very much so."

At that, she rushes toward us as much as her ailing body will allow and pulls on Tag's arm until he bends enough that we are both within kissing distance. She presses her lips to both of my cheeks then to both of Tag's, her powdery lilac scent enveloping us in a cocoon of maternal love.

"Be good to each other, babies," she warns mildly, just before my phone rings from my pocket to interrupt.

Tag sets me on my feet and I dig out my cell. "It's probably my parents," I explain, checking the screen to see whose call I missed.

"Talk to them," Tag says, giving me a quick peck on my forehead. "I'll catch Mom up and then meet you upstairs. I'll bring our bags up in a few."

I nod, hitting Dad's number and heading for his office. He answers on the first ring. "Hey, Dad, we're back. I just wanted—"

"Are you alone?" he interjects, his voice dripping with restrained urgency.

"Yes, why?"

"Weatherly, I have to tell you something, but you have to promise me that you won't let on like you know just yet. I need to talk to Donald and see what our options are."

Donald? Donald is Dad's lawyer.

"Talk to Donald? About what?" There's a pause that really isn't all that long, probably, but my father's behavior has managed to marinate the seconds in trepidation. "Dad, what is it?"

"We had an investigator look into Tag. Just as a precaution."

My heart sinks. I can feel it thumping in the pit of my stomach, stirring up enough dread to make me queasy.

"And?"

"One of the first things that he found was a tie to a shell corporation. The same corporation that tried to buy Chiara." I say nothing. My mind is spinning too fast for me to respond to him right away. "We refused, of course, but he must've hired someone who knew his way around business holdings because he somehow managed to discover that neither me or my company holds the majority of the interest in Chiara."

"Wait. What? You don't hold the . . . Then who does?"

"You do. I put sixty-two percent of the stock in your name when you were just a little girl. When I saw how much you loved it there, I wanted it to be part of my legacy to you, and part of your future. She was to be a gift to you on your wedding day. I didn't mention it because, obviously, you didn't marry someone I approved of, but it seems he already knew. The second offer, that time from another shell company between him and someone named Kiefer Rogan, was directed to you as the primary shareholder. But still, he didn't give up. He just changed his tactics."

"Dad, what are you saying?"

"I'm saying that Tag tried to buy Chiara. And I'm saying that when his offer was refused a second time, he didn't give it up. He found a way to get it anyway. By marrying for it."

My head is pounding so hard I have to sit down and rest my head in my hand. I know what he's getting at. The knowledge of it, the understanding of it is glaring at me, laughing at me, screaming at me like a living presence in the room. A cruel, vicious, inescapable presence that lurks in every dark, dusty corner.

"Are you absolutely certain about this, Dad? I mean, I know you don't approve of Tag, but—"

"Weatherly, I would never make something like this up because I disagree with your choices. You're my daughter, *my child*. I'll do everything in my power to protect you. Even if that means protecting you from yourself."

"Is that what this is? You think I've made a mistake and you're trying to—"

"I'm not trying to do anything. These are the facts. I'm simply informing you that your husband had an ulterior motive for marrying you and I'll be damned if I'm going to let him worm his way into getting what he wants at the expense of my daughter."

His voice is angry, but I know it's not all because of me. William O'Neal is likely much more upset that someone has nearly gotten the best of him in a business deal and he never saw it coming.

He didn't see it coming and neither did I.

Ohgod ohgod ohgod! How can this be happening? How can this be true?

I feel like a child who has walked outside her charming woodlands cottage and stumbled onto a bloody battlefield. Inside my bubble there was this surreal sense that all these unexpected things were working out so perfectly. But now I've been pushed out the door by my father, pushed out into a reality that tells me I've been a pawn all along. The realization is beyond devastating.

"Weatherly, listen to me. You *cannot* let on that you know just yet. You have to let me get together with Donald on this. Damage control is imperative."

I feel sick. Literally sick. My stomach can't decide if it wants to hurt or swim, and my chest feels tight with carefully bottled emotion. And I can hardly think past the black hole of devastation that's sucking at my heart, threatening to pull me into weightless oblivion.

"I won't say anything, Dad. But what am I supposed to do? I mean . . ."

I don't know how to assimilate this information. Yes, my relationship with Tag began as a farce, but somewhere along the way, it became very real to me. I fell in love with him, with the way he looks at me, the way he laughs with me. The way he makes me feel. The way I can see our future in his eyes. A future spent raising our children between the rows of grapes at our favorite place in the world. And now, to find out that he was playing me the whole time just to get his hands on Chiara . . . I don't know what I'm supposed to think, what I'm supposed to do. How I'm supposed to act.

"You keep your chin up. You're an O'Neal. And nobody pulls a stunt like this with an O'Neal. He'll pay, sweetheart. He'll pay."

Although he can't see it, I give my father a watery smile. While I appreciate him championing me, I don't want revenge. At least not yet. Right now, I just want to crawl into a hole and die. Only I can't. I have a husband who I'm supposed to be making a new life with. Enjoying. Getting to know on a deeper level. That sounded a whole lot different ten minutes ago. Ten minutes ago, it sounded wonderful to spend more time watching Tag tease and care for his mother. Ten minutes ago, it sounded rewarding to see how Tag would introduce me as his wife to his closest friend. Ten minutes ago, it sounded exciting to see how my husband will manage the vineyard during harvest season. Ten minutes ago, I was deliriously happy to be a part of his future. But now . . . now it just sounds heartbreaking. It sounds like a list of things I'll never get to see because he isn't who I thought he was. He was just a dream.

How will I be able to look at him without feeling betrayed? How will I be able to let him touch me without feeling dirty? How will I be able to spend time with him without feeling devastated?

I can't. I can't stop the way I feel. My only option is to try and control the way I express it. I can feel all the awful things; I just can't show them.

For the first time in my life, I have found a use for the cool, emotionless way in which I was raised to comport myself. I'll be involved because I have to be. I'll be detached because I *need* to be. For self-preservation. That's the best that I can hope for.

Tag appears in the doorway, a grin on his face and our luggage in his hands. *All* of our luggage. I look down at his long fingers, fingers that have teased and thrilled me more times than I can count in the last weeks.

A near-crippling wave of sadness floods me. I try not to let it show on my face, but I'm not quick enough. I wasn't expecting him to show up before I was ready to face him.

I know he knows something's wrong. His expression turns to one of concern and he drops all our bags on the floor and ambles in to me. "What's wrong?" he asks when he kneels down to put himself at eye level.

Fighting back tears, I shake my head and point to the phone. I see his lips thin in anger. That's fine if he thinks my father has said something to bother me. Whatever he thinks, whomever he blames will be a perfect and convenient red herring that I can use until this gets resolved.

"I'll just talk to you later, Dad, okay?" I say into the phone.

There's a moment of silence during which my perceptive father is no doubt deducing that my abrupt ending is a result of unwanted company.

"We'll talk soon," he says in his clipped way. All business. That's my dad. But after his pause, he adds something else. Something long overdue and as rare as a night-blooming orchid. "Love you, Weathervane."

Tears flood my eyes. I'm already emotional, but to hear my father say that, something that he hasn't said to me in years, is my undoing.

"Love you, too," I respond brokenly.

I hear the click of the line just before I let my phone fall from my ear into my lap so that I can cover my face. I wish Tag would just leave me alone in my grief, but he doesn't. Instead, he scoops me up with a gentleness that burns my poor heart like hot wax to new skin, and carries me silently up the stairs. He doesn't ask questions. He doesn't pry. Obviously, he's drawing his own conclusions about my distress. He just takes me to our room—what used to be only *my* room and has ceased to feel like that since the first time we made love in it—and lays me on the bed. He pushes the hair back from my face and kisses my forehead. And my eyelids. And my nose.

"Whatever he said, I'm sorry. I never wanted our marriage to bring you pain," he says kindly.

Liar! I want to shout. But I don't. I let my eyes tear and my chin tremble and I just nod at him, keeping my mouth shut until I can say the word aloud. However long that might be.

With a sigh, I turn onto my side, away from Tag, until I hear him creep quietly out the door and pull it shut behind him.

TWENTY-FOUR

Tag

"Is she okay?" my mother asks when my foot hits the bottom step.

"I don't know."

Mom's brow furrows into a frown. "Do you think she knows?"

"No, there's no way she could. I think her asshole of a father said something to upset her." I run my fingers through my hair, getting angrier. "I just wish I could do something about it."

I feel protective of my wife. Men like William O'Neal don't deserve the love of women like Weatherly. He doesn't deserve to be able to hurt her, to be able to affect her the way he does. He shouldn't be allowed to dictate her life, to manipulate her the way he does. And yet he does. As wrong as it feels that he gets some part of her heart, he does. He has it. And he obviously doesn't give a damn how he treats it. Seething, I grit my teeth. I could happily wrap my hands around his throat and throttle the shit out of him for whatever he said to upset her.

But then that would be hypocritical. I'm hurting her, too. Maybe even worse than he is. She may not know it yet, but *I* do. *I* know I'm keeping things from her, things that would possibly change the way she feels about me. Even though I'm doing it for the right reasons, it still churns like acid in my gut that I have to. This is not who I am. I don't hurt people and not give a damn about it later. Even the women I've been with, I've always treated with respect. That's who I am. That's who I was raised to be. That's who I *want* to be. The type of man who deserves the love of a woman like Weatherly, not the kind who breaks her heart and then walks away with some of the pieces stuck to his shoe.

Small, cool hands grip my forearm, jarring me from my thoughts, and I look down into my mother's worried eyes. "She's in love with you, son. You take care with her. She trusts you and you're . . . you're . . ." Her eyes well with tears.

"Mom, I'm not going to hurt her. I will make this right."

"You're lying to her. You're already hurting her. You just don't know it."

"She'll understand when it's all said and done. She's not a cold woman. She'll understand. And then she'll forgive me once she realizes why I've done the things I've done."

"That's a big gamble. If you break her heart, you might not ever get it back."

It's my turn to frown. Although my insides clench at the thought that she might hate me when this is over with, however small the possibility, I still think Weatherly will understand when I tell her everything. She'll understand why I had to keep some things to myself until just the right time.

But hearing my mom tell me that I might not ever get my wife's heart back gives me pause. I haven't had it nearly long enough. I'm not ready to give her up yet. Maybe ever. But the problem is, I've come this far, *too far*. How can I make it right without going back in time and being honest with her from the start?

That's the rub. I don't think there *is* a way. I think I've come too far to turn back now.

"But it's already done. How the hell am I supposed to change it *now*?"

Immediately, I feel guilty for snapping at Mom. She doesn't deserve that. She's just trying to help. Hurting *her* was never part of my plan either. Everything I've done, I've done for her. So she'll never have to leave her home, so she'll never have to worry about medical care. Whatever happens to me in my life, with all the crazy turns it's taken, she'll be okay. Even if I lose everything, she'll be taken care of for the rest of her days.

"You could tell her. Before it's too late."

I bite my tongue, agitation and frustration welling up inside me. I was going to tell her that morning on the balcony, but other things got in the way, other things like her little moans and the hot, wet feel of her body gripping mine. After that, I just didn't think about it again. Weatherly and her delectable body are very distracting.

But they're not distracting me now. Damn it. And I get the

sinking feeling that my window has closed. But maybe I should try anyway.

"Let me get a few things in order, then I will. I'll tell her."

"I just hope she understands. Trust and honesty are so important in a marriage. I just wish—"

Guilt and the fear of losing Weatherly forever is making me feel defensive, like I need to explain to my own mother that I'm not the monster here. I still feel like the bad guy. At least Weatherly was honest with me. I can hardly say the same.

"Ours wasn't a regular kind of marriage, Mom. You can't forget that she originally agreed to this out of convenience, too. She's not the clueless, innocent here. We *both* did what we had to do," I defend vehemently.

"But you knew her reasons. You didn't give her that same courtesy."

"I couldn't. And you know why."

"You *could've*. You could've trusted her. But you didn't."

"I couldn't risk you, Mom. You know that." I feel like my mistakes are crowding in on me, a jury ready to convict. An executioner ready to cut Weatherly out of my life.

"I begged you not to do this."

"Well, I did. I did what I thought was best and I suppose I'll have to deal with the consequences, too. Now, if you'll excuse me, I have to go to town. If Weatherly comes down, tell her I'll be back before dinner."

And with that, I walk off. I leave my mother behind. I leave Weatherly behind. But I take all my messed up feelings over this

with me so I can sort through them and figure out how the hell
to turn this around.

The warm August sun is low on the horizon when I pull back into
the drive. I fully expect to smell food when I walk in, as Mom
called a couple of hours ago and said she wanted to fix us a special
dinner tonight. To celebrate.

But I smell no dinner. I hear no voices. It's just quiet. Oddly quiet.

I walk through the first floor, looking for signs of life. I find
none. The kitchen is dark except for the single light that shines over
the island. I take the stairs two at a time and find that our bedroom
door is still closed. I knock softly, but get no response, so I knock
again.

"Weatherly? Are you all right?"

Still no response, so I open the door and peek inside. I can see
the outline of her on the bed. It doesn't look like she's moved since
I left. Alarm streaks through me. I push the door the rest of the
way open and walk quietly to her side.

"Weatherly?" I whisper.

I can see the side of her face now. Her eyes are open and she's
staring at the wall, at nothing. I can see the dying, orangey light
revealing to me what she won't. It shines on the wet tracks streak-
ing down her cheeks. It sparkles in the damp spikes of her lashes.
She's been crying. Again. Recently.

Gently, I slide my hands under her shoulders and knees and
lift her into my arms. I cradle her against my chest as I turn to sit
on the bed. She's limp, but stiff, too, in a way. She keeps her arms

down at her sides, doesn't attempt to put them around my neck or touch me in any way.

My stomach feels heavy. Something is very, very wrong.

"Talk to me, baby," I say against her hair. The endearment just slips out, but it feels right. *She* feels right. In my arms, in my life.

She makes no move to speak, just stares straight ahead. I brush a silky curl away from her throat, but she still won't look at me.

"Weatherly, you're scaring me," I tell her. And I mean it. This isn't like her. What the hell happened?

I feel as much as hear her sigh. She swells and then shrinks in my arms. "Just let me sleep tonight. I'll be better tomorrow."

I don't know how much to push if she doesn't want to talk about it, so I stand and turn again, putting her right back where I found her. I bend to kiss her cheek and then she rolls away from me, goes back to staring at nothing.

TWENTY-FIVE

Weatherly

I wake to the feel of Tag's weight bearing down on the mattress and, a few seconds later, his arm sliding around me to drop over my waist. His body heat almost burns me from behind. My body wants to move toward it, to sink into it, but my brain keeps me perfectly still. It's the same war that I've been fighting for hours now. My brain and my heart can't agree on anything. And my body . . . well, it's just a damned unruly traitor.

I don't move a muscle until I feel the steady puff of Tag's breath against my neck grow deep and even. Only then do I relax enough to fall back to sleep.

In my dreams, lips that feel like heaven are kissing my neck. I arch my back and press my hips into the rigidity prodding me from behind. A breathy sigh tickles the hair by my ear and the hardness presses back. Heat pours into my belly, saturating the place where my thighs are squeezed together.

A warm hand glides over my hip and pulls my nightgown up to my waist. A rough palm settles on my stomach and inches its way down. Down, down, down to the ache that never seems to abate.

Long fingers cup the inside of my thigh and lift my leg, setting it on a firm, slightly hairy one. The cool night air hits the damp material of my panties and I groan softly. The hand shifts and I feel the *snap* of elastic breaking. Silk parts, leaving me open to the insistent fingers that find my core. I gasp at the first contact. A gentle exploration of my folds proves that I'm wet, more than ready for whatever my dream lover has in mind. A naughty explicative is growled into my ear and then the hand disappears. There is movement behind me and then something broad presses into my entrance. I tilt my hips back toward it, craving fulfillment on an unconscious level.

I feel hands again, teasing and taunting, pinching my nipples as the smooth head rocks between my legs. I whimper, desperate to know the pressure of it inside me, filling me up.

The palm skates down my stomach again, finding my clit and rolling it gently between skilled fingertips. I reach back and dig my fingernails into a firm, muscular butt cheek, pulling it toward me, begging for more. And I get it. All at once, he dips down just enough and then pushes up and into me, stealing my breath.

Teeth and tongue are at my ear, fingers and palm are at my mound, heat and strength are at my back. And the voice, the voice I'll never forget is ringing out into the dark. "Jesus Christ, you feel so good!"

And that's what brings me awake. Fully awake. To Tag touching me, making love to me, thrilling me. From dream to reality, Tag owns my body. It seems that's a fight I'm destined to lose.

So I give up fighting. I place my hand over his and I urge him on me, his fingers playing, his palm massaging, all the while his long, thick cock is sliding in and out, in and out.

When my breath starts coming in erratic bursts, Tag picks up his pace, pushing me relentlessly toward a release that I'm losing control over. I bite down on my lip and I push it back. I fight it with everything that I have, somehow reasoning that if I can keep from letting go, I might stand a chance of surviving Tag Barton.

But he's not satisfied with that. As if sensing that I'm holding back, Tag pulls out and sits up in bed. He looks down at me, his gaze eating me up before he even touches me again. I squeeze my eyes shut, unable to resist if I can see his gorgeous face and his gleaming eyes. I see the want there. I see the passion that's only for me, but it's all a lie. A lie that hammers ten-inch spikes into my heart. So I block him out the only way that I can.

Tag gently rolls me fully onto my back and parts my legs. He runs his hands from my knees to my groin and follows them with his lips. They continue up my body, stopping only to pay homage to my navel and my nipples before I feel them at my throat. Still, I don't look at him. I can't.

He goes still after he settles between my legs. I feel him throbbing at my entrance. I feel my entrance lapping at his crown, begging him to come inside.

"Look at me, Weatherly," he orders softly.

I squeeze my eyes shut tighter.

He shifts on top of me, rubbing the head of his cock between my folds, a move specifically designed to drive me mad. I grit my teeth and pray for strength.

"Please look at me. I want to see your eyes," he pleads, dragging his lips over my chin and my jaw, to my ear. "Please."

There's something earnest in that one word. It sounds different. It *feels* different, different even from the first one in the sentence. It seems . . . desperate. Maybe that's why, against my better judgment, I open my eyes.

I'm held the moment I meet his gaze. His gray eyes are deep, shadowy pools of mercury that suck me in and steal my will, destroy my resistance. With our gazes locked, he slides slowly into me, a sweet promise made without words. His eyes never leave me, penetrating me deeper than his body. All the way to my soul. "I think I'm falling in love with you, my fair Weatherly."

I gasp, his words so close to the ones I've waited and longed to hear from him. They melt into my blood as orgasm spreads through my body, his confession an accelerant to the fire in my belly. Like a blazing heat, it starts at the place where we're joined and radiates outward, suffusing my every cell, warming my every muscle.

I groan at the feeling, unlike anything I've ever experienced. Rather than violent and explosive, as it normally is, this is deep and steady. Reverent almost. It pulses gently through me with a ceaselessness that rocks me to my very core.

Tag doesn't take his eyes off me. Not when his breath hitches, not when his body jerks, not when his muscles quiver. We savor every second, every subtle nuance together, locked. Joined.

And when the heat starts to wane, when the ecstasy begins to abate, Tag leans forward to brush his lips across my cheek, capturing the single tear that escaped from the corner of my eye.

When I wake again, Tag is gone. I feel him as if he were still here, though. My body remembers every touch. My heart remembers every word. If only I could believe either.

I think I'm falling in love with you, my fair Weatherly.

God, how I wanted to hear those words a day ago, a week ago! But now? I can't help wondering if somehow he knew how much I wanted to hear those words and he's using them against me, another manipulative tool designed to get something from me.

My eyes burn with unshed tears as I'm overcome with that feeling of loss again. I grieve what was. Or what *I thought* was. I grieve what will never be. I mean, where could we possibly go from here? He married me to get Chiara. To my soul, that feels like he married me to steal from me.

Searing pain pulses through my chest. The truth hurts so much. But I have to push back the pain. I almost blew it yesterday. I can't let him know that I know, which means that today I have to act more normal. Starting now.

I shower and dress and make my way to the kitchen. It's empty, but there is a basket of warm muffins, covered with a towel and a note from Tag. *Enjoy, beautiful. I'll be back before lunch. T.*

I bite into a moist blueberry muffin and pour myself a cup of coffee from the still-warm pot. I don't taste either. I might as well be eating cardboard and drinking wet air. I glance at the clock on the wall. It's just after eight, nowhere near lunch. I perk up as my brain starts to form an idea. A plan. Maybe during his absence, I can find something to use *against him*, or something to help us. To help *me*.

After I brush crumbs off my shirt and rinse out my mug, I sneak back up the stairs to the room that Tag moved into the day that I arrived here. When he was forced to move out of mine. I can't be certain that he'd even keep anything incriminating here, but if by chance he *did*, I intend to find it.

Only not in the bedroom. I find some clothes, some personal hygiene things that have not yet made it into "our room" and a few other uninteresting odds and ends. Nothing important or telling. Or helpful.

As I make my way back down to the first floor, I rack my brain for other places he might've left things. I can't believe that there wouldn't be *anything* of a business nature here. Not one scrap of paper, not one note. A laptop or computer. There *has to be* something somewhere. I just have to find it.

I meander through the house, hoping I'll be inspired, but I'm not. I head outside and into the grass, following the curve of the yard around to the back of the house. I see the caretaker's quarters with its open front door, although I don't see Stella. She might be resting. Tag kept on the housekeeping services, just to a lighter degree, while we were gone. I imagine he might keep them on full time so that Stella doesn't have to work in her condition.

As I eye her little place, I wonder if he'd have kept important things there. I can't imagine why, though, since he wasn't actually staying there with her.

Then I remember the cabin. The one that's being renovated. The one that he was staying in intermittently before he took up residence at the main house. The remodeling was confined to the bath and kitchen, with only painting to take place in the other areas of the small structure. Nothing that would necessitate Tag moving *all* his stuff out. Maybe he left some things there. In a desk, maybe, or a cabinet or a drawer. If he did, it'll be locked, no doubt. It would have to be, what with the way it was renting out to perfect strangers there for a while. But only important things are locked. And what I'm after would definitely be considered an important thing.

I turn and walk in that direction. According to Tag, the renovations came to a standstill because the old family friend who was acting as contractor was involved in a car accident. He had to postpone work for three months while he completed physical therapy after his knee surgery. I think that was only about two months ago, not long before I arrived, so the cabin should still be vacant. Private. Searchable.

I feel paranoid, like someone could but look at me and know that I'm up to no good. I glance guiltily left and right as I traverse the shaded path that leads to the cabin. I find no one watching me, but it does nothing to calm my nerves.

I breathe a sigh of relief when I reach the big oak that stands guard over the quaint little cabin. It has two small dormers and a rustic front porch that make it perfectly suited to the mountainous backdrop. The inside will be state of the art after the remodel is complete, but it will still retain all of its traditional vineyard charm.

The front door is unlocked, so I push my way in and close it behind me. It takes my eyes a few seconds to adjust to the dim light, but when I do, I can see what great work has been done thus far.

The kitchen has been outfitted with stainless steel appliances, tile backsplash and a skylight, and there are two slabs of granite resting on the island, as though someone stopped mid-project expecting to return the following day. Only no one did.

I take a minute to look around. It's been years since I've been inside this place.

My casual browsing comes to a screeching halt when I reach the bedroom. Beneath the plastic sheeting, the same kind that has been placed over all the furniture, I see a small desk pushed into a corner. The construction dust is hardly noticeable, which is in sharp contrast to the thick coating that covers every other piece. Someone has come to this desk recently. Or maybe often. They've peeled back the sheeting to look underneath. I just hope whatever drew them here is still present.

Carefully, I fold the sheeting onto itself, revealing the wooden desk with its four drawers and matching chair. A laptop rests, closed, on the surface, making me wish that I had more time. I'll need to have a better idea of where Tag is and when he left before I attempt to break into his computer. For now, I'll have to settle for going through the drawers.

There is a key lying at the edge of the laptop, in plain sight. Even though it's a long shot, I grab it and see if it fits the master lock for the desk.

And it does.

I pause, frowning. If he left it unlocked, or the key so easy to find, there can't be anything of import here. But then I reason to myself that since the cabin has been empty of both guests and contractor for two months, maybe Tag just left it unlocked because he was the only person here.

Until me. And he probably never thought poor little rich girl, Weatherly, would ever catch on to his ruse.

Whether my logic is flawed or not, I know it won't hurt to at least look while I'm here. So that's what I do.

Going through the drawers, I flip through notebooks and papers, files and folders. There are all sorts of things about the running of Chiara, things any caretaker might track, but nothing suspicious. I find information about the passing of Joseph Barton, Tag's father. The death certificate, the obituary, some pictures of their family in the early years. Nothing that I need, though.

I'm about to give up when I see an envelope sticking out from underneath that stack of papers. It's simply labeled *Jameson Gregory Randolph III.*

The hair on the back of my neck stands up when I read that name. Jameson Randolph is the owner of Randolph Consolidated, the company that has been staging a hostile takeover of my father's company. Why in the world would Tag be in possession of something that references him or belongs to him?

A week ago, I wouldn't even have considered going through Tag's things this way. A week ago, I had *no reason* not to trust him and *every reason* to give our marriage a real shot. But today isn't a week ago. Today everything is different. Today I don't have the luxury of trust. That's why, with trembling fingers, I turn over the envelope and reach inside for the contents.

There are two letters inside, one on plain, white copier paper, the other on thick, creamy stationery. I unfold the white one first.

Dear Mr. Barton,

My name is Franklin Evans. I am the lead attorney for Randolph Consolidated as well as the personal counsel for Jameson Gregory Randolph, Jr. I realize this will come as a surprise to you, but I beg you to read the enclosed letter in its entirety and then call me at my home number, listed below. There are some very important matters that we must attend to regarding the death of your father and his estate.

I look forward to hearing from you,
Franklin J. Evans, Esq.

I set the first letter in my lap and unfold the second, my heart thumping heavily against the inside of my rib cage. Some primal, intuitive part of me knows that I will not like what I find within the rich, vanilla folds of the second letter, but I have to know. The gloves have come off. The fight has gotten dirty. And in a battle like this, information is power. I've heard my father say that all my life, but I never thought it would hit so close to home one day.

Tag,

This is probably the first you've heard of me and I'm not going to apologize for that. Your mother and I made the decision jointly to keep you removed from my world, to let you grow up outside the dog-eat-dog business that she hated so much. I doubt she ever even told you about me, but I'm your father. Your biological father, that is.

I met your mother many years ago when she was working as a maid here at my home. I was married, but she was young and beautiful and I was accustomed to taking anything I wanted whenever the mood struck me. But your mother was different. She wasn't like the other women I'd grown used to. She was kind and wholesome, too good for a man like me. That's why when she told me she was pregnant, we decided to part ways. She could never have been happy here and I wanted to do right by her for once. That's why I let her go.

I didn't know it at the time, but my wife was barren. It wasn't a concern until I had my first heart attack just over a year ago. Since then, I've been trying to convince Stella to tell you about me, but she refused. She wanted to honor the memory of the man you've always known as your father. I understand that, but I find that I can't abide by her wishes any longer. I have an empire that I'd like to see live on after I'm gone, a legacy that should be passed on to the next generation of Randolphs. I don't want those greedy bastards on the board to take control, so I have to bequeath my shares and all my personal holdings to someone. I'd like that person to be you.

I don't expect that I'll be alive very much longer. This might even reach you after I'm gone. I just ask that you at least hear what my man, Franklin, has to say before you walk away from your inheritance.

Although you didn't know it until now, on the day of your birth, you became Jameson Gregory Randolph III. Regardless of the name your mother gave you, your blood is Randolph. Live up to it.

Sincerely,

There's simply an illegible swirl where a name should be, as though Tag's father signed this as a business memo. I can't even imagine receiving a bomb such as this. A letter out of nowhere, changing my entire history. And, likely, my entire future.

My heart is torn, part of it feeling great sadness and empathy for Tag, the other part feeling even more betrayed than I did a few minutes ago. His deception runs deeper than I thought and it's even worse than my father suspected. The man I know as Tag is the person behind all of my current misery. He's the face behind the company that's threatening my world. He's the reason for . . . everything. He's the reason I was being coerced to marry Michael. He's the reason my father closed my trust fund. He's the reason my family stands to lose everything Dad worked so hard for. He's the reason my soul is shattered.

On the flip side, he's also the reason I found hope, the reason I fell in love, and the reason I want to go back to bed and never wake up. For a split second, he was everything good. And now, he's everything bad. How could this be? How could I be so blind?

A crushing sensation settles over my chest, as though Tag physically kicked me right in the vicinity of my heart. With heavy limbs, I replace the envelopes, taking great care to put the key where I found it and roll the dust cover back into place.

Numbly, I make my way out of the cabin and back to the main house. When I get back to my room, I pull out my other suitcase and start filling it with the remainder of my belongings. I never unpacked from our honeymoon, so there isn't that much to gather. I stop at the small desk that sits in one corner of my room and I scribble a note for Tag.

I want a divorce.

Clear. Simple. Honest.

I leave it on the bed and carry first one bag and then the other down to the garage, stowing them in the backseat of my car. My chin trembles as I start the engine and back out into the circular drive. As far as I know, I might never see Tag Barton again. He has what he wants. Or at least he thinks he does. He might let me go and never even try to find me and explain.

I close my eyes against the pain.

He's taken so much from me, even if he never manages to get Chiara legally. He still stole it from me. It was a place of such peace and refuge for me, a place where I could come to remember better days, but now it will never be the same. He might as well have burned it to the ground and left only the ash.

Because of that, part of me is dying as I shift out of reverse and into drive. To make my way forward. Forward, away from the vineyard. Forward, away from Tag. Forward, away from all the hope and possibility that was just within my grasp, but then so cruelly ripped from it.

I begin the drive back to Atlanta, scanning the lush vineyard through watering eyes as I say a silent good-bye to Chiara and all the false happiness I found here. Despite the cold, hard facts, I know that I will never be the same after the last couple of months. I'm leaving a big piece of my heart on this mountain. A big piece that's been crushed into tiny slivers left to mingle with the dirt and die in the warm night.

When my front tires hit the main road, I dial my father's number. His gruff voice is anything but comforting and I almost hate to give him the satisfaction of being oh-so-right. But he's more equipped to deal with treachery of this magnitude. He's lived and breathed this kind of business for as long as I can remember.

"Look into Jameson Randolph's son, Dad. I think you'll find a trail that leads back to Tag. I'll call you in a few days."

I hang up before he can ask questions. I hang up before he can hear me fall apart. I turn off my phone so that I can grieve in peace. And I do. All the way back to Atlanta.

TWENTY-SIX

Tag

Even before I see the raised garage door and empty bay where Weatherly's car was parked, I know that something is wrong. I can feel it, almost smell it in the air like a storm is coming.

I park at the top of the circle and take the front steps as well as the inside steps two at a time. I know before I enter the bedroom what I'll find. Weatherly is gone.

After I check the bathroom and find that, indeed, all her toiletries are gone as well, I see the note lying on the bed. It's short, to the point and bothersome as hell.

I told her I was falling in love with her last night. Why would she leave? I thought she'd *like* hearing that. She told me she loved me on our wedding day, for God's sake. I would've thought she'd be pleased to hear that I have feelings for her, too. Feelings far beyond just the physical.

Now I know without a doubt that I should've told her sooner. But because I didn't, because I didn't tell her everything, I never felt right about telling her how I really felt about her either. Knowing what I knew. Knowing what I was keeping from her. On some level, maybe I was trying to save her from falling for me when she didn't know the ugliest parts. Maybe I was afraid she'd stop loving me if she found out. Maybe I'm not the man I thought I was, the man I *hoped* I was. Whatever the reason, my inability to confess my full feelings for her might well have cost me *her*.

I shake my head, throwing off that reasoning.

No, it can't be that. Weatherly isn't the type to run because of something like that. She wouldn't throw away what we have just because I can't say the L word yet. She's not that fragile. No, it has to be something else. Something has happened. That's the only plausible excuse. I know . . . *I know* . . . that Weatherly loves me. I can see it in her eyes, feel it in her touch. Women can't fake shit like that. And even if they could, Weatherly couldn't. She's not that kind of woman. She's *real*.

So then why is she gone? Why now? Why without a word? Jesus H. Christ, what the hell happened?

I think back over every word, every minute of the less-than-twenty-four hours we've been back and the only thing I can figure is that her father said something to upset her. Upset her enough to want to leave me. And divorce me.

I want a divorce.

I bound back down the stairs. I don't pack a single belonging. I head straight for Mom's place.

The front door is open, so I swing through the screen just enough to talk to her where she's sitting in the small kitchen.

"Will you be okay if I'm gone for another day or two?" I ask, suddenly feeling guilty for leaving her again. But this is something I have to take care of. I have to find Weatherly and bring her back here. I can't figure out how to help her if she's in Atlanta, hiding things from me. Her place is here. At Chiara. With me.

She raises her eyes to mine. I see the concern in them, but I don't see pain. She just looks tired, as she so often does. "I'll be fine. Are you going after her?"

"Yeah. How did you know she was gone?"

She shrugs. "Besides hearing her drive off, I just had a feeling that she would leave."

I frown at that. "Well, I'm gonna bring her back and figure this out. I just have a feeling it's something I'll have to do there. I don't expect her to answer her phone. Not after the way she left."

"No, I wouldn't expect so."

"The food service people will still be cooking for you. And cleaning up. Whatever you need. I know I told you they were contracted through our honeymoon, but I didn't give them an end date for their services. And I won't. So use them, okay? Don't be stubborn and try to do everything for yourself."

"I'm not—"

"Mom," I interrupt, giving her a withering look. "Don't even try it. We both know you're stubborn, but I don't feel comfortable leaving if you're not going to use them. It's either use them or I'll be forced to stay and you'll ruin my chances with Weatherly. So which will it be?"

Her smile is small and sad. "A ruthless negotiator, just like your father."

We both know that's not the best of compliments, considering that my *real* father was a sharklike businessman.

"Hey, if it gets me what I want . . ." I say with my own shrug.

"That's just what he would say."

Normally, I'd take exception to that, but I don't have time to debate the despicable traits that I inherited from my father. I've got a wife to find and bring home.

"Promise me, Mom."

Her sigh is weak but audible. "Fine. I promise. But *you* have to promise *me* something."

"Like what?"

"Promise me that you'll tell her the truth. All of it. Promise me that you'll do your best to let her in. She's good for you. I can see it. And she could mean the difference between you turning out like your biological father and you living a good, happy life that would make any mother proud."

"So you're saying I'm destined to be an awful person if I can't get her back?"

"No, I'm just saying that a life without love leaves room to love the wrong things. Money, power, influence. Those kinds of love can destroy you."

"You know I'm only interested in one thing, Mom."

"But don't let your determination to have your way cloud your view of right and wrong."

"Are you saying that it already has? Is that what this is about?"

"I didn't say that."

"You didn't have to."

Although her expression is grieved, she doesn't try to argue with me. That alone is answer enough.

"I'll have my phone with me at all times. Call if you need anything, okay?"

"I'll be fine."

"And remember your promise," I tell her as I back out the door.

"Remember yours."

As if I could forget.

TWENTY-SEVEN

Weatherly

I've been home less than two hours when a knock sounds at my door. There's only one person it could be and I really don't feel like dealing with him. But if I don't do it now, he won't let me rest until I do. One can only avoid William O'Neal for so long.

I swing open the door to my father's angry red face. "I'll sue that son of a bitch! If he thinks he can get away with this, he has no idea who in God's great kingdom I am," he says as he storms past me.

With a sigh, I close the door behind him, bracing myself for a furious tirade. "You can't sue him for being a liar, Dad. It's not illegal. If it were, half the people you do business with would be in jail."

I don't add that he, too, would likely be imprisoned.

"Don't tell me what I can and can't do! I employ some of the most vicious lawyers on the eastern seaboard. I can do anything I damn well please."

I resist the urge to roll my eyes. This is typical O'Neal temper rearing its ugly head. Reason and rationale go right out the window when he gets like this. He just wants someone's blood and he wants it now.

I swallow my sigh, but I can't keep the sadness from my voice. Not completely. "Maybe Donald will have some suggestions. Have you talked to him since I called? Did you give him this new information?"

"Yes. He's looking into things from his end, but I've also reached out to a contact I have on the Randolph Consolidated board of directors. If this little asshole wants to play hardball, he can see firsthand how the big boys play."

"What are you planning, Dad?"

"I did a little digging after we got off the phone. It seems that all the stock was left to Jameson Gregory Randolph III. While Tag's blood might be Randolph blood, his legal name isn't. Stock has to be transferred to a living heir or recipient. If Tag hasn't made some other legal arrangements to take over Jameson Junior's holdings *as Tag Barton*, he might not have a leg to stand on."

"So he'd have nothing, then?"

My father's smile is smug and mean as hell. "Not a damn thing except a job at a vineyard, which he'll lose, and whatever meager savings he's managed to amass on his own."

I should be thrilled at the prospect of Tag being destitute after what he's put me through, after what he attempted to do to me and my family. So why am I not? Why do I feel like this is taking things too far? He had no such qualms when he lied to me to get what he wanted. Why should I have any qualms about hurting him?

It does bring rise to one confusing question, though. "Dad, if Tag has controlling interest and all the wealth that goes along with being the sole heir of Jameson Randolph, why would he marry me for Chiara? Why would he even want it when he's already got so much money? He could buy ten vineyards."

"Because he's a greedy, soulless bastard, just like his father."

That's a pat enough answer, but I'm not buying it. It makes no sense that Tag would go to such extremes for a modest vineyard. On top of that, the Tag who I came to know and fall in love with was anything but greedy. Of course, I obviously had no idea who he *really* was, so what the hell do I know?

That brings me back to the present, to my current predicament.

"Well, whatever happens from here on, I'm out. I just want the divorce and Chiara. The rest is between you two."

I'm not sure I'll ever even visit my family's vineyard again, but this is more about the principle of the thing. One day I may change my mind. One day, when all of this is behind me and my heart is hopefully healed, I might want to revisit the place that I've loved for so much of my life.

But right now, I can't see that day arriving. I can't imagine how I'll be able to look at Chiara the same way again. I can't imagine how I'll be able to go there without seeing his face, feeling his touch. I also can't imagine how I'll ever get over falling in love with Tag Barton.

What began as a hideaway became my burial ground. And the man who felt like my biggest blessing had now become my biggest curse.

TWENTY-EIGHT

Tag

One of the benefits of being the surprise heir to a Fortune 500 company is the breadth of resources available. Money can buy the best when it comes to that. I had to make but a single call and fifteen minutes later I had Weatherly's well-hidden address on my phone. Information has always been valuable—in life, in the Army, in personal affairs. Never has it been so welcomed, though. I feel relief, as though I'm back in control, knowing that Weatherly can't escape me. Can't hide from me. If I couldn't find her, couldn't get to her . . . that would be a problem.

I slow to a stop in front of the beautifully landscaped high-end patio homes. They look like Craftsman bungalows in an exotic rainforest or something. The surroundings are exquisite and lush, totally befitting of a woman like Weatherly. I can picture her here just as clearly as I can picture her covered in mud, lying beneath me between the rows of grapevines at Chiara. I'll probably never be able to get that out of my mind—her creamy skin covered with my muddy handprints, her delectable body coming to life at my touch.

I get out and walk purposefully to the door that should belong to Weatherly. I'm not letting her go so easily. Whatever it is that her father is up to, she needs to know that I'm not going away without a fight.

I ring the doorbell and knock twice on the door, anxious to get this straightened out and head back home. I couldn't be more surprised when William O'Neal answers the door, thunder on his face.

"What the hell are you doing here, Randolph?" he spits venomously.

For the first time, my pulse stutters. He just called me Randolph.

He knows. And if he knows, Weatherly knows.

Shit!

That's what this is all about.

TWENTY-NINE

Weatherly

I watch Tag's face as my father's words sink in. I see the guilt wash in like a pale, frothy wave. If there was ever a teeny tiny part of me that thought maybe he had intentions of coming clean eventually, that teeny tiny part just died a teeny tiny, miserable death. It's clear that Tag didn't want me to know.

"Jesus, Weatherly," he begins, pushing past my father. I stop him in his tracks.

"Don't. Just don't. Whatever you came here to say, it doesn't matter." I didn't imagine that it would be so hard to say those words. My throat constricts as though it's trying to close in around them, to stifle them. To keep me from uttering them. To keep me from ending things. Forever. "This is over. And you need to leave."

"Weatherly, whatever you think—"

"It's not a matter of what *she thinks*, you son of a bitch! It's a matter of what *she knows*.

"Listen, O'Neal," he says, whirling angrily toward Dad. "I get that you're her father and all, but she's a grown woman. This is between Weatherly and me. It's none of your business."

"None of my business? *None of my business?*" Dad hisses through gritted teeth. "You've been trying to take everything from me and my family, you marry my daughter for her vineyard, and you think *that* is none of my business? You couldn't be more wrong."

"I didn't . . . It's not what . . . This is all a big misunderstanding. If you'll give me a few minutes with Weatherly—"

"She doesn't want a few minutes with you, or didn't you hear that? She's done with you. And when *I* get done with you, you'll wish you'd never met the O'Neals."

"Look, do what you want. *Think* what you want. I don't give a shit. She's the one I care about. *She's* the one I need to talk to. I need to tell her that I tried to buy Chiara so that my mother would always have a home. So that she wouldn't be uprooted in her condition. She's dying, for chrissake. I didn't want her to have to move when you found out she could no longer be your housekeeper and your cook."

"I would never have—"

"Don't give me that load of crap! You're a ruthless businessman who sees only bottom lines. You don't see people or lives or futures. You see dollar signs. And she would be a liability in your eyes. Don't pretend to be someone you're not, *O'Neal*!"

"However you try to paint this, you're still the bad guy here.

You lied to my daughter. You tricked her into marrying you so that you could get your hands on her property. Well, I've got news for you, smart guy. Chiara is protected. It doesn't convey through marriage. It—"

"You think I don't know that? You think I didn't do my homework? That I can't afford to hire a fleet of lawyers to research this, to find a loophole? I knew exactly what I was doing when I married your daughter. I knew what I was doing when my company donated five million dollars to her charity, too."

My heart flutters at his words. "That was you?"

Tag turns to me now. His face softens and I'm reminded again of how amazing he can be, of how happy I was with him. For a while. Before he broke my heart.

"Of course it was me. I knew it meant a lot to you. And I figured you'd marry Michael if you had to, just to save those kids."

"And you couldn't have that, could you?" my father sneers. "You couldn't risk anyone getting to it through my daughter before you."

"I can't deny that. I didn't want anyone else involved with Chiara, anyone who might influence Weatherly. Anyone who might pose a threat to the only home my mother has known in nearly thirty years. But donating to Weatherly's charity is hardly the act of a monster."

"Then why marry her? Why do this to her if your intentions were so pure?"

"At first, it was just a stall tactic. I had to buy some time. When she told me about Safe Passage, I knew that could be the answer. She wouldn't *have to* marry then. I could buy Chiara from her and my mother would be safe. I knew she would never make Mom leave. I knew she wasn't *like you*. But then . . ."

My father glares silently at Tag, waiting. I'm the one who prompts him when his pause drags on.

"But then what?"

"But then I started to really *want* to marry you," he says quietly, his smoky gray eyes sucking me in, fogging my resolve.

"If what you say is true, then why hide who you were? Once you made the donation, why hide that you're Jameson Randolph's son?"

"I knew she'd hate me. I knew this would happen. And I didn't want it to."

"Just how long did you think you could keep it from her? How long did you think you could hide it?"

Tag shrugs. "As long as I needed to. It's surprisingly easy to cloak ones identity when money is no object."

"So you'd have lied to me forever?" I ask, the tiny kernel of hope I'd begun to foster shriveling up inside me.

"Honestly?" he asks, stepping closer to me. "If I thought telling you the truth could cost me *you*, then yes. I'd have lied to you forever. I didn't realize until recently that I'd do just about anything to have you in my life. To make you happy. And I knew this would make you hate me."

I don't know how he can make the confession of willfully lying to me sound so much like a confession of love, but I'm struggling to retain my anger. My father must see that, too, though. And he takes measure to restore it.

"If you think for one second that your smooth talking will get you out of this, you're a bigger fool than I thought. You manipulated my daughter. You used her, lied to her and just admitted to having no problem with doing it forever if it suits your purposes. The best thing you can do for yourself is leave her the hell alone. This is going to get ugly enough for you as it is. You can trust me on that."

Tag is still watching me, his eyes pleading with me, as my father stomps to the door and jerks it open.

"I suggest you do the smart thing and get out of here before I call the police."

"I'm her husband," Tag informs in a husky voice. It's a statement of fact, yes, but it also has a possessive ring to it that stirs something primal in me. It's as though he's saying that I'm his and that no one can do a damn thing about it.

The words . . . the tone . . . the look in his eyes . . . Chills spread down my back.

"Not for long," Dad growls. "Now get out!"

"I'll need to hear her tell me that, if it's all the same to you."

He's standing so close. His scent is so achingly familiar. There are still parts of me that gravitate toward him, that want to lean in to him like a freezing person might lean in to heat.

But he hurt me. He lied to me. He manipulated me. Those are facts, too. I'm not sure I will ever be able to trust him again. Not after this. No matter how much my heart wants me to.

"You need to go, Tag. It's for the best. This was a mistake, right from the start."

"You don't mean that," he says, his voice low. "You *can't* mean that."

"What did you expect, Tag? You lied to me. Right from the beginning. How did you think this would end?"

"I didn't. I didn't expect it to end. I didn't want it to. I know I didn't tell you on our wedding day, but I thought this would be forever. I . . . I know now that I should've told you, but I thought I made that clear in every second that we spent together." He moves in close, his voice reduced to a breathy whisper that my father would have no hope of hearing. "Every touch," he says, raising his hand as if to touch my face, only to let it fall away before he does. "Every kiss." His eyes, his tortured, tortured eyes drop to my lips before they close, as if it's too painful to look at them. To remember.

"Stop, Tag. I can't . . . This is just . . . You need to leave." The tremor in my voice is an almost palpable ripple in the air.

I pray to God that he doesn't know how hard this is for me, how close I am to just falling back into his arms. I'm on the verge of throwing all caution to the wind—again—and giving in. No matter how bad that would be for me, no matter how deeply I could be hurt. In moments like this, when everything between us is sizzling to the surface and emotions are running high, I think I might give up anything—any amount of future pain and heartache—to be with him for just one more day, just one more night.

I've never been happier than when I was in his arms.

But I've also never been *unhappier* after making these recent discoveries.

His eyes open and his expression falls in the subtlest of ways. "I'll go. For now. But I won't be far. I won't *ever* be far. You're mine, fair Weatherly. You might not believe that right now, and I've done a shitty job of telling you, but I love you and I'm not giving up."

He places a chaste kiss on my cheek, little more than warm breath and warm lips, before he turns away and strides back across the room.

"This isn't over," he tells my father as he passes.

"It was over before it began."

Tag pauses, stares at my dad for a few seconds and then glances at me over his shoulder. His eyes hold mine for a heartbeat and then he's gone, leaving me arguably more miserable than I was before he came.

I never dreamed days could be so long and exhausting. And not in a good way. Not in the way days felt long when I was with Tag, as though we had all the time in the world. Not in the way I felt limp and satisfied after making love with him for an hour, as though my muscles had turned to jelly. No, these days are painful. Agonizing. Humiliating. Never ending.

Somehow, word about Tag's identity leaked out and made its way around our circles. I'm sure my father had something to do with that.

For the last thirteen days, there has been a mixture of outrage, disgust and pity. The outrage coming from most of Dad's associates. The disgust has been primarily with my mother and her friends. And the pity . . . well, that's been coming from my friends. I've been getting calls and visits, but the one common factor that every caller and visitor shares is pity. It's in the voices, in the eyes, in the tentative smiles. They're fairly dripping with it, as if to say, "Poor Weatherly. She fell in love with a man who was just using her."

And they're right. All of them. I let first my attraction and then my love for Tag blind me. I was so desperate to find love *on my own* that I didn't think about ulterior motives, even though I had one myself. Sort of. But mine didn't hurt anybody. And he knew what it was. I can't say the same for his. Tag's are *still* hurting me. And he's not helping.

In between visits and calls, I've had deliveries. Dozens of them. Flowers, candy, expensive jewelry, all with similar sentiments on the card—*I'm sorry, Please forgive me, Don't give up on us, I love you.* At first, it was as though Tag was just lashing out with his money, but then, with later deliveries, I began to see the heart behind the gifts. It was subtly personal for a day or two. Wildflowers from the forest near the waterfall where he proposed, a basket of grapes from the field our cabin overlooked, earrings that match my engagement ring, bread from a little bakery we found on our honeymoon. The gifts haven't stopped. Not for one day. They only seem to be getting harder to ignore, especially when my delivery came on Tuesday and I began to realize what our time together meant to Tag. Every moment, it seems, made an impression on him as well. The evidence came to my front door that day and every day since.

It was in the form of a picture. It was a photograph taken at Chiara, showcased beautifully in a heavy silver Tiffany's frame. It wasn't the frame that stopped my heart, though. It was the picture itself. The shot was taken at sunrise after a rain, in between the rows of grapevines. The earth was dark and wet, and there were puddles that held water, reflecting the fiery orange of the rising sun. I took one look at it and I knew which row it was. I knew why he took a picture of that exact puddle. There was a handprint in the mud, possibly the one that Tag left there as he drove his body into mine that first time. Chills spread over my skin when I saw it. I stared at it for at least a full minute before I sat down in the floor, leaned up against the front door and cried.

That wasn't the only picture either. I've gotten eight so far. All of them have come in stunning frames, some even encrusted with jewels, jewels that I'd be willing to bet are real. But they've never impressed me. No fancy frame could do that. No jewelry or flowers or candy could do it either. Only the personal gifts, only the meaningful pictures.

Every day Tag has told me that he loves me. Not in words, but in the beautiful hues of a sunrise, captured at different spots throughout the Chiara lands that have special meaning only for us. Each of them has chiseled away at the ever-widening crack in my heart until it's now an all-consuming chasm.

I might've weakened by now if it weren't for my parents, my mother especially. In her artful way, she tells me what's going on in the outside world. She keeps me informed of the fallout from Tag's audacious maneuver. He's the talk of the town in our circles, which means I am, too. In ways I never wanted to be. The elite Atlanta corporate world is divided—those on the O'Neal side and those on the Randolph side.

According to Mom, "people" are calling Tag the only man worthy of the Randolph name. They're saying he's a bigger asshole than his father. More cunning, more ruthless. His name is the worst kind of curse in my family and it gets worse by the day.

Some of the local papers have even begun to pick up on what's going on, citing the whispers of a new corporate magnate on the scene. And evidently Tag is making this name all by himself. Randolph blood really must run in his veins. Turns out my hot-blooded winemaker is nothing more than a cold-blooded shark.

THIRTY

Tag

I rented a little office in Enchantment when I found out about my real father all those months ago. I knew I'd need a place to conduct business that was unrelated to Chiara and my life there. Maybe that was a by-product of the way *I* felt—somehow separated from my life there, as though my biological father drove a wedge between the past and the present.

In some ways, Chiara and my childhood there felt like a lie. At least for a while. It got easier with time, and even easier once Weatherly came along. She's why I've rented yet another office space, only this one in Atlanta so that I can be close to her, even though there doesn't seem to be a need to be right now.

I've called several times. She won't answer. She hasn't said anything about the gifts I've been sending either. Not that I'm really surprised. I guess I just hoped.

Since that first day at her place, the proverbial shit has hit the fan. News quickly spread about Jameson Randolph's heir and his merciless business ethics. Little do they know that the only business transaction I've been behind since my father died was the bid for Chiara. The board of directors has been at the helm of Randolph Consolidated—ostensibly in an effort to give me time to get adjusted—and that's been okay with me. On any given day, I'd rather be working the fields at Chiara than dealing with a bunch of assholes in expensive suits. Chiara was real. They weren't.

Until now. Now, nothing seems quite right. Nothing seems to fit. Not even Chiara. Without Weatherly, I feel like a ship lost at sea. I'm sort of aimless. Restless. Part of me wants to go back to Chiara and resume my life there, but I know that when I get there, it'll be empty without her. Besides, I wouldn't feel right going back there and picking up life where it was before her. Chiara is hers. It didn't convey in marriage. I know she would never make Mom leave, but it wouldn't be right for me to go back like none of this happened. Mom is safe. That's all I care about. That and Weatherly. I'm not sure I even want to go back there yet anyway. Not even to visit. Without my wife, it's a totally different place. *Since my wife*, it's a totally different place.

There's a knock at the side door, the one that leads to the private apartment behind my new office. Only a few people know I'm back here, but I don't hesitate to answer it. Since the threats to our team were neutralized, we are all back to life as usual. Well, as usual as it can be for three ex–Special Forces guys trying to make something of their lives.

Today, I don't have to wonder who's visiting. Something in my gut tells me who I'll find at the door, so I'm not at all surprised when I swing open the panel and find Rogan leaning against the jamb.

"You look like hammered shit, man," he says, scrunching up his face in disgust.

"Thanks. That's what I was really needing to hear today, dickweed."

I back up so he can come in, which he does. He slaps my cheek as he passes. "Forget how to shower and shave?"

"No. I just didn't feel like doing either one."

"I can smell. I mean, I can tell." He throws a grin over his shoulder at me. I punch him lightly in the right kidney as a reward. "What the hell did that girl do to you, Tag? I've never seen you like this, bro."

"Like what?" I ask, heading to the fridge for a couple of beers. He doesn't really need to answer my question. I already know what he means. I've wondered the same thing myself, wondered how the hell she worked her way under my skin and into my heart this way. It's like one day I was fine and the next day, *BAM!* I hardly recognize myself.

"Pussy-whipped."

"I'm not pussy-whipped."

"You are *so* pussy-whipped. You think I don't know what it looks like? What it feels like?"

"What? Pussy? I sure as shit hope so."

He gives me a withering look and takes the proffered beer. "You know damn well what I mean. And I'm not busting your balls. Been there, man. In fact, now I'm quite happily pussy-whipped."

"It's not like that," I tell him, feeling pissy that he reduces it to sex when it's so much more than that. "I've had tons of women. At least twice what your pretty-boy ass has had. This is different. It's more than that."

"Calm down, calm down," Rogan says, holding out one hand like I'm a wayward kid he's trying to soothe. "I didn't realize you loved her, dude. Why didn't you just say so?"

"I thought it was fairly obvious."

Rogan grins. "It is. I just like giving you a hard time. Next to Jasper, you're about the hardest bastard to read of anyone I know. But *this* I could see. Hell, I saw it the day you brought her to my house."

"You did?"

He nods. "Yep."

"Then why in God's name didn't you tell me?"

He shrugs. "I knew you'd figure it out eventually. And I didn't want to miss all . . . *this*."

"Thanks a lot. You've been a great friend, asshat," I tell him derisively.

"A good friend is there when things are good, but a great friend comes around when the world falls to shit. That's why I'm here. Your world fell to shit. I came to help you pick up the pieces."

"I appreciate it, Ro, but there's not much you can do on this one, I don't think."

"Maybe not by myself, but you can't forget that I have help. Valuable help."

"What kind of 'valuable help'?"

"I have the help of a woman." He winks at me and takes a long draw from his beer.

My curiosity is piqued. A woman's perspective might actually be beneficial. "Maybe you're not so useless after all."

"Right?"

"So what does Katie say about all this?"

"She asked what you'd done. I told her. She cursed you for the sake of all women for about ten minutes, but then she told me to tell you to figure out what's standing in your way."

I feel deflated. That's no help at all.

"Lies. The past. Things I can't change. But I already knew that."

"She thought you might say that. She said to ask you if there was anything you could do to prove yourself wrong."

"To prove myself wrong?"

"Prove yourself wrong. Or maybe it was to prove yourself worthy. I can't remember now."

I grab a handful of nuts from the bowl on the bar behind me and throw them at him. "Useless. Asshat."

I still can't help smiling when he starts laughing.

"Seriously, though, man. Go see her. Let her see how miserable you are. If that doesn't snap her out of it, then . . ."

"Then what? I'm screwed, right?"

"You might be."

"I'll go by again, but I'm not holding my breath that she'll even open the door. No, Katie's right. I need to prove myself to her. I just don't have a damn clue how to do that."

"It'll come to you, Tag. But until then, go see her. It can't hurt."

I hope not. She doesn't need any more hurt from me.

THIRTY-ONE

Weatherly

I can't imagine being any more uncomfortable. My father was supposed to bring by the divorce papers that his attorney drew up for me. When I heard the knock at the front door, I assumed it was him, so I opened it without checking. I just stood there with my mouth hanging open for a good ten or twenty seconds when I saw Michael Stromberg standing on the stoop.

"I'm sure you'll be happy to get your hands on these." His smile was wide and smug when he handed me the envelope. "Your father asked me to drop them by. He had some errands to run. May I come in?"

My father didn't have errands to run, unless ill-timed matchmaking can be considered an errand.

"Of course," I said politely, stepping back to allow him to enter. It wasn't until I opened the envelope and saw the black-and-white evidence of the dissolution of my marriage to Tag that I felt my insides begin to crumble. For the thousandth time. I didn't know it could keep on hurting, or even hurt worse than it already had, but it could. And it did.

My mind was battered with questions, the same questions I'd asked myself a million times, all without answer. How could something so perfect have been nothing more than a lie? How could something so right have turned out so very, very wrong? How could I be losing the one thing I always wanted—the man of my choosing, someone to love, someone to grow old with? Someone who was mine. All mine. Someone who was with me for no other reason than love.

Only that was never really the case with Tag. He had as much reason to marry me as Michael did, if not more. It was that realization that cut through me, all the way through me, like a sword separating bone from tissue, blood from vessels, heart from chest. It severed the last thread of hope I'd managed to preserve, and without it, I was lost.

That was half an hour ago. Despite my despair, I've had to sit and make polite conversation with Michael this entire time. I nearly sigh in relief when the doorbell rings. I don't care if it's just the deliveryman bringing me another bittersweet gift from Tag. I'm happy with *any* interruption.

Until I open the door and find Tag standing on my stoop this time. At the sight of him, my stomach clenches into a tight knot and my heart pounds so hard I can feel the pulse of it in my toes.

"Hi," he says, stuffing his hands in his front pockets. He looks as though he feels awkward. Under different circumstances, I might call his gesture adorable. It reeks of insecurity and desperation, something that seems foreign on Tag. It probably seems foreign *to* Tag, too. I doubt he's found himself in many situations where he isn't in complete control. I imagine this is hard for him. And it damn well should be.

"Hi," I reply evenly. "What are you doing here?"

"I, uh, I just wanted to stop by and see you."

"Tag, you shouldn't be here. I told you—"

"I know what you told me, but I can't live with that, Weatherly. I love you. I'm *in love* with you. I can't just give up without a fight."

His words please some pathetic part of me that seems impervious to the deception he perpetrated against me. It loves him without condition, without reservation. Still. Always.

"It's too late for that. You should've fought when there was still something left to fight for," I tell him, my anger rising. I hate that he can still make me feel regret and sadness and heartbreak. I hate that I can't be cool and calm and unaffected. I don't know what's showing on my face, but my insides are a mess. They were the instant I laid eyes on him, and they will be for hours after he's gone. And as long as he continues to be a presence in my life—whether through visits or gifts or messages or whatever—I'll never be able to heal enough, to make myself strong enough to put him behind me.

"You know, when I was in Delta Five—that's the Special Forces team that I was a part of—they used to call me the brave one. I was always the first one in, always the one rolling, balls out, into our mission. I wasn't afraid to die or get shot or get stabbed or burned or whatever. I knew I could handle whatever came my way, even death. My parents had bred that into me. To go after what I want, to be fearless and bold. And I always did. I was never afraid of losing. Until now. Until you. I'm brave enough to face knives and guns, death and torture, discovery and capture, and the only thing I've ever known that scares the living shit out of me is losing you."

When I open my mouth to stop him, he keeps going, giving me no chance to speak.

"I know that might not mean much to you, but it means everything to me. I screwed up. I admit it. But I never saw you coming. I never thought I'd meet someone like you, someone who could bring me to my knees with a look or a touch. I wasn't prepared. But now I am. *Now I am.*"

My muscles are shivering, my insides quaking. My mind is swirling with emotions and words, choices and consequences. Can I trust him? My heart tells me that I can, but it's led me astray before.

I want to trust him. I want to believe his words. More than I ever thought I could want anything. Except the man himself.

But I never saw you coming. I never thought I'd meet someone like you, someone who could bring me to my knees with a look or a touch. I wasn't prepared. But now I am.

My heart taps frantically against my ribs, words perched delicately on the tip of my tongue, but before I can respond, a voice sounds from over my right shoulder.

"Won't he take 'no' for an answer, Weatherly?" Michael asks in a haughty voice. I don't have to turn around to know that he's wearing a self-satisfied smile. He was just waiting for the day when he could best Tag.

Tag's eyes, which had clicked to a stop over my head, drop from Michael back down to me. They've gone from warm, soft gray to hard, icy steel. "What the hell is he doing here?" His words are clipped. His voice is low. His demeanor is as ominous as a storm cloud.

Again, before I can answer, Michael speaks up, coming to stand close at my back. "I came to bring her divorce papers. Unlike you, I'm welcome here because I haven't been deceiving her all this time."

"Michael, please," I shoot back over my shoulder in irritation. He's only making a difficult situation even more so.

"Don't pretend like you've got Weatherly's best interests at heart, you greedy bastard. At least I'm in love with her and not trying to make her a miserable trophy wife with a powerful father and a big bank account."

"I can see why she's had enough of you and your lies. As it is, it'll take me months to make her forget your filthy touch, but I assure you, I'm just the man for the job."

I don't know what Michael is doing behind my back; I only know that I don't see the explosion until it happens. Suddenly I'm pushed rather gently to the side and Tag is roaring past me, grabbing Michael by the front of his crisp, white, four-hundred-dollar shirt and hauling him up against the wall hard enough to make plaster sprinkle from the ceiling and pepper my hardwoods.

"If you so much as lay a *finger* on her, so help me God, I'll burn your life to the ground and then throw you in the fire." Tag's chest is heaving. "And if you think I'm bluffing, try me. If you think I'm afraid of you, *try me*. Try me. Please. I'm begging you. I know more about killing people and hiding it than you know about expensive cigars and cheap whores."

I'm quietly holding my breath, uncertain how to respond to this, when Tag surprises me by planting his fist in Michael's stomach. I hear the sickening thud ring through the room. I hear Michael's garbled grunt when he bends forward and then crumples to his knees. Tag, as if he has to finish making his point, puts his foot on the side of Michael's face and pushes until Michael falls over, curled on the floor in the fetal position.

I'm standing, stunned and speechless, when Tag comes to me. He doesn't touch me, but I get the feeling he wants to. Not in anger, but in desperation. He raises his hands twice, but then lets them fall limply to his sides.

"I love you. I love you, damn it! The real, deep, forever kind of love. Can't you see that? God! *God*," he says, gritting his teeth and clenching his fists. "It makes me crazy to think of . . ." With a barely human growl, he spins away from me and stalks to the door. His breath is coming in harsh pants that stretch his shirt across his back, and I can practically feel him trying to control his rage. He swings the door open, but then pauses on the threshold. He just stands there as though he's trying to collect himself. After he's taken several deep breaths, I hear his voice again. It's a plea full of quiet torture and immense regret. "I'm sorry, Weatherly. I didn't come here for this. I can't . . . I just don't . . . I love you. That's all I can tell you. I love you and this is killing me."

And with that, he turns and walks out the door, pulling it shut behind him.

I love Tag. That's the plain and simple truth. I don't want to. I tried not to. But I can't seem to stop and it won't go away. With every day, I mourn the loss of him a little bit more. And this apartment . . . now it's filled with his words, his confession, his gifts, his desperation. I can feel them like a tangible presence, even when my eyes are closed. It's getting harder and harder to breathe every day. Every single day.

Besides that, there are the circumstances of our union—as well as our breakup—and the fact that they're looming around every corner. I know that the only thing that I can do, the only way that I can survive, is to cut ties and start over. I have to get out of here. Away. Way away. However I can. It's the only thing that will save me at this point. I can't be here anymore. In this world. So close to Tag in so many ways, yet so far from him, too.

I refuse to ask my father about my trust, about whether he's decided to change his mind. I don't need his money when it comes with conditions. Instead, I spoke to a realtor yesterday about selling my place. It should give me enough money to relocate and start over, to buy a modest little house somewhere else. Anywhere else. I have no real ties here. My parents aren't involved in my life in any way that necessitates me being local. They have a way of keeping tabs on me no matter where I'm located. The only other thing keeping me here is Safe Passage. I've good people in charge there, though, so I believe the kids and their best interests will be in good hands until I feel like I can come back here and pick up life again. If that ever happens. Until then, they'll be fine.

The last loose end is Chiara. I know Tag can't take it from me. My father had that tied up long ago to prevent *anyone* from being able to take it. Tag just didn't know that. There's no way he could've. But that's not the point anymore. His mother's home—*his home*—meant enough to him to go to all this trouble. And I would never want to hurt Stella. She's always been good to me and she deserves to be able to live out the rest of her life, however short or long that might be, in her home. But at the same time, I want nothing to do with it. Everything surrounding Chiara is too painful now, too bittersweet. I'll never be able to move on if I don't let it go and, by extension, let Tag go. So I'm going to sell it to him. Like he wanted. Only I will insist that it be put in Stella's name. She'll undoubtedly will it to him when she passes, but at least I'll have that satisfaction in the meantime.

I haven't told Dad yet. I even used a different attorney to have the paperwork drawn up. As soon as it's ready, he'll call Tag and present the offer—the *only* offer. He can take it or leave it. I have a feeling he'll take it, though. And then we'll be over. Officially. Truly. Definitively.

And I'll be alone.

THIRTY-TWO

Tag

"You need sleep, son," Mom says, rubbing my back as she passes. I'm slumped in a kitchen chair with my throbbing head in my hands.

"No shit," I mutter.

"Language." Her soothing circles become a stinging slap before she walks away. "Have you talked to her?"

"Not since I put Michael on his ass. She probably hates me."

"Whether or not you've earned it, I can't see Weatherly hating you. I knew when I saw you two together that she loved you. And real love, *true love* doesn't die that easily. Even when we want it to."

"I just don't know what else to do, Mom. I've told her how I feel. I've apologized every way I can think to apologize. I've begged. I've pleaded. I don't know what else I can do to convince her that I love her. That I need her."

"She doesn't trust you, you know."

I resist the urge to repeat my previous "No shit." "I realize that. But I can't very well earn back her trust if she won't see me, if I can't be around her."

"No, but you can show her that she's worth more than anything to you."

"I have. Or at least I've tried."

I sit up and lean back, letting my head drop onto my tense shoulders. After a few seconds of silence, I see Mom's face pop into my field of view as she bends over me, a stern expression in place.

"Try harder."

"How?"

Her smile is confident and amused. "It'll come to you."

THIRTY-THREE

Weatherly

I'm waiting with my bags by the door for the courier to arrive. He's bringing me some paperwork to sign. Tag accepted the offer, but evidently he has a caveat of his own, one that requires my attention before I leave. It's my last piece of business in Atlanta. From here, I'm going to Missouri. Someplace distant. Someplace different. Someplace I can hide until I heal. *If* I heal.

At the ring of the bell, I open the door, smiling politely at the older gentleman. With his ruddy complexion and slicked back hair, he looks like he should be delivering body parts to those who made the mistake of offending the mafia. I wonder if he'll have a thick Northern accent when he speaks. He says nothing, though, simply hands me a packet, which I take. "Thank you. I won't be a minute."

"Take your time, ma'am," he says in a decidedly Southern way, tipping his head and smiling. The gesture transforms him from a burgeoning criminal into a pleasant, competent courier. It's amazing how that works.

I take the packet to the table and open it, spreading out the papers and looking for the brightly colored tag that indicates where my signature is needed. When I find it, I read the caveat and stop, my pulse picking up speed to a near gallop. Tag's one request is that I bring the papers to him to sign. Personally. At Chiara. Today.

Shit.

I was really hoping to get out of here without seeing him again. It sets me back almost to square one when I see him, when he says things that I long to hear him say. But at least this will be the last time. After today, I can move forward consistently, heal a little more each day. I hope. I'm hoping that out of sight really *is* out of mind. And heart.

I sigh. I suppose leaving tomorrow won't be that big a deal. I wanted to drive to Missouri. Take my time. Think. Just be . . . away. I was planning to stay in a hotel until the movers could pack and move my things to my new place. One day's delay won't change any of that. The *type* of delay, however, might change what I think about on the trip tomorrow.

Actually, it won't. I have no doubt that I'd have thought of Tag ninety percent of the time anyway. Now I'll just have fresh images, fresh words to dwell on.

Fun, fun.

I straighten the papers and stuff them back in the envelope. I take a twenty out of my wallet and head back to the door. When I swing it open, the man is still standing there on the stoop; he moved away from the door just enough that he could stand in the bright morning sunshine. His head snaps around when he hears the door and he smiles reflexively.

I hand him the money. "Thank you for bringing these. It seems I'll be delivering them myself, so I won't have further need of your services."

He nods and discreetly accepts the money as he takes my hand in both of his. "Thank you, ma'am. Enjoy the rest of your day."

I watch him walk off, feeling suddenly anxious about what the rest of my day might hold. I haven't heard from Tag since the offer was made two days ago. In a way, I expected that I might. But then again, I knew I wouldn't. This is what he wanted all along. What's left to say?

That's why I'm nervous about meeting him at Chiara. But I will. I have to get this sewn up before I leave. That's why I pull myself to my full height and square my shoulders. I have to do this and I have to do it now.

The over-two-hour drive only makes matters worse. By the time I get to the winding road that starts up the mountain toward the vineyard, my palms are sweating and I'm nauseous. The *idea* of leaving Tag behind, of making our "end" final, wasn't nearly as upsetting when I was safe at home. At a distance. It seemed like a nebulous thing. But now, knowing that I'll be laying eyes on him for the last time in just a few minutes . . . it's almost more than my poor heart and nerves can handle. This is not the eventuality that I hoped we'd have. I never saw this coming.

I barely feel the warm wind whipping through my hair as I start down Chiara's long, beautiful drive. I'm hardly aware of the lightly scented air or the familiar rows of grapevines that are flying by. I have only one thought, and I'm less than five minutes from him now.

I slow nearly to a stop when the house comes into view. There are four shiny black cars in the circular drive. My heart sinks. I had thought Tag would try once more to tell me that he loves me, that he made mistakes where we are concerned, but I suppose he really *is* getting the only thing he wanted now. Those cars look like they belong to businessmen, men like my father and Michael and their lawyers. All the ingredients to settle up a matter such as this, when all Tag had to do was sign the papers.

Dread floods the back of my throat like bile, and I swallow hard. Whatever lies ahead, this will all be over soon and I'll be on my way to a new state, a new home and a new life. One day, all this will be a vague, unpleasant memory.

That's what I tell myself as I pull to a stop, as I shift into park, as I get out of my car and again as I mount the steps. I take a deep breath and reach for the door handle, ready to face the inevitable, but it swings open before I can, startling me.

Tag is standing just on the other side of the opening, his gray eyes unreadable. My heart lurches in my chest when his lips curve into a polite smile. *Polite.* He's not even going to pretend that there was more to us than this.

"Come in," he says, holding the door as though this isn't still my home.

An unbearable sadness drips through my veins like slow-moving cold water. I return his polite smile and step inside, my stomach turning over miserably when he holds out an arm directing me toward the dining room. I'm not surprised to see a few people, businessmen, who I don't know. I am, however, surprised to see my father here. His expression is carefully blank when his eyes meet mine.

I frown at him as if to ask why he's here. He merely shakes his head in one small, short gesture. I'm even more apprehensive now. This was supposed to be an easy transaction. Not . . . *this*.

I feel Tag's hand at my lower back and I jerk involuntarily. Not because he scared me or because I'm repulsed by this touch. Quite the opposite, in fact. It feels like electricity. Like heaven. Like home. Like no touch for the rest of my life will ever compare to it.

If I were a lesser woman, I might dissolve into a puddle of tears, but instead, I square my shoulders and meet every curious eye in the room, nodding to each of the gentlemen as I go.

"Gentlemen, this is Weatherly O'Neal Barton. Weatherly, this is Tom Geffen, my lawyer. To his left is Gerald, the head of the Randolph Consolidated legal department. Beside him is Fritz Montgomery, the largest shareholder at Randolph Consolidated besides myself, as well as a board member."

"Gentlemen, it's a pleasure," I say demurely, my insides a jittering mass of jelly contained only by the clenched muscles of my abdomen. I can do this part. I was *bred* for this part—to face men like this.

"I'll leave you to finish up. There's something I need to discuss with Weatherly."

With the pressure of his hand guiding me, Tag urges me on through the dining room and into the kitchen, toward the back door. He opens it for me as well. I walk through without question. Although I'm curious as to what he has to say and why he needs privacy to say it, I'm happy that *our* business doesn't involve all those men. Somehow that was very upsetting. Very impersonal, as though we hadn't spent countless hours wrapped in each other's sweaty, naked arms. At least this way, that is somewhat preserved. Even though it's a painfully poignant reminder of what I lost. What I actually never had.

Tag leads me wordlessly through the grass, along the path that fronts the oldest field of grapevines. He continues on and we walk for several minutes, always in complete silence. Then my stomach starts to tighten in a different way. I realize that he's heading toward the unfinished cabin, the one that's little more than four walls and a roof. The one that we spent so many wonderful hours inside, making love and talking.

My throat burns and tears sting my eyes. I didn't expect him to bring me here. I wasn't prepared. I wasn't prepared for any of this.

It takes us about ten minutes to reach the cabin. When we do, I'm surprised to see that there are windows installed and a door in place. I want to ask questions, but I don't. He's obviously been busy, having people finish what he had married into.

I gulp when he stops at the bottom of the steps and turns toward me. He says nothing, just stares down into my face, his gray eyes shining like silver smoke in the dazzling sun, shining with what I now recognize as love. Bright, beautiful love. Gently, he takes my hand and leads me up to the door. He twists the knob and pushes it open, gesturing for me to precede him, so I do.

The interior of the cabin is finished as well. It's furnished sparingly, the biggest additions being a wall that separates the living space from the bedroom and a big, four-poster bed that faces the floor-to-ceiling windows overlooking the lower vineyard.

There's a small mahogany table and chairs right inside the kitchenette area. On its top burns a candle that smells like bougainvillea and sunshine. It has a vaguely familiar aroma that eases the tension in my shoulders despite my heightened anxiety. I note the labels on the coffee and bottles of wine that decorate one end of the countertop—Italian. A bittersweet pang registers somewhere in the vicinity of my broken heart.

I move on, determined to keep my composure. I reach out to touch the glassy surface of the tiny bar as I pass. It, too, reminds me of something I found at our little piece of heaven in Italy—the enameled lava stone that covered the kitchen island and every surface in the bathroom.

I pass through the living room, taking in the cozy loveseat that faces the empty fireplace and the rich bearskin that stretches out between them. Then, because it's the last thing to see, I make my way slowly toward the bed.

I frown when I see the duvet up close. It, too, looks remarkably like the one from our villa in Tuscany. I run my hand over it, chills breaking out down my arms at the feel of it. It even *feels* like the one from our honeymoon. Memories, happy memories, roll through my mind. The grief that follows them nearly brings me to my knees. I gasp involuntarily as I struggle to hang on to what little bit of composure I have left.

"Yes," Tag says quietly from behind my left shoulder.

"What?" I ask, my trembling voice making less noise than the breeze pouring through the open windows.

"Yes, it's from our villa."

Pressure builds inside me. It starts directly over my heart and radiates outward, like a starburst, consuming my entire chest in a blaze of fire. "Why?" I ask, not trusting myself to say more.

"I wanted to surround myself with every little piece of you that I could find. I ended up here. In *our* cabin, with things from *our* honeymoon. Bits of you, *memories* of you everywhere I look."

"Why?" I ask again, my chin trembling with unshed tears, my heart trembling with unrealized hope.

"Because you're the only thing that's ever made me truly happy. You're the only woman I'll ever love. And if you still won't have me, I'll take whatever parts of you I can get my hands on, even if it's a comforter that felt the brush of your skin or a chunk of stone that held your hand."

"You got what you wanted. You don't need me. You don't need *any of this.*"

"You're wrong. I need you more than I need to breathe. More than I need to see or hear or walk. I'd give up everything I am for one more day with you. Just. One. More. Day."

I feel the tears ease from my lashes and work their way silently down my cheeks. How can I ever believe him? How can I ever believe that it's *only me* that he wants, and not some commodity or possession that he can get through me?

The answer is that I can't. I can't believe him. I will always wonder and there's nothing he can do to change that. His wounds cut too deep.

"It's easy to say that when you have everything."

"I *did* have everything," he corrects.

My frown returns. What is he playing at now? "What's that supposed to mean?"

"Those men up there? They're here to finalize a deal."

"What kind of a deal?"

"The kind that merges your father's company and mine. The kind that gives you everything I have, including Chiara. Because you're my wife. And I don't want it if I can't have you. I don't want any of it."

I'm afraid to turn toward him. I'm afraid I'll see that this is a joke. I'm afraid I'll see, once again, that he's trying to deceive me.

But Tag won't leave me with my fear. His big hands come to my shoulders and urge me to face him. And what I find when I do is sincerity. And desperation. And something that looks an awful lot like love.

"I made the biggest mistake of my life when I didn't tell you about Chiara, when I didn't tell you who I was. This stuff . . . *all this stuff* came between us. My lies came between us. I knew you'd never believe my words again, so I'm trying to show you in the only way I know how—by giving you a multibillion-dollar offering. By laying everything I have and everything I am at your feet and begging you to forgive me. To come back to me. To love me again." Tag drops to his knees in front of me and takes my hands in his. "I promise you won't regret it. I'll do anything. Anything, Weatherly. Just ask it. Just say the words and it's done. Whatever it is."

I'm overwhelmed. I'm almost afraid to believe what's happening, to believe what he's saying. "Tag, I—"

"Please, Weatherly," he interrupts brokenly, squeezing my hands and bringing them to the center of his chest. His face is crushed, his eyes dull and pleading. "Please don't say no. I swear to God I don't think I can survive it if you leave me again. I'm nothing without you. This life, this life that I've always loved, is shit without you. If you want to kill me, if you want me *to die*, this is how you do it. You walk out that door. You walk out of my life. But you might as well take mine when you go, because it won't be worth a damn without you in it."

My heart is pounding. My vision is filling. My soul is aching. "I'm afraid, Tag. You hurt me so much and I . . . I . . ."

"I know, baby. I know I did. And I'll spend the rest of my life making it up to you if you'll just let me. If you can just be brave. Brave enough to trust me. To try again. Just this one time, be brave enough to take a chance on me, knowing all there is to know. I wasn't brave enough to tell you the truth and risk losing you, but I lost you anyway. Be braver than me. Risk for me. I promise you won't regret it. Please, Weatherly."

As I stare down into his gorgeous face through a galaxy of sparkling tears, I'm torn. My heart is telling me one thing, my head another. Despite their very different urgings, I know which one I'll follow. It's the one I *have to* follow. The only choice I have.

"I'm only saying yes because I have no choice," I tell him quietly, warmed by the heat of his hands where they hold mine.

Tag's expression falls. "You always have a choice, Weatherly. I would never force you to do something you didn't want to do. I just thought . . . I guess I hoped . . ."

His voice trails off as he drops his head, his fingers loosening their hold on mine. When he releases them, I reach down and curl them into the front of Tag's shirt. Surprised, he glances up at me just as I'm dropping to my knees.

"You listen to me, Tag Barton. No one can force me to do something that I don't want to do. Not even William O'Neal. But this," I tell him, tugging until he leans forward and his belly is pressed to mine, "this is what I want. It's what I *need. You* are what I need. I've never been so miserable . . ." I close my eyes at the mere memory of the pain and heartache I've suffered these last weeks.

Hands cup my face and I crack my lids to find Tag's fierce face less than an inch from mine. "Never. Again," he growls.

"Never again what?"

"Never again will I hurt you. As long as this heart beats, as long as these lungs breathe, you won't be hurt again. Not by me, not by anyone. You're mine. And what's mine, I'd die to protect."

"You can't save me from all the hurts of the world, Tag, but you can save me from yours. Please. Please, please, please don't disappoint me. I don't think I could take it again."

"I won't. Ever. I'd do anything for you. Anything." When I say nothing, his grip tightens. "Do you understand that, Weatherly? Do you really know what it means to me when I tell you I love you? When I tell you that I can't live without you?" He seems almost desperate again, desperate to make me understand what's in his heart.

The thing is, I know exactly what he means.

"Yes. I do."

"Then you know that when I give you *me*, when I make you this promise, I make it on everything that's ever mattered to me.

You're safe with me, Weatherly Barton. You won't ever have to be brave again. I've got you. I've got you," he whispers, his voice laced with emotion.

"Never? Not even for, say, childbirth?" I ask, giving him my first real smile since that fateful day when we got back from our honeymoon.

Tag's face softens, so much so that it brings tears to my eyes. "Childbirth? Children? With *me*?"

"Yes, with you. Only with you. I'd love to have some."

Lips brush mine in the sweetest kiss known to man. Tag then winds his arms around me and crushes me to him in an embrace that tells me finally . . . *finally* everything is going to be all right. I know now—as surely as I know my name and my birthday and that I fell in love with a man the first day that I met him—I *know* that my husband will make sure of it. Because he's brave enough to love me. And I'm brave enough to love him right back.

EPILOGUE

Weatherly

Five years later

The afternoon sun is pouring onto the patio. I take another sip of water, wondering if this was the best idea. In my condition, getting overheated probably isn't a good idea. But when I hear the delighted squeals coming from the water, followed closely by a deep chuckle, I remember why I'm out here, why I wouldn't miss this.

Tag is in the pool with our daughter, Willow. Since I'm so close to delivery, I can't play with her as much as I'd like. Tag makes up for it, though, by taking her on four-wheeler rides through the grapevines and watching her while she climbs trees. And by throwing her around in the pool at least twice a day.

It didn't take me long to figure out that he was going to be an amazing husband. Once we managed to put all our issues behind us and move forward, he threw himself into it with gusto. I was a little nervous about how he'd do with a baby, but I needn't have been. He's exceeded my expectations and then some. He can be so gentle, yet so playful. He's every little girl's dream daddy, I'm sure. He would've been mine, for sure.

My own father has come around quite a bit since the birth of our daughter. It's like he realized he was being given a second chance to make different choices and set different priorities, and he did. He and Mom come to visit at least once a month and stay for a week. It's not Tag's *favorite* week, but they get along a lot better now that there's no room for a hostile takeover in their relationship. The merger of a part of each of their companies worked out better than anyone could've anticipated. Dad's money is safe. Growing, in fact. And Tag's is, too. Not that he cares as much about it as my father does his. It's nice to have a fortune, but our life is pretty simple. We're happy spending our time here at Chiara, with each other and with our child. And soon, there will be another little laugh to add to the mix.

As if in agreement, I feel a tight squeeze low in my abdomen. It steals my breath for a second. I breathe through it, thinking that it's just a Braxton Hicks contraction. I realize that it might be more than that, however, when five minutes later another one seizes my uterus. And another one five minutes after that.

"Uh, babe?" I call out to Tag when the third one eases.

He glances over at me, his face still wreathed in a gorgeous smile. "Beautiful?"

"I think you might need to cut the swimming short and call my parents." I do my best to get out of the lounger gracefully, but I know it's no use. At this point, the best I can do is lumber.

When I straighten, I see Tag's smile fade. He stills, his long fingers unmoving where they're wrapped around Willow's waist as he was preparing to pick her up and throw her. "What's wrong?"

"Whassa matter, Mommy?" Willow chimes in, her tiny hands resting over her father's much larger, much tanner ones.

"I could be mistaken, but I think we might be making a trip to the hospital."

With lightning speed that one wouldn't expect from a man as big as my husband, Tag hauls himself and our daughter out of the pool. He runs, dripping wet, a giggling child in his arms, over to me to help.

"Don't worry about me yet. I'm fine. Go get some dry clothes on both of you and bring my suitcase to the car. I'll meet you there."

"You got it, Mrs. Barton."

They disappear in a swirl of excited whispers that include something about momma and a baby brother. I smile as I waddle my way across the patio and out to the garage. I have to pause twice, once to catch my breath and once until a contraction passes. This one seemed like it might be less than five minutes from the last one. Quite a bit less.

"Better hurry," I call out to no one in particular. My labor with Willow was brutal, but surprisingly short, especially for a first child. I can only imagine how quickly our son might get here once he gets started.

I press the button to open the garage door. The cool interior air brings attention to the wetness between my legs. "Oh shit, oh shit, oh shit," I whisper, rarely ever using that kind of language now that little ears hear every word we say. And often repeat them.

Another contraction hits and I cry out. That can't have been more than two minutes at the most. *Ohmigod, ohmigod, ohmigod!*

Sweat breaks out across my upper lip and a sense of panic starts to erupt in my chest. If this is real labor, which it seems to be because it's escalating, we won't have time to make it down the mountain.

My mind races as I run through my options, wishing I'd listened to Tag about staying in Atlanta for the last month of my pregnancy. I wanted to be here, though. Our home. And Willow loves it here so much. Just like I did when I was her age. I didn't think it would be a problem, but what if I *am* in labor? What if I *can't* make it down the mountain? What if I've risked the safety of our son?

The thought is agonizing. It brings with it a searing pain to my heart. Behind my eyes, too, as tears rush in.

I hear the scuffle of feet behind me seconds before I feel Tag's hand at my lower back.

"You coming? Or are we going without you?" he teases. When I turn to face him, his expression falls and turns to one of alarm. "What's wrong?"

"I don't think I'm going to make it down the mountain," I say in a trembling voice, all the while silently praying that God protect my baby from my own stupidity.

"Wh-what do we do?" he asks, his words hushed, his eyes full of fear.

"Let's go back into the house. We can do this. Right?" When the color leaves his face, I prompt, "Right?"

"Yes. Yes!" he replies, his second response more certain that the first. He sets Willow on her feet. "Walk behind us, cricket. I'm gonna carry Momma."

That's the only warning I get before he sweeps me off my feet and walks briskly back to the house. He takes the front steps two at a time, pausing to look back for Willow, who is running as fast as her little legs will carry her. Tag starts toward the stairs, but I stop him.

"Maybe we should do this in the living room, near the kitchen. Just in case we need things from there."

He changes his direction, taking me to the couch and depositing me gently on the cushions. When he straightens, he takes his phone out of his pocket. "I'm calling 911."

"Okay," I say, breathing through pursed lips as another contraction squeezes my uterus. "Oh God! Call your mom, too. Maybe she'll know what to do."

He tells the 911 operator what's going on and where we're located, then hangs up and dials his mom, who is only a few dozen yards away at her house. "Mom, Weatherly's in labor. We can't make it down the mountain. Can you help?"

Her response must've been short because Tag hangs up within seconds. My contraction has eased and my brain is working a little more clearly.

"We'll need towels and boiling water," I tell him. "At least that's what they always need in the movies. Maybe you should Google midwifery," I suggest.

So he does. He's still spouting off all sorts of facts when Stella arrives. She's cool and collected and takes charge immediately.

A sense of hopefulness and peace settles over me and I think that, if the paramedics don't get here in time, my child and I will be in good hands.

I never imagined I'd be here, that I'd be lying in a hospital bed after having delivered my baby at home with the help of my husband and my mother-in-law. Yet here I am. Tag is in the rocking chair in the corner, rocking our son, Jenner, as he sleeps. He's humming quietly, a look of perfect happiness on his handsome face. All I can see from the bundle in his arms is the one chubby hand that still holds his father's finger. He went to sleep clutching it. As long as I live, I don't think I'll ever forget this picture.

Stella took Willow with her to meet my parents at the hotel so they can rest. It's been a stressful couple of days and none of us have had much sleep. I started bleeding uncontrollably after Jenner was born. I'd lost an alarming amount of blood by the time the paramedics arrived. They rushed me here, where I underwent emergency surgery to remove some parts of the placenta that weren't delivered properly. That's what led to the postpartum hemorrhage. I must've scared the life out of Tag. He hasn't left my side. Asleep or awake, evidently he's been with me from the moment I went into labor until right this minute. I can tell that he's tired, and that he's in desperate need of a shave, but otherwise, he looks like the happiest father in the world.

As though he can sense my eyes on him, my thoughts on him,

he lifts his head and captures my gaze with his own. We stare at each other for countless seconds until he gets up and walks to the bedside.

He bends to press his lips to my forehead, still cradling the sleeping Jenner. "You're my life. You know that, right?"

I nod, emotion clogging my throat like cars on a congested interstate.

"Thank you for marrying me. And forgiving me. And for the gift of our children," he says softly. "But most of all for your love. You're making me the man I've always wanted to be."

"You've been that man all along. I saw him from the start."

"Thank you for not giving up on me."

"I didn't have a choice. I love you too much."

"You could never love me too much. It's impossible."

"I don't know. Sometimes I feel like I couldn't be me without you."

"It's only fair. I *know* I wouldn't be me without *you*. When you started bleeding," he says, his voice cracking and his eyes filling with tears. "Shit! I just . . . I couldn't . . . There was nothing I could do except hold your hand. And it was so cold . . ."

Tag drops his head to my chest, right over my heart, and I run my fingers into his silky hair.

"I'm not going anywhere. And next time, we'll stay in Atlanta."

He raises his head and locks his shining eyes onto mine. "Next time? You mean this didn't scare you out of having more?"

I shake my head confidently. "No. These are little miracles of our love. I'd have a dozen of them if I could."

His smile is happy again. Excited, even. "Well, you know, we could start working on that. I mean, I *am* your husband and I guess it's my duty to . . . you know."

"Yeah, I guess you'll just have to suffer through . . . you know," I say with a grin. Nothing seems to impair our sex life. It's even more amazing now than it was in the beginning. And it was pretty damn amazing then.

"I love you, Weatherly Barton."

"And I love you, Tag Barton."

When he leans down to press his lips to mine, our son whimpers in his arms, his grayish blue eyes opening to lock on to mine. Tag scoots into bed beside me and I'd swear for a second that I could see Jenner smiling up at me.

If you missed the first book in the Tall, Dark,
and Dangerous series, turn the page for a preview of

STRONG ENOUGH

Available now from Berkley

PROLOGUE

Jasper

Seventeen years ago

"What's he gonna do, Mom?" I try to wriggle away from her, but she holds me too tight. I feel like something bad's gonna happen, but I don't know why. "Maybe I can make him not be mad. Let me go!"

"Shhh, baby. It'll be okay. You have to stay here with me or he'll take you, too."

My heart's beating so hard it hurts, like it did that time when Mikey Jennings punched me in the chest. Not even my mother's arms around me makes the pain go away, and her hugs usually make everything better.

My eyes water as I stare out the window. I can't blink. I'm afraid to. I don't want to see what Dad's going to do to my older brother, Jeremy, but I can't look away either.

The longer I watch, the less I can move, like my feet are glued to the floor and my arms are strapped to my sides. It feels like I can't even breathe. I can only stare at the cold, gray water and the two shapes moving closer to it.

I see Jeremy's fingers clawing at my dad's hand where it pulls him by his hair. It's not doing him any good, though. Dad isn't letting go. Jeremy's feet sometimes drag along the ground, his ratty tennis shoes kicking up mud and grass, but my father never slows down. I can tell by the way his other fist is balled up that he's mad. Madder than usual, maybe.

Jeremy got in trouble at school again today. They called Dad at work instead of Mom, so she didn't even know until Dad brought Jeremy home. By then it was too late.

"No kid of mine's gonna act like a monster. There's something wrong with you, boy," Dad was saying when they walked through the door. Jeremy was in front of him. Dad pushed him so hard, my brother fell and slid across the kitchen floor.

There *really is* something wrong with Jeremy. The doctor said so. He said Jeremy needed medicine, but Dad doesn't care. It just makes him mad, makes him lose his temper with Jeremy even more.

I was standing at Mom's side when Dad stopped in front of her. He put his finger in her face until it almost touched her nose. His eyes were that red color all around the edges like they are when he's getting ready to whip Jeremy. "You'd better hope this little shit doesn't turn out the same way." He slapped me in the side of the head when he said it. It made my ear sting like a bee got me, but I didn't even say "ouch." I didn't say *anything*. I knew better than to open my mouth. "One's enough."

Dad went and grabbed Jeremy by the back of his shirt, pulled him up to his feet and threw him out the kitchen door. Jeremy fell again, but that didn't stop Dad. He followed him into the yard.

"Get up, you worthless little asshole," he yelled. There was something not good in Jeremy's eyes when he looked up. Then I saw him spit on Dad's work boots. I knew he shouldn't have done that. I knew it even more when Dad kicked him in the ribs. Now we're watching my older brother get dragged away for punishment.

Rather than stopping at the old stump that he bends Jeremy over to whip him, Dad keeps walking right out into the lake. He doesn't even stop at the edge.

My eyes hurt while I watch, but I can't close them. Something about this time looks different. Feels different. Something about the hot tears streaming down my face tells me that this time *is* different.

Dad's boots splash through the shallow water. He drags my brother behind him like he does a bag of trash when he's loading up the truck to go to the dump. Jeremy falls and gets back up, falls and gets back up. He's fighting for real now. He's kicking and hitting. I see his mouth open wide like he's screaming, but I can't hear it. The only thing I can hear is my heartbeat. It's like drums in my ears, it's so loud.

Dad stops when the water is up to his waist. He pulls Jeremy to him. I see his face from the side, my father's. It's so red it looks purple. Veins are standing out all down his neck. My brother's face is almost white, like he's wearing ghost Halloween makeup. His eyes are dry, though. He stopped crying over the stuff Dad does to him a long time ago.

Dad yells something at Jeremy, his mouth stretching so wide it looks like he could eat him. Like a snake, just swallow him whole. Jeremy just stares up at him with his pale face. Dad shakes my brother hard enough to make his head snap back, and then he dunks him under the water.

I suck in a breath. I've never seen Dad do this before, no matter how mad he gets at Jeremy. Something in my chest burns while I watch Dad hold him under, like *I* can't breathe either. Like air is stuck in there, burning. Just like I'm stuck in *here*. Hurting.

I taste salt from my tears. I lick them away, ashamed to be crying. Something starts pecking the top of my head. A wet trail, like snail slime, slides down the side of my face. I wipe it away and look at my hand. It's just water. Warm water.

Tears. But not my tears. They're Mom's.

I count. *One Mississippi, two Mississippi, three Mississippi*. I wonder how long Jeremy can hold his breath. My head feels like it might explode.

Four Mississippi, five Mississippi, six Mississippi.

Air and sound push past my tight throat to make a weird garbled scream. It lands in the quiet room like a crack of thunder. It's the only noise I make. It's the only noise I *can* make.

I watch Jeremy's hands, beating against my dad's wrist. Dad never budges, though, never lets up. His arm is straight and ruthless, holding my only brother under the water.

Mom's arms squeeze me tighter. It's getting even harder to breathe.

Seven Mississippi, eight Mississippi, nine Mississippi.

I count, even though time stopped moving. When I get to

twenty Mississippi, I start over at one, start over for Jeremy, to give him more breath. To give him another chance. But he doesn't use it. He can't. His time already ran out. Like his breath did. I know it when I see his hands drop away. They fall into the water and float, like there's nobody attached to them. Like my brother just . . . left.

Dad lets him go. Sort of pushes him out into the deeper water. Jeremy just drifts there, like he's playing dead. Like he used to do when Mom took us swimming on summer afternoons when our father was at work.

I don't watch Dad walk out of the lake. I don't watch him walk across the yard. I don't even look up when he walks through the back door. I just watch Jeremy, waiting for him to move, waiting for him to wake up.

"Get your purse. We're going out to eat. The boys can have a sandwich here."

Boys? Does that mean Jeremy's okay?

I start toward the door, but Mom grabs me. "Jasper, be a good boy and get my purse for me, sweetie. It's beside the front door."

Her eyes are different. They look scared and they make *me* scared, so I just go get her purse and bring it to her like she asked. When I hand it to her, she takes it and pulls me against her. I feel her arms shaking and when she lets me go, she's crying. But she's smiling, too, like she's not *supposed* to cry. None of us are supposed to cry.

"You sit right there in front of the television, okay? Don't you move a muscle." Her voice is warning me about something. I don't know what's going on, but I'm afraid. She's afraid, too.

"Okay."

I turn on cartoons and sit on the couch until I hear Dad's truck start. When I do, I get up and run as fast as I can, through the kitchen, out the back door and across the yard toward the lake.

It's raining now and the grass is slick. I fall twice before I can get to the edge of the water. When I do, I holler at my brother.

"Jeremy!" He doesn't move. He just floats on the surface like my green turtle raft does. "Jeremy!"

I look back at the house and then back to my brother. I know nobody can help me. Nobody will stand up to my dad. Not even my mom. If I don't help Jeremy, he'll die.

My hands are shaking and my knees feel funny when I step into the water. It's so cold it stings my skin, like when I fell off my sled last winter and snow went up my pants leg. I couldn't get it out fast enough. It was so cold it almost burned. But this time, I keep going no matter how much it hurts.

When the water is up to my chin and my teeth are chattering so hard I bite my lip, I think about turning back. Jeremy is so far away, I can barely see him and I can't catch my breath enough to holler for him.

"J-J-Jer—" I try again.

I paddle out farther. My arms and legs weigh so much I can hardly move them through the water. It's like trying to run in cold, thick soup. I fight to keep my chin up, gulping down the water that laps into my mouth.

I swim and swim and swim, watching the back of Jeremy's head until he's close enough for me to touch. It's raining harder now. Big, fat drops are splattering on the back of my brother's neck, and it's running down my forehead and into my eyes.

I grab a handful of his dark hair and raise Jeremy's face out of the water. His eyes are open, but they aren't looking at me. They're looking at something else, something I can't see. I take his arm. It's cold and feels kind of like that fish Dad brought home and made Jeremy skin.

My stomach hurts and my eyes burn. I feel like somebody's squeezing me around the middle, squeezing me so hard I can't even cry.

I take my big brother's hand and I pull him toward me, toward shore. He floats pretty easy, so I swim a little and tug, swim a little and tug.

After a while, it gets harder and harder to move, harder and harder to keep my face above the water. The shore, the grass, the back door of my house . . . they're all getting farther away, not closer. I'm scareder than I've ever been before. Even scareder than that time Jeremy made me watch *The Evil Dead*.

Jeremy seems heavy now, like he's trying to drag me down every time I pull on him. "Swim, Jer, swim," I mumble through a mouthful of water. "Please."

I go under. When I try to scream for help I know won't come, water goes down my throat. I try to cough, but I can't. There's no air.

I can see light above me and I use my heavy arms and legs to crawl toward it. When I finally get my face out of the water, I grab for my brother's hand. I hold on to it tighter than I've ever held on to anything before, even my favorite G.I. Joe soldier.

I paddle as fast and as hard as I can, pulling Jeremy behind me until I can touch the squishy bottom of the lake. I pull and tug and drag me and Jeremy to the shallowest part of the water and I roll him over.

His lips are blue and his face is still so white. But it's his eyes that scare me the most. They don't look like he's awake. But they don't look like he's asleep either. They sorta look like mine feel—scared. Like he saw something that made him want to hide, but he didn't get away fast enough and now he's just . . . froze.

I shake his shoulders. I scream my brother's name. I cry even though I don't want to.

I give in and pound on his chest. I know that if he gets up, he'll punch me in the back of the leg until I say "uncle," but I don't care. I just want him to get up. But he doesn't. He doesn't get up. He doesn't move at all. He just slides in the mud until he's back in the water.

I try to reach for him, but my feet slip and I almost fall in. That scares me so bad I scream my head off. I can't go back in. I won't come back out if I go in the water again. I just know it.

Don't make me go back in! Don't make me go!

But what about Jeremy? What about my brother?

I cry as quiet as I can as he floats away from me again. I watch his white ghost face until the only thing I can see is black. And nothing else.

ONE

Muse

I shake out the three-hundred-dollar sweater I just folded for the third time and I start over. Somehow keeping my fingers busy seems to calm my brain. It gives me something to think about other than the man I'm waiting on and how worried I am about taking this step.

When the icy blue cashmere is folded perfectly—for the *fourth* time—I lay it on top of the others in the stack and check the time on my phone again.

"It's almost noon, damn it!" I mutter, as if my friend Tracey Garris can hear me all the way across town. She's the one who knows this guy. I should've gotten more information from her, but she was in a rush this morning and she's in a meeting now, so I'm stuck waiting. Information-less. I only know what she muttered so briefly before she hung up, something about a guy coming by and his name being Jasper King.

I let out a growl of aggravation and grab another sweater, flicking it open with enough force to cause one sleeve to snap against the table like a soft crack of thunder. For some reason, I feel a little better for having taken out a bit of my frustration on *something*, even if that something is an innocent piece of very pricey material.

Rather than climbing right back onto a ledge of frustration, I purposely tune out everything except the words of the song playing overhead, "If I Loved You." It always reminds me of Matt, the guy I left behind. The guy who should've hated seeing me leave. The guy who *would've* hated seeing me leave *if* he'd loved me like I wanted him to. But he didn't. He let me go. Easily. And now, even after eight long months, it still makes my heart ache to think of him.

I don't shy away from the pain. In some twisted way, I bask in it. Like most artists, I welcome all kinds of emotions. Good or bad, they inspire me. They color my life and my work like strokes of tinted oil on pristine white canvas. They make me feel alive. Sometimes broken, but still alive.

After I finish the sweater, I move through the store, lost in thoughts of my ex and how much it hurt to say good-bye. I'm straightening a rack of ties when the chime over the door signals the arrival of a customer. I catch movement in my peripheral vision and absently throw a polite greeting in that direction. "Welcome to Mode: Chic," I say, feeling both resentful and relieved at the interruption.

I get no response, so with a deep sigh I even up the last row of ties and smooth my vest before turning to find my visitor. When my eyes settle on the interloper, all thoughts of Matt and the past and every trouble in the world melt away for the time it takes me to regain my breath.

A man is standing behind me. I didn't hear him approach, didn't smell cologne or soap, didn't sense the stir of the air. He was just coming through the door one second and looming right behind me the next.

He's tall, very tall, and dressed in black from head to toe. Other than his lean, dramatically V-shaped physique, that's all I notice about his body. It's his face that captivates me. From an *artist's* standpoint, he reminds me of a bronze sculpture, something strong and ancient that was carved by the talented hands of Michelangelo or Donatello, Bernini or Rodin. From a *woman's* standpoint, he's simply breathtaking.

His face is full of angles and hollows—the ridge of his brow, the slice of his nose, the edge of his cheekbones, the square of his chin. Even his lips are so clearly defined that I find myself wanting to stare at them, to reach up and touch them. Find out if they're real. If *he's* real. But it's his eyes that I finally get stuck on. Or maybe stuck *in*. They're pale, sparkling gold, like a jar of honey when you hold it up to the sun. And they're just as warm and sticky, trapping me in their delicious depths.

Despite all my worries, worries that have consumed me for several days now, I am only aware of the raw, primal power that radiates from him like heat from a fire. He doesn't have to say a word, doesn't have to move a muscle to exude confidence and capability. And danger. Lots and lots of danger.

I don't know how long I've been staring at him when I become aware of his lips twisting into the barest of smiles. It's minimally polite, but somehow anything more would seem a betrayal of the intensity that oozes from his every pore. The tiny movement is potent, though, and I feel it resonate within every one of my female organs like the echo of a drumbeat in the depths of a hollow cave. *God, he's gorgeous.*

As much as I enjoy the rubbery feel of my legs, the tingly fizz in my stomach, I pull myself out of the moment. Not necessarily because I want to, but more because I have to. I'm at work. Men don't come in here to be ogled. They come in here to be outfitted.

Unless they come here to see me. The thought hits me like a slap. Could this possibly be the bounty hunter Tracey was telling me about?

"Pardon me," I eventually manage, taking a step back as reality and worry and purpose crash back into my mind in a multicolored tidal wave. "How may I help you today?"

Dark head tilts. Tiger eyes narrow. Silence stretches long.

I wait, part of me hoping this is the man who will help me, part of me praying he's not.

When he finally speaks, it's with a voice that perfectly mirrors what he physically projects—dark intensity, quiet danger. "I need to be measured for a suit."

I let out a slow breath, oddly more disappointed than relieved. "I can do that for you." I take yet another step away, clasping my hands together behind me, determined to find some equilibrium in his presence. I glance at Melanie, the other person working the store today. She's the owner's daughter and for the fourth hour straight, I find her holding down the chair behind the cash register, typing into her phone. I should probably tell her that I'll be in the back getting measurements, but I obtusely decide to let her figure that out for herself when she can't find me. It won't take her long to realize I'm gone when someone else comes in and I'm not out here to do her job for her. "This way," I say, turning toward the rear of the store.

All business now, I ask questions as I make my way toward the dressing rooms. Even though his rich, velvety voice warms my belly, I find it easier to concentrate when I can't see the man following quietly along behind me. He answers all my queries politely, seemingly oblivious to the way he affects me.

I take him to the larger dressing room, the one with a platform that rests in the center of a crescent of mirrors. It has enough space for a desk and computer to one side, so we use this room to measure for tailored clothing. That and for special fittings like bridal parties and other groups.

I glance to my left as we enter the scope of the mirrors. My gaze falls immediately on the figure behind me. I look quickly away, but not before I notice the lithe way he moves. With the fluidity of the jungle cat his eyes remind me of.

Like a tiger. Surefooted. Silent. Deadly.

Without turning, I sweep my arm toward the dais. "If you'll stand there, I'll get the tape and be right with you." I don't doubt that he's following my instruction, even though he doesn't respond. I still can't hear him, still can't even detect a disturbance in the air, but now I can *feel* him, as though my body has become perfectly attuned to his within the five minutes he's been in the shop. It's beyond ridiculous, but it's the absolute truth. I've never been more aware of a man before. Ever.

I busy myself gathering the cloth tape, a small notepad and a pencil, doing my best to keep my mind on the task at hand until I'm able to control my thoughts to a small degree. Those wayward thoughts scatter and my mouth goes bone-dry when I turn and see him standing on the platform, muscular arms hanging by his sides, long, thick thighs spread in a casual stance. It's not his posture that catches me off guard. It's his eyes. Those intense, penetrating eyes of his. He's watching me like a hunter watches prey. I feel them stripping me bare, asking all my secrets, exposing all my weaknesses.

"Ready when you are," he murmurs, startling me from my thoughts.

"Right, right. Okay," I say, dragging my gaze from his and focusing on his body. As disconcerting as it is to appraise him so openly, it's not nearly as disturbing as eye contact, so I go with it.

As I take him in, I realize that he's a magnificent male specimen. I'd wager that his dimensions are perfect for every kind of clothing, from formal to sleepwear. And, dear God, I can only imagine what a striking figure he'd make in a tuxedo. He'd look like a model. For guns, maybe. Or bourbon. Something dangerous and thrilling or smooth and intoxicating.

I clear my throat as I approach, careful of my feet as I step up to stand beside him. I sense his eyes on me as I move, making me feel clumsy and slightly off balance.

I lay the pad of paper on the thin podium to my right and I clamp the pencil between my teeth as I stretch the tape out straight. With movements that I'm relieved to find swift and sure, I measure his neck and over-arm shoulder width, his chest and arm length. I jot down the numbers then make my way to his waist, cursing the fine tremor of my hand when my knuckles brush his hard abdomen.

I note his measurements, mathematical proof of the flawless way he's put together. What I don't write down are things that no numbers could convey. I don't need to. They'll be seared in my brain for all eternity, I think.

Wide, wide shoulders, the kind a girl can hang on to when she's scared. Strong, steely arms, the kind that can sweep a woman off her feet. Long, hard legs, the kind that can tirelessly chase down what he wants.

It's when I get to his inseam that things get . . . tense. Surprisingly, despite all the other worries that hover at the back of my mind, I can't overlook the heaviness that presses against the back of my hand as I measure. My belly contracts with a pang of desire that rockets through me. *Good Lord almighty!*

I snap into a standing position, turning away to write down the last of his measurements before he can see the blush that heats my face. Normally, I'd love all these "feels," but not now. Not today. Not like this. It seems like a betrayal.

Without another word or glance, I take my pad and step off the platform, moving to the computer to enter them into a New Client form. My pulse settles more and more the longer I keep my eyes to myself. "What's your name, sir? I'll set up a profile for your order." Still, I don't glance back at him. I keep my gaze glued to the lighted screen.

"King," he replies, his voice so close that I jump involuntarily. I don't turn when I feel his hulking presence behind me; I just stiffen.

I type in the name. It's as I'm hitting ENTER that it clicks. *King. The last name of the bounty hunter Tracey told me about.*

I whirl to face him, ready to pin him with an accusing stare, but I stop dead when I see that he's not looking at me. He's looking down at what he's holding. Between his fingers is the pencil that was stuck between my teeth. I can see the tiny bite marks as he rubs over each one.

I watch him move his thumb over the indentions, gently, slowly. Back and forth, like an intimate caress. It's hypnotic. Erotic. A fist clenches low in my core, causing me to inhale sharply at the sensation. It feels as though he's rubbing *me* with those long fingers. Touching me, arousing me. It's so physical, so tangible, so *real* that I have to reach back to steady myself against the edge of the desk.

"What sharp teeth you have," he says quietly, Big Bad Wolf-style. When he glances up at me, his eyes are a dark and serious amber. "Do you bite?"

"No," I whisper. "Do you?"

"Only if you ask nicely."

TWO

Jasper

I watch her lush lips part, her breathing already shallow. She's off-kilter. Just the way I like. "Are you Tracey's friend?" she asks, finding a coherent thought and clinging to it.

"I am," I reply, reaching around her to lay the pencil on the desk. The action brings my face to within an inch of hers and our arms brush. I hear the soft gasp of her inhalation.

"Why didn't you just tell me? You didn't have to pretend to be a customer."

Anger. It rushes in to clear away the cobwebs. I can see it in the way her sleepy green eyes start to flash like two fiery emeralds.

"I wanted a few minutes alone with you before you went on guard. Like you are now."

"Why? Am I being interviewed or something? I thought *I* was the one hiring *you*."

"You are. But I like to know who I'm working for when I take a job like this."

While the look on her face says she doesn't approve of my tactic, she's too curious to let it go. "And?"

"And what?"

"And what did you find out? What do you *think* you figured out about me in ten minutes of silence?"

I hold her gaze for long, quiet seconds before I speak. I sense how uncomfortable it makes her. I'm used to it. Such directness makes *most people* uncomfortable, but that doesn't stop me. Keeping others off balance is always a benefit to me. "I don't need to *interrogate* you to learn things about you. Being *with you* is enough."

"Yeah, right," she scoffs, trying for casual.

"For instance, you're a hard worker who takes her job seriously, even though I don't think it's really the job you *want to be* working. You're good at this, but you're not quite at home here, which tells me that this isn't permanent. You looked sad and distracted when I came in, like you might be missing someone. Maybe *that* is where home is. And then there's the fact that you're trying to hire me. I'd say that accounts for the worried frown I keep seeing between your eyebrows."

Her mouth drops open for a few seconds before she snaps it shut. "Is that all?" she asks sarcastically, pulling her vest tighter around her middle like she feels naked. I'm used to that, too. No one likes to feel exposed, like their secrets aren't theirs to keep anymore.

"No, that's not all, but I doubt you want to hear the rest."

She eyes me warily for a few seconds before she raises her chin, eyes locked bravely onto mine. "Of course I do."

She's courageous. Ballsy. I like that.

"Well, just off hand you have a good eye for color, which makes me think you're artistic. Artists are usually very . . . emotional. I'd say that when you're not consumed with concern you have a tendency to throw yourself into the way you feel regardless of potential outcomes."

"You can't possibly know that."

"I can. And I do. Just like I know you wash your hair in something that contains lilac." Her eyes widen, but she says nothing so I continue, leaning in ever so slightly. "And then there's the fact that you're attracted to me. You don't want to be. You probably even think that you *shouldn't be*, but that's like catnip for you, isn't it?"

She's shaken. Visibly shaken, but I don't back off. I don't give her a centimeter of the space I can see that she needs. I want her this way—off balance, uncertain. She's the kind of woman who would rather *feel* than *think* if she has a choice. And that's good for me. Not only will it serve my purposes *very* well, it's also sexy as hell.

Her cheeks blaze with a rush of blood and I think about running my finger over her skin to see if it's as silky as it looks. But I don't. At this point that would be too much. I'm nothing if not intuitive. And controlled. In my line of work, I have to be.

I actually smile when she steps out from between the desk and me. I can see by her expression that she's choosing to ignore my assessment altogether. It's much easier than trying to deny the truth.

"You, um, you said 'take a job like this.' A job like *what*? I thought this is what you do."

I cross my arms over my chest. "My jobs aren't *exactly* like this, but they're close enough. The main thing is that I . . . find things. And I'm damn good at it. So tell me, beautiful, what can I find for you?"

New York Times and *USA Today* bestselling author **M. Leighton** enjoys letting her mind wander to more romantic settings with sexy Southern guys, much like the one she married and the ones you'll find in her latest books: the Tall, Dark, and Dangerous novels, including *Tough Enough* and *Strong Enough*; the Wild Ones novels; and the Bad Boys novels. When her thoughts aren't roaming in that direction, she'll be riding wild horses, skiing the slopes of Aspen, or scuba diving with a hot rock star, all without leaving the cozy comfort of her office.